"We're good together, Teressa. We could work with that."

She leaned into him, her body warm and pliant. "It's not that simple—"

Dusty brought his mouth down on hers again before she could say anything else. What did he have to lose? Maybe he could even convince her they deserved a chance.

He stiffened at the thought. What was he doing? She'd just given him a legitimate out, but he'd been so...consumed with kissing her, he hadn't been paying attention.

He dropped his arms, noticing with satisfaction her lips were red and swollen. "You're a great kisser," she said.

He wiggled his eyebrows, pleased by her compliment. "I have other hidden talents."

She put her hand on his chest and pushed him back. "There are children in the house."

"Right. Kids." And she was the mother of his child, not one of his here-today-gone-tomorrow dates. She deserved respect and consideration. She deserved someone a lot better than him.

Dear Reader,

To Be a Dad is Teressa and Dusty's story. They first appeared as secondary characters in *When Adam Came to Town* (Harlequin Superromance, September 2013), and readers have often asked if I would write their story.

I love both these characters. Teressa is so brave and feisty, and Dusty has the biggest heart in the world, and as I wrote (and rewrote) the story I realized they were much more complex than I'd initially realized. Which, of course, made them more interesting.

It was a pleasure spending time with Teressa and Dusty, as well as revisiting the fishing village of Collina. And before you ask, because readers have commented how they'd love to visit Collina, it's a fictitious village. The Bay of Fundy is real, though, and it's possible to find villages similar to Collina by the bay.

I hope you enjoy reading *To Be a Dad*. I love to hear from my readers. You can contact me through my website, www.katekelly.ca, or email kate@katekelly.ca.

Kate Kelly

KATE KELLY

——

To Be a Dad

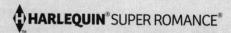

Recycling programs
for this product may
not exist in your area.

ISBN-13: 978-0-373-60866-9

TO BE A DAD

Printed in U.S.A.

HARLEQUIN®
www.Harlequin.com

ABOUT THE AUTHOR

Kate Kelly has had a love affair with books her entire life. Writing came in fits and starts, and she didn't take it seriously until her forties. Now she can't get along without it. She finaled in the RWA Golden Heart contest and won the RWA Daphne du Maurier contest. She has the good fortune to live on the east coast of Canada with her husband (the children have flown away). She writes, grows herbs and perennials, and sails when the wind blows her way.

Books by Kate Kelly

HARLEQUIN SUPERROMANCE

1751—A DELIBERATE FATHER
1875—WHEN ADAM CAME TO TOWN

Other titles by this author available in ebook format.

To my amazing daughters-in-law, Josie and Naomi

To Martina, the best mother-in-law ever

To my sister-in-law, Tina, and my niece, Jennifer

And, as always, to my guys, Adrian, Reed and Rei

CHAPTER ONE

TERESSA WILDER DEPOSITED her armload of groceries on the kitchen counter and listened to the cadence of her mother's voice as she read Sarah and Brendon a bedtime story. As a single mom, she didn't know what she would have done the past six years without her parents' support. Unfortunately, her mother never let her forget the sacrifices she'd made to help her.

Two children from two different fathers, and now...

She grabbed the small white bag from the pharmacy, slipped down the hall into the bathroom and tucked the bag under a stack of towels. No sense in dropping the *P* bomb until she knew for sure. Her legs gave out, and she dropped down onto the toilet and covered her face with her hands. Who was she trying to kid? She was a baby-making machine. Hence her six-year-old daughter, Sarah, and three-year-old Brendon. She was probably the only almost-virgin with two kids. She could kiss goodbye her lifelong dream of escaping her hometown and becoming a chef in Paris.

"Teressa?" Her mother tapped on the door. "The children are asleep. Are you all right?"

No, but she would be. She was an expert at sucking it up. "Of course. Be right out." She flushed the toilet and splashed cold water on her face before returning to the kitchen.

She stopped in the doorway to watch her mother put the groceries away. "Don't bother with the groceries, Mom. You've helped enough for one day. Thanks for looking after Sarah and Brendon."

She tried to be as independent as possible, paying rent to her parents for the tiny carriage house that hid behind her parents' big, old family home, and she worked full-time as a cook at the local café. *Her* café. She may only own a third of it, but having worked there for five years she knew the business better than her other two partners, Sylvie Carson and Adam Hunter.

"You can't leave chicken at room temperature too long."

Teressa bit back the retort on the tip of her tongue as her mother stashed the chicken breasts in the refrigerator. Her mother meant well, it was just… She was tired and needed to be alone. And she knew more about chicken than her mother, Sylvie, Adam and the whole damned town.

"Dad's probably wondering where you are. I'll put the rest away."

Her mother, whom she'd for some reason started

to think of by her name, Linda, made one of her sounds of disapproval that she so excelled at. "Dad's asleep in front of the TV by now. That man." Her mouth twisted into a bitter shape.

"Maybe he should have a checkup. How long has it been since he's seen a doctor?" Her mother was convinced Teressa's father was the laziest person in their village, but Teressa worried he was the unhappiest. She hadn't a clue how to help him, because he'd disappeared behind a wall of silence years ago.

"You know your father and doctors. He'd have to be half-dead before he went to see one. There's nothing wrong with him that a real job wouldn't fix." Linda sniffed her indignation. "Well, if you're sure you don't need any more help, I'll be off."

Teressa scooted over to the door and held it open. "Thanks again."

Linda zipped up her fleece. "They're my grandchildren. Of course I'm going to help. Good night, dear. And don't stay up too late. You look a little peaked."

"Good night, Mother." Teressa let the door swing shut as she went back to the groceries. Did people still use terms like *peaked*? How about *devastated*? *Bummed out, desperate? Stupid?* Yeah, definitely *stupid.*

What had she been thinking, having wild, totally out-of-control sex with Dusty Carson? God, he was so hot, there were days she could barely stand to be in the same room with him. Unfortunately, he was also irresponsible and immature. As friends they got along great. And as lovers, too. If their one time together was any indication, there were certainly no problems there. But as partners? Okay, maybe once or twice she'd imagined them together, but her daydreams never lasted because she was talking about Dusty. Mr. Party Boy. His head was as far from marriage and responsibility as it could get. She frowned. Strange that she'd never wondered why he avoided serious relationships.

She banged the cupboard door shut at the same time the phone rang. Checking the display to make sure it wasn't doofus-man, she scooped up the phone. It was Anita Carson, doofus-man's sister-in-law. Teressa didn't make friends easily, but Anita, Cal Carson's wife, was the kind of person who slipped under Teressa's defenses without her noticing. They were slowly becoming good friends, although they were polar opposites. Anita was cool, always unfailingly polite and had a husband who would walk over coals to get to her. Teressa blurted out what was on her mind more often than not and was certain there wasn't a man on earth who would care enough to take on her and her tribe of children.

"Hey," she croaked into the phone.

"Teressa? Anita here." Teressa heard the hesitation in Anita's voice. "Did you pick up the test while you were in town?"

Teressa tucked the phone under her ear and maneuvered a carton of milk into the refrigerator. "Yup."

"And?"

"And nothing. I just got home. I haven't had time to take the test." In the tiny village of Collina, New Brunswick, it was next to impossible to keep a secret, and telling Anita she might be pregnant was the same as telling the entire Carson clan. But a part of her had instinctively known she needed help this time, and it wasn't likely to come from her mother, so she turned to her new friend for help.

"Would you like me to come over?"

"Yes. No. I don't know." She closed her eyes and massaged her right temple. "I guess not. If I'm pregnant, I'm going to be a mess, and if I'm not I'm going to be a mess, only a happy mess."

Anita was silent for a minute. "I think I should come over. See you in a few minutes."

Resigned, Teressa finished putting the groceries away and slipped into the kids' bedroom to check on them. As usual, the sight of them asleep softened her knot of anxiety. They may have started out as "mistakes," but they were the best mistakes she'd ever made. She picked up Sarah's rag doll from the floor and tucked it into bed beside her tiny daughter.

Sarah had inherited Teressa's red hair, but instead of being heavy and straight like hers, it corkscrewed out of her head in zany curls. Teressa had talked her into growing it long, hoping the weight would help straighten it, but that idea wasn't working out so well. It wouldn't be long before the insults started coming Sarah's way on the playground. At least she could teach her daughter how to stand up for herself. As a child, it hadn't taken Teressa long to realize that following her mother's advice—to ignore what the other kids said and take the high road—wasn't going to cut it. She'd gotten as good at handing out the insults as receiving them. She kissed her daughter's forehead and moved across the room to Brendon's bed.

As usual he'd kicked off all his blankets. He had his father's blond curls, and her brown eyes. She put her hand on her stomach. Would this baby have Dusty's coloring? Dusty had blond hair and blue eyes so beautiful she could spend hours looking at him. He wasn't movie-star gorgeous; he was a fisherman, after all, and his face was lined from years spent on his boat, and from laughing. Dusty laughed a lot. Often just thinking about him made her smile, but not tonight.

Being a Carson meant something in the small fishing village of Collina. Not that the Carsons were rich. But Pops Carson was as close as they got to a mayor around here, and everyone respected the family. Growing up, she and Dusty hadn't run with the same crowd, because he was four years older than she was. But once they hit their twenties, age didn't matter as much anymore. She and Dusty had flirted with each other off and on, but once she had Sarah, Dusty switched to big-brother mode, which was his way of telling her they could be friends, but that was it. For all his crazy and wild ways, he'd become her sounding board and good friend. For the past three years she'd buried the physical attraction she had for him, until a few months ago when they'd both started spending time with the new guy in town, Adam Hunter. Unfortunately, Teressa had confused her friendship with Dusty as something more than physical attraction, and now there was a good chance their relationship was going to be put to the test because chances were she was pregnant.

When she heard a knock at the door, she pulled the blankets over her three-year-old son and dropped a kiss on his forehead. She should have told Anita not to come when she'd called earlier to ask if she could drop by. Anita was so reserved Teressa hoped some of her restraint would help keep her own emotions under control. But Anita would insist Teressa take the pregnancy test tonight, and she wasn't sure she was ready. She didn't think she'd ever be ready for a third child.

"What's that?" Teressa asked as she entered the kitchen.

"A bottle of nonalcoholic bubbly." Anita stashed

the bottle in the refrigerator between the milk and the orange juice. Anita was tall and willowy, her long blond hair falling in a perfect curtain across her back. She used to have the perfect figure but had lost too much weight last summer, unlike Teressa, who had noticed lately that bits and pieces were starting to sag and shift, like those half-deflated balloons people tied to their mailboxes.

Two years ago, Cal and Anita had eloped before anyone from the family or the village had met Anita, and Cal, in his usual impervious way, presented his bride to everyone, expecting them to love her as much as he did. It had taken a while for folks to warm up to Anita because she was so different from the rest of them. But in the past few months, Teressa had been enjoying getting to know her better.

"I'm going to need something stronger than fake champagne to lift my spirits, girl," she admonished Anita.

Anita crossed her arms and tried to look stern, an almost impossible accomplishment for someone with Bambi eyes. "Have you done it yet?"

"No."

"Where's the kit?"

"Bathroom."

"What are you waiting for?"

Teressa's shoulders slumped. "I just... It's not that easy."

Anita's voice softened. "Whatever you decide, I'm behind you one hundred percent."

Teressa wrapped her arms around her waist. "It's not that I don't want the baby." That wasn't the complete truth. She did, and she didn't. Already having two children, she understood what an incredible gift it was to have a child, and she knew in her mother's heart terminating a pregnancy was not an option for her. But bringing up three children by herself? She wanted to cry every time she thought about the work and the responsibility.

"You're a wonderful mother, Teressa. Anyone can see that. If you're pregnant, and you want the baby, we'll all help in any way we can. I know you don't want to hear it, but I think Dusty is going to be a great dad."

"I just bet he's jumping up and down with joy right now."

"I imagine he's scared. Almost as scared as you."

"Scared he'll get stuck with me and my brood."

"Maybe." Anita shook her head. "But he cares about you, Teressa."

"If this were a few years ago, and it was just about Dusty and me, maybe we'd have a chance. But I'm twenty-eight years old, too old to get stars in my eyes. And I travel with a posse these days, in case you haven't noticed."

"You're arguing to avoid the inevitable. Go." Anita pointed toward the bathroom.

Aɴɪᴛᴀ ᴛʀɪᴇᴅ ᴛᴏ ignore the sadness that tugged at her heart as she watched Teressa disappear into the washroom. Sadness for her friend because her life had always been so hard, and sadness for herself because more than anything, she wanted to have Cal's baby. But Cal, afraid of history repeating itself, refused to start a family, and the miscarriage she'd had a few months ago had only confirmed his fears.

Once Teressa was out of sight, Anita sank onto a kitchen chair. She'd insisted on coming over tonight against Cal's wishes. Teressa deserved to have someone to hold her hand for this. Anita just wished there was someone stronger than her. She sighed and leaned back.

Everything was a test these days. Was she strong enough to stand by her friend without breaking down and tell her of course she was lucky to have a third child while Anita longed to have just one of her own? Could she fit into a community that was as alien to her as her father's world of rules and rituals would be to almost everyone living in Collina? Could she become a strong woman like Teressa and her sister-in-law, Sylvie? She wanted so much, but mostly she wanted a family of her own, and she was going to do whatever was necessary to make that happen.

She straightened when she heard a truck pull into the driveway. She'd found the courage to leave her old life and follow Cal to Collina, and she'd find the courage to prove to her husband she was emotionally and physically ready to have a child.

THE HALLWAY FELT miles long as Teressa trudged toward her future. The past few weeks, she'd been playing a mental game, trying to trick herself into believing she wasn't pregnant when she knew she damn well was. Of course she was! She'd never caught a break.

Her life had derailed almost before it had started. When she'd become pregnant with Sarah, she'd had to forego the opportunity to attend the chef school she'd been accepted into and had gone to work as a sous chef in the local café she now owned in order to support herself and her new baby. She'd been there ever since, and yes, Dusty and Sylvie's father, Pops, who had owned the café for years, had been more than good to her. But no matter how kind and generous he'd been, Collina was still a small fishing village on the edge of the Bay of Fundy, and Paris was a million miles away.

She stopped and peeked into the kids' bedroom again. Angels, both of them. She could do this. There was room in her life for a third child. But that was all. Forget a husband or boyfriend. Romance? A serious career? Who had the time or energy?

She closed the bathroom door and pulled the

pregnancy test out from under the towels. The moment of truth had arrived.

"WHEN DID YOU turn into such a slob?"

Good question. Dusty stuck his hands in his back pockets and rolled back on his heels. "Been a little preoccupied lately."

"Is that what you call it." His older brother, Cal, shoved two empty cases of beer out of the way with the toe of his boot. "How can you live like this?"

"I didn't ask you up here for advice on house-cleaning."

Cal studied his face. God only knew what he saw. Pure terror? "Has she taken the test yet?"

"I don't think so. Anita just went over there. She'll call when they know. So." He looked around his cluttered house. As usual, Cal was right. He was a pig. "Where do we begin?"

"We?"

"Come on. I need help. We all know that Teressa's going to have to move out of the carriage house. It's already too small for the three of them. I have to at least offer her a place to stay, I guess. It's time I started fixing up the house, anyway. I'm getting tired of living like I'm at my hunting camp."

"Okay, let's start here." Cal dug his jackknife out of his pocket and sunk the blade into the wood trim around the large living room window.

"Hey! That's not helping," he protested. He'd

thought he'd got a great deal when he'd bought the house a few months ago, but he had a feeling he was about to find out exactly why the bungalow had sold for such a low price. Cal had tried to warn him to have the house assessed, but Dusty's knee-jerk reaction of telling his older brother to mind his own business had kicked in and the house had been an impulse buy all the way.

His ever-efficient brother pulled a notebook out of his jacket pocket and started writing. "The wood's full of rot. It's gotta go. And those carpets are gross. Some of that new click flooring would clean this room up, and it's not expensive." He stopped writing and smirked at his brother. "Best of all, you can install it yourself."

Great. How was he supposed to fit in reno work during lobster-fishing season? He was on his boat twelve hours a day because of the high tides. Collina got close to fifty-foot tides locally, five times higher than the rest of the Atlantic coast. Most ports along the bay drained out with the tide and filled up when the water rolled back in. Once he went out on the rising tide, he couldn't return until the tide rose again. It wasn't easy fishing on the Bay of Fundy, but it was one of the richest fishing grounds on the east coast of Canada. Plus, he'd grown up working on the bay and knew its moods and the riches beneath its surface.

Cal gave Dusty's shoulder a brotherly punch. "I'll

help when and where I can. So will Pops. Matter of fact, we'll have to watch how much he does. The doc says he still has to be careful. Heart attacks at his age are no picnic. I imagine Adam will lend a hand, too."

Cal continued talking as he wandered into the kitchen. "This is where you're going to need my expertise. Plywood cupboards went out with the sixties."

"Right." A ball of iron settled in Dusty's stomach as he eyed the rust stains in the old white enamel sink. "Where the hell do I start?"

"I'll go through the house and make a list of what needs to be done right away. If you want to get any renos done, you're going to have to make room in here. I suggest you start carting everything out," Cal said.

Dusty looked around, bewildered. "Everything? I just moved in."

Cal took his elbow and pointed him toward the mountain of empties sitting by his kitchen door. "You moved in months ago. You've got to clean this crap out of here. Come on, I'll give you a hand."

Dusty welcomed the straightforward work of hauling what was basically trash out of his house. Maybe he had let things get a little out of control around the house. The work prevented him from thinking about his real problem. Teressa. In one way or another, Teressa had been a problem forever.

He was crazy about her, and he couldn't stand her. That was maybe putting things too strongly. But she came with so many problems attached, she scared him. First, the kids, and—okay, he liked kids well enough. But man, kids that didn't go home at the end of the day? He worked hard, and when he got home he liked to kick back, drink a few brewskies and watch a game if it was hockey season or hang out with his pals. If Teressa lived with him—and face it, she had to move somewhere because where she was now wasn't big enough even without the baby, and if there was a baby—she wouldn't tolerate a bunch of guys hanging around.

He stashed an armload of empties in the back of his truck, pulled out his cell phone and checked that it was turned on. If he and Teressa had a kid he wanted to take care of it. His mom had died when he was young, but Pops had been a great dad. Still was. Not wanting to worry him, Dusty hadn't told his father about the baby yet.

If there was a baby.

On top of the kids—and don't get him started on the other fathers—there was Teressa. He sat on the tailgate of his truck and stared off into space. She was crazy sexy. If they had all these kids and babies and things, they'd never have time for sex again. That just plain sucked.

As for getting married and building a life together? Loveless marriages worked sometimes, didn't they? His own parents' marriage may well have been a marriage without love. His mother had died in a car accident while running away with her lover when he was thirteen years old. It had hurt like hell knowing his mom didn't love him enough to stay, but now, looking at the tragedy, he realized Pops must have suffered the most of all.

If he married Teressa, and she screwed around on him because she didn't love him, he didn't think he could handle it. He'd always assumed he'd get married someday, preferably to a sweet woman who was crazy about him and liked having a fisherman for a husband. Teressa didn't think much of his job or of him, or Collina as far as that went. She'd never stopped dreaming of moving away. He couldn't imagine living anywhere but Collina and working on the water.

The only thing they had going for them was their friendship. Teressa was a good enough friend that she didn't mind telling him off when he needed it. Like when Pops had his heart attack and Dusty had unraveled. Teressa pointed out that it wasn't about him and told him to grow up and think about Pops. Her little speech had been exactly what he'd needed to ground him. She almost always gave him what he seemed to need, whether it was a slap up the side of the head, or a good laugh, or the ear of a good friend.

"Hey, bonehead. This is your mess, not mine.

Get the lead out," Cal called from the doorway of the house as he ambled toward Dusty.

Dusty pushed away from the tailgate. "How do you suppose people have sex if there are all these kids around?"

Cal grinned. "They don't. Ever again." He pounded Dusty on the back. "That's good, considering how easily Teressa gets pregnant. I can see it now, you two and twenty kids."

"Not funny."

"Sorry. Tell you what. If you and Teressa do hook up, Anita and I will take your kids for a night here and there."

His kids. Jesus.

"You okay? You look like you're going to hurl."

No, he wasn't okay. He may never be okay again. What did he think he was doing? There were days when Teressa acted like she didn't even like him. And there were days when she pissed him off royally.

He'd been waiting half his life to make love to her, and when the opportunity suddenly presented itself a few weeks ago the last thing on his mind had been birth control. If she was pregnant, what did that mean? Would he be expected to marry her and inherit an entire family? Did he even want a family right now? He was so mixed up, he felt as if his head was going to explode.

"You need to talk, Dusty?" Cal looked concerned.

Dusty shook his head. "I can't think straight. I like Teressa, but she drives me nuts. I even like kids, and her kids are great, but that doesn't mean I want an instant family."

Cal frowned. "You're not going to want to hear this, but I've gotta tell you, bro, *like* is not going to be enough to get you through the rough times. I *love* Anita, I'd die for her, and still sometimes I can't breathe and have to get out of the house and away from her. I know this is a lot to take in, and you have my full sympathy, but you and Teressa have to sit down and talk. I think you, not Anita, should be over there holding her hand right now. I tried telling Anita that, but she's got ideas of her own these days. Why don't you go?"

"Right now?" What if Teressa wouldn't let him in the house?

"Tell Anita I could use her help here."

"You're probably right. I should be with Teressa." He remained glued to the spot.

"About time. Good luck, bro. Call later if you need to talk."

"Yeah. Thanks, Cal." Dusty climbed into his truck and started the engine and backed out of his yard. He concentrated on the road in front of him, feeling as if he was one step removed from every-thing around him. No more avoiding the truth. The hour of doom had arrived. Time to pay the piper. Man, he wasn't going to hurl, was he? For damned sure he made himself sick.

Think of Teressa. Think of what she's going through. He swallowed the acid in his throat, rolled down the window and sucked in a lungful of cold November air. This was Teressa. They'd known each other forever, and they'd work things out. Everything was going to be all right.

Maybe.

CHAPTER TWO

TEN MINUTES LATER, Dusty stood outside Teressa's door and watched his breath plume in the frosty air. It was only a week into November and already it felt like winter. The temperature on the water, as always, was at least ten degrees colder than on land. He'd have to dig out his long johns, that is, if he could find anything after his brother finished ripping his house apart.

He was stalling. Hard to pretend otherwise. Although he had mixed feelings about going through that door, no way was he going to leave Teressa to face another pregnancy on her own. Aside from everything else, she was his friend, and she'd had a hard life up 'til now. It wasn't in him to turn his back on a friend in need. Plus, her getting pregnant was as much his fault as hers. Teressa loved children, and he suspected she'd never consider terminating the pregnancy. Truth be told, the thought of doing such a thing made him feel queasy, but it wasn't his decision to make.

When he shoved the door open, Anita pivoted

around, frowning at the intruder. That was pretty much how he felt, like an intruder.

"Hey." He stayed by the door, figuring Teressa would fly into the room and kick him out any second.

"You came!" Anita made it sound as if he'd shown up at some kind of social function.

"I thought I should be here." It came out as one word: *IthoughtIshouldbehere.*

His sister-in-law studied his face. "I think Teressa will be relieved to see you."

"You think? Cal says to tell you he's at my house, and he needs your help."

His big brother, the tough guy no one could get close to, had fallen head over heels in love with Anita. How had Cal done that? How had he let down his barriers and exposed himself? Anita seemed like a nice person. Dusty was almost certain she loved his brother, but Cal and Anita had had problems lately, and neither one had confided in anyone what those problems were. Which proved, just because you loved someone and got married, there were no guarantees that everything was going to work out.

He trusted Pops and, he supposed, Cal and Sylvie. But Teressa's moods were too mercurial to make it easy to trust her. Nine times out of ten she came out swinging. The one thing he did trust about Teressa was that she always tried to be fair. Or almost always, at least.

Anita grabbed her jacket from the back of the chair and shrugged into it. "She's pretty high-strung tonight."

"I figured."

Anita tilted her head. "If you don't mind my asking, are you going to ask her to marry you?"

"I don't even know if she's pregnant yet."

"You realize that she'd probably say no." She stood with her hand on the door knob.

"I figured." Had he? Really?

"Maybe you better—"

"Anita? Go, okay? I'll take it from here."

Anita came back into the room and surprised him when she rose on tiptoe and kissed his jaw. His unshaven jaw. Christ, he couldn't even get that right. "You're a good man, Dusty Carson," she said.

He swallowed hard. "Thanks."

"Call Cal later if you need someone to talk to," she added on her way out the door. She stuck her head back in. "Take your boots off," she hissed. "You don't want to upset her."

Dusty breathed more easily when he heard Anita pull out of the driveway.

Teressa had probably heard the vehicles coming and going, too, so he might as well go and find her. He pulled off his boots and left his jacket on a hook by the door.

Her bedroom was empty, and he kept on going, but hesitated at the kids' room. Should he check on them? Would he wake them if he opened the door? After a second of listening and hearing nothing, he continued on. So, she was in either the bathroom or her closet of a living room. The bathroom door was closed. He considered knocking, but went with his gut. If he knocked, she could tell him to get lost before he had a chance to talk to her.

When he opened the bathroom door, Teressa was sitting on the toilet, staring at her hands in her lap. A flat plastic stick sat on the edge of the sink. She looked so scared it reminded him of the Halloween when she was twelve, and he and a bunch of guys had hidden in a hedge and jumped out at her. She'd peed her pants right there on the sidewalk in front of everyone. She hadn't talked to him for a year after that. Hell, no wonder she didn't trust him. At sixteen, he should have known better.

Dusty squatted down in front of her. "Are you okay?"

"Couldn't wait for the bad news, huh?"

"So, are you…?" The words stuck in his throat.

"I don't know. I can't look."

Dusty picked up the plastic stick. "This it?"

"Yup."

"What am I looking for?"

"Two lines."

"Two lines means you're pregnant?" His hand shook.

She continued staring at her hands. "That's the way it works."

"You're pregnant."

Teressa groaned and listed to one side.

Dusty squatted down on his haunches again and slid his hands along her thighs. "It won't be so bad. We'll do this together."

Her head snapped up. "Really? You want to be pregnant for the first trimester or the last?"

Usually, right about now, he made some smart-ass comment and they got into it. He took a breath, counted to ten. "I want to be with you during the whole thing." He swallowed his panic. "All of it. The pregnancy, the birth and all the years to fol-low."

She pushed his hands away and stood in front of the sink. "Don't do this."

"Do what?"

"Be nice to me. It makes everything so much harder."

He stood and looked over her shoulder at her re-flection in the mirror. "I'm trying to make things better."

"I don't deserve better."

"What are you talking about? You think you

got pregnant by yourself? We're in this together, whether you like it or not." He rested his hands on her hips and pulled her back into him. "Far as I'm concerned, you deserve the best."

He nuzzled her neck, inhaling her sweet scent, found her earlobe and nipped it. He could seriously get used to this if they were married.

She stiffened. "What do you think you're doing? Stop."

Not exactly the reaction he was looking for. "Why? You can't get pregnant again. We might as well take advantage of the good parts."

"So, you're in this for the sex?" she hissed.

He raised his hands as if she'd pointed a gun at him. "No. You're…you're twisting it around." Right, and that lump in the front of his jeans was just a stick. Log. Whatever. "All I'm saying is…" *Shut up, man.* "I think you're a really attractive woman, and no matter what happens in the next year, I'll still find you attractive."

She flicked her long red hair over her shoulder, and he watched it sway across her back, remembering how it felt against his chest their one mad night together. He chanced a glimpse in the mirror and caught the shadow of sadness in her eyes. Okay, maybe he was going about this the wrong way. As usual.

He put his hands on her shoulders and gently

turned her until she stood in the circle of his arms. "Give me a chance, Teressa. I won't let you down."

She closed her eyes and sunk into his embrace. He was always startled by how fragile she felt in his arms. Not that he got to hold her often, but, yeah, in his mind she resembled an amazon warrior. In reality she was a slender woman with too heavy a burden to carry.

She rubbed her cheek against his shoulder and pulled away. "Thanks. I needed a hug."

"Always glad to be of service." He watched Teressa's open expression shut down at his flip answer. Would he ever learn to think before he opened his mouth? He cupped her face before she could move away. "I'm serious. I want to be a part of your life." Now was probably a good time to mention marriage, but he wasn't ready to go there yet. Wasn't sure he ever would be.

"Come on." He tugged on her hand.

She snatched her hand back. "I'm not going to bed with you, Dusty Carson."

Great start to a…whatever the word was for what they had. He should give up while he was ahead. Determined to push forward, he took her hand again. "I want to talk to you about…things. Let's go into the living room."

"What's wrong with the bathroom? You got something to say to me, this is as good a place as any."

"You're just being contrary." He slipped his arm around her shoulders. "Come on, Tee. We'll be more comfortable on the couch."

She shrugged him off, her lip curling in disdain. "Is this your sad attempt at seducing me? 'Cause in case you haven't noticed, it's not working."

"I'm not trying to seduce you."

"You yell like that, you're going to wake the kids up."

Dusty scrubbed his hands over his face. He should get the hell out while the getting was good. But no way would he leave Teressa to face having another child by herself. He'd do the right thing if it killed him. "Okay. You want to do this here, we'll do it here. Sit." He pointed at the toilet.

"What is your problem?" Teressa sat, for the first time looking a little curious.

"Mommy?" A small, worried voice sounded through the door.

Teressa started laughing. "You're going to want to let Brendon in before he gets hysterical."

It was a sign. He and Teressa weren't supposed to take their relationship a step further. If they were, everything would have gone smoothly. Hell, who was he kidding? Nothing had ever gone smoothly between them.

He yanked open the door and glared down at the tiny boy hopping from one foot to the other.

"Dusty!" Brendon blinked like he was going to cry. "I gotta pee."

"Okay." He stepped into the hallway, but his heart thumped over when he glanced back at Teressa. Her laughter had morphed into tears as she scooped up the pregnancy stick and tossed it into the trash.

"Mommy, are you sad again?" Brendon hugged her leg.

"No, baby. I'm just tired. Good on you for getting up to go to the bathroom." She sidled past her son. "Dusty will help you, okay? I have to take care of…something."

Again, Brendon had said. *Are you sad again?* He knew Teressa struggled with her life as a single mom, but he had no idea how much.

Tears pooled in Brendon's eyes.

"What's your problem?" Dusty barked.

"I can't reach."

Squatting down, Dusty mentally kicked himself as the kid started crying in earnest. "What do you need, Brendon?" Other than a kind, caring adult.

Brendon gulped back tears. "My potty."

Potty. Right. He opened the only closet door and grabbed the white plastic potty. "You don't pee standing up yet?" There was so much he didn't know about kids. He placed the potty in front of Brendon and backed off to give him some privacy. Nothing turned the tap off faster than another guy watching you take a leak. When he glimpsed back to make sure Brendon was okay, the kid was sitting on his potty, staring up at him.

"Will you teach me to pee standing up at the toilet?"

Dusty folded his arms over his chest. "Now?"

Brendon shook his head from side to side. "Tomorrow."

"Sure."

Dusty fidgeted as he waited for Brendon to do his thing. Where had Teressa gone? They hadn't even had a chance to talk about the baby. *Oh, my God.* His lungs collapsed, and he gulped for air. He didn't know if he wanted to laugh or shriek with horror. In a few months, he was going to be a dad.

"You done yet?"

"Guess so." Brendon pulled up his bulky pajama bottoms. The kid was wearing diapers. Why wear diapers if you didn't need to?

"Okay, see you, bud."

Brendon's bottom lip trembled. "Mommy always tucks me in."

"I knew that. But we've got to be quiet, because we don't want to wake up your sister."

When he scooped the little boy into his arms, Brendon held himself stiff as a board. He smelled good, though, like little kid and sleep. He laid Brendon in his bed and pulled the covers up to his chin.

"Dusty?" he whispered with his eyes closed, his body still stiff.

"What?"

"Promise."

"Promise what?"

"You'll teach me how to pee standing up."

"If you're still awake when I get back from fishing."

He watched Brendon as his face softened into instant sleep. *Kids.* They were amazing. He didn't know the first thing about them, though. How did you know if you were being a good dad or not? There had to be some kind of manual on how to bring up a kid. He needed to start reading up on the subject, but the idea that he was actually going to be a dad felt so unreal, as though someone was playing a really bad practical joke on him. He wished he could go to sleep and wake up to find he was still a free man.

But that wasn't going to happen. He was officially going to have a child of his own. Well, Teressa was going to have it, and the child would be theirs, not just his. He tiptoed out of the bedroom and went in search of the lady in question. He found her in the kitchen, unloading the dishwasher. She didn't look at him when he walked into the room.

He grabbed Teressa, pulled her into his arms and, before she could say a thing, he kissed her.

And kissed her. And kissed her. She tasted so sweet and sexy at the same time. He loved how soft her mouth felt, how good she tasted.

And he liked how she clung to him, as if she needed help to stand up when he finally lifted his mouth from hers.

"No." Her voice sounded husky, the same way brandy felt as it slipped over his tongue. No to him? To them? To sleeping together?

He kissed her again, brought his hips hard up against her, so she could feel what she did to him. She trembled in his arms. He liked that, too.

"We're good together, Teressa. We could work with that."

She leaned into him, her body warm and pliant. "It's not that simple—"

He brought his mouth down on hers again before she could say anything else. What did he have to lose? He loved kissing her. Couldn't get enough. Maybe he'd even get lucky and convince her they deserved a chance.

He stiffened at the thought. What was he doing? She'd just given him a legitimate out, but he'd been so…consumed with kissing her, he hadn't been paying attention. Time to cool things down.

He dropped his arms and stepped back, noticing with satisfaction that her lips were red and swollen. "You're a great kisser," she said as she wiped the back of her hand against her mouth.

He wiggled his eyebrows, feeling inordinately pleased by her compliment. "I have other hidden talents."

She snorted. "I'm well acquainted with your *talents*."

"I wouldn't say you were *well* acquainted." A corner of his mouth hitched up. "I'm thinking we could use a little refresher course."

She put her hand on his chest and pushed him back. "There are children in the house."

"Right. Kids." And she was the mother of his child, not one of his here-today-gone-tomorrow dates. Somehow that changed everything. She deserved respect and consideration. She deserved someone a lot better than him.

Teressa leaned against the counter for support and rubbed her arms, feeling cold and yes, lonely, damn it. There was no doubt she and Dusty were physically compatible. But she'd known that already. She had the opposite problem, actually. It was difficult being around him and not jumping into those heavily muscled arms of his. Dusty had earned his muscles from honest work, just as he'd earned those sexy crinkles at the corners of his eyes from squinting into the sun. Heaving heavy lobster traps was man's work. She knew because she'd tried working on one of the local boats one summer. She did the job, but that was all she'd done that summer. Work and sleep. She had immense respect for fishermen.

She eased farther away from him, not that there was much room in her tiny kitchen. Tiny kitchen, tiny house and in her parents' backyard. Her parents meant well, but she was too old for them to be monitoring her every move. Her mother was likely wondering right this minute what Dusty was doing there so late in the evening. Teressa closed her eyes. Wait until she found out. There was a scene she refused to think about until absolutely necessary.

But she had bigger problems to deal with at the moment. First, she had to keep enough distance between her and Dusty so at the very least, she couldn't smell his scent of clean soap and ocean and wind. She could become addicted to that smell if she let herself.

And second, she needed to save him from his good intentions. Dusty had an active imagination and left to himself, he'd…heaven knows, decide marriage was the answer to their problems? She needed to hang on to the small bit of independence she still had, because she refused to become that poor woman Dusty Carson saved.

She smiled across the kitchen at him. "We're friends, Dusty. Good friends. Let's leave it at that."

The stress lines that bracketed his mouth softened. "I would if I thought that would be okay, but living here isn't going to work, and you know it.

Your mother is going to have a fit when she hears you're pregnant again," he said before she could brush off his concern. "And the house is too small. You're going to have to move somewhere, and I've got a house big enough for all of us. It just needs some work. Which I'm doing," he added in a louder voice when she opened her mouth. "And where else is there to move to in this village? If you and the kids move in with me, everyone's happy."

"Everyone? Really?" What about them as a couple? "This isn't one of your larks, Dusty. If I ever decide to live with someone, it's going to be because I can't live without them. For now I'm fine right where I am. I appreciate that you want to 'fix' things, but living together will only make matters worse."

"You mean I'll make things worse."

"It's not easy living with children, because they have to come first. Always. It's not like you didn't have a life before this. Have you given any thought to what you'd be giving up by taking us in?"

He looked at the floor. "Sort of. Not really." He sighed. "Maybe you're right. But what about you? What do you want to happen?"

She studied the handsome man standing in her kitchen. She'd forgotten that he'd always been the peacekeeper in his family. But now he was considerate, as well. When had that happened?

She sighed. What did she want? How long had it

been since someone asked her that question? And Dusty was right. She had to be practical; her family needed somewhere to live.

She still wasn't certain Dusty was the answer to her problems. As a matter of fact, if she was certain about anything, it was that moving in with him would cause more problems than it would solve. But she should at least show him the courtesy of considering his offer. It couldn't have been easy for him to come here tonight.

She sat at the table and motioned for him to do the same. "This is just a wish list, okay? I don't expect anything."

He nodded.

"I want a house big enough for my kids and me. But if I ever decided to move in with you, yours needs to be fixed up. I'm not being mean," she rushed to explain, afraid she'd insulted him. "It's just, your house is kind of…it needs help."

"Yeah, I got that. And I'm already working on it. But I'm going to need your help. You have to tell me what to do. What colors you want the walls, that kind of thing."

Unexpectedly, her nerve endings tingled with excitement. She'd lived in her parents' house before moving a few feet away into their carriage house. She'd never had a place, not even an apartment, to call her own. Not that Dusty's house would be hers.

But she'd have some say in how to decorate her living space for the first time. That could be fun.

For heaven's sake, talk about grasping at straws.

"Is that okay with you?" he asked, frowning.

"Yes." Realizing he was doing all the giving here, she smiled for his benefit. "I've never had the chance to decorate before."

He blazed a returning smile that turned her insides into mush. She blinked and looked away. She shouldn't have smiled at him.

"I'll be honest, Teressa. I don't have tons of money, so the house won't be as fancy as Cal and Anita's. But I've got some. Like if you want to buy a new stove and stuff. We could do that."

Oh, hell. He was going to do his nice-guy act, the one that made her temporarily forget how irresponsible he was. Like the time he'd promised to help her paint the table and chairs in the café, then blew her off when an old girlfriend showed up. She and Dusty had been having one of their good days, teasing each other and laughing a lot while painting the chairs outside in the sunlight when a petite, perfectly put-together blonde chased Dusty down at the café. The blonde had fluttered her fake eyelashes once at him, and he was gone. He hadn't even apologized for leaving her with a half-finished job.

She needed time to think things over. It was too much of a gamble to trust her heart—or those of her children—to him, and she knew better than to depend on anyone too much. Hadn't she learned over and over again that way led to heartbreak?

She hadn't been in love with either Sarah or Brendon's fathers, but she'd been willing to try with Corey, Sarah's dad. Until she realized Corey had no intention of giving up the parties and settling down. At twenty-two there was nothing more boring than watching people get drunk while you remain stone-cold sober. Was that going to be a problem with Dusty, too? Everyone knew how much he loved to party. Why did she have to fall for the good-time guys? Why couldn't she have dated an accountant?

"Let's put the housing issue on hold for now. Like I said, we're fine here at the moment. We need to talk about our relationship." She darted a look at his face as it hardened.

He leaned back and stretched his legs out in front of him. "Okay."

"Can we…can we take it slow for a while. See how things go?"

"You mean no sex."

She nodded. Was that what she meant? She wasn't sure.

"Do I get a say in this?"

She scratched at a nonexistent spot on the kitchen table. "Not really."

"You're not attracted to me?"

She couldn't hold back her smile. Life would be

easier if she could lie to him and say she wasn't. "That's not the problem. It's just…sex complicates things, and with the children involved, I think we should take everything slowly."

"So that means we could possibly have sex in the future."

"Something like that."

"Okay."

She sat up straighter. That had been an easier win than she'd expected. "Who have you been having sex with?" It hadn't occurred to her that Dusty might have a girlfriend stashed away in the city, but it made perfect sense. He was a good-looking guy and fun to be with most of the time.

"There's no one else."

Right now. The words stood between them.

She watched him carefully for a telltale sign that he was lying, but he continued looking at her with a straight expression on his face. *Right now* was a start, she supposed.

"I've got a request," he said.

"What?" she asked suspiciously.

"We have a date once a week."

"A date?"

"Yeah. Once a week, you and me spend time together alone. Like go out to dinner. Or rent a movie and stay home and watch it together. Alone."

"What about the kids?"

"We'll find a babysitter."

She searched for the problem or hidden agenda and came up empty. "Okay."

"And you gotta wear sexy underwear every day."

She half rose out of her chair. "What?"

Dusty grinned. "I don't have to see it if you don't want. But I like imagining you wearing lacy things under your clothes." He glanced at her from under his lashes. "I always have."

Heat spiked through her as she held on to her chair with both hands. How was she supposed to respond to a request like that?

"Don't be ridiculous," she snapped. "I don't have any sexy underwear. I'll be wearing a nursing bra in a few months, for Pete's sake."

Dusty made a low humming sound as his gaze flicked over her breasts. A blush burned a path right up into her hairline.

"Forget it. All of it. Go home. Now." She pointed a shaky finger at the door.

He caught her finger, kissed the tip and laughed. "Come on, you're tougher than that. What else is on your wish list?"

If only he knew how vulnerable she was when it came to him. She didn't feel nearly as tough as she needed to be. "My wish list." She massaged her temple. "I'd love to have a few minutes every day to myself."

"Like when you come home from work?"

"Exactly. I'd love to be able to sit down and do

nothing for say, fifteen minutes. Just…sit." She leaned forward. "What do you want?"

"I don't know." He looked down at the table. "I know this probably sounds corny, but I guess I want you to be happy. I know our situation isn't ideal, but I assume from the way you're talking you want to keep the baby. Who knows? Maybe we'll surprise each other."

He sounded so sad. Not at all like the Dusty she knew. She looked away and stuffed her knuckles in her mouth, the urge to cry overwhelming. She was all messed up in her head and her heart, but she'd never intended to hurt Dusty.

"I want you to know I'm very fond of you, Dusty."

He patted her hand and took it into his. "I care about you, too. We're going to be all right, Teressa."

She blinked back tears. "I hope so." She leaned across the table and kissed him. If she wasn't careful, she'd end up as just another in the long line of broken hearts Dusty had left behind him.

CHAPTER THREE

DUSTY SCRUBBED AWAY the residue of a hard day's work. It was an unseasonably warm day for November, and he'd overdressed, anticipating a biting north wind. Instead, he'd spent the day sweating and stripping away one layer of clothing after another. Not much he could do about his underwear, though. His deck hands, Josh and Andy, had teased him about his red long johns.

He and Teressa had managed to keep the news about her pregnancy a semisecret for two days now. *Semi* because his family knew about it, but Teressa had begged for a few more days before she broke the news to her mother.

Mrs. Wilder was a gnarly person to handle. He didn't know exactly what her problem was, other than she looked as if she had a broom handle stuck up her... Hell, he had to stop thinking like an adolescent, especially about the grandmother of his child. But there was no denying she was a bitter woman. He didn't remember her being uptight when he was a kid, but kids saw the world differently than adults.

For the past two nights he'd worked hard emptying his house of anything that absolutely didn't need to be there. It looked empty and rough at the moment, but slap down some new flooring and a fresh coat of paint on the walls and things would start to come together. That's what he kept telling himself. Where he'd find the time to accomplish all that, he had no idea. Because regardless of what Teressa said about how she was fine where she was, eventually she was going to need a bigger place, and houses didn't come up for sale all that often in Collina. Plus now that he'd started working on his house, he was getting into the renovations in a big way.

As soon as he ate, he planned to head over to Teressa's to nail down a time that they could go to Lancaster together to buy some paint. His bank account already had a huge dent in it, because Cal had purchased a bunch of building and plumbing supplies. Good thing Dusty had a solid line of credit, and that it was one of the better fishing seasons. If he was careful, he might almost pull this off. Although Teressa had been pretty clear on not moving in with him, the fact was her place would be too small once the baby came, and he thought he should at least offer her the option of moving in with him. He gulped for air. It was the right thing to do. No matter how many times he repeated that thought to himself, it didn't get any easier to swallow.

Dusty heard a knock on the door as he stepped out of the shower. He wrapped a towel around his waist and stuck his head out into the hallway that led to the kitchen. "I'll be out in a minute."

"No hurry, son. You've done a lot of work the past few days."

His father, Pops. The man he most admired in the whole world. Cal had given Pops the lowdown, and Dusty had talked to him briefly on the phone, but he hadn't heard from his father since. He grabbed a fresh pair of jeans and a T-shirt, pulled them on and ran a hand through his wet hair as he hurried down the hallway.

"There you are." Pops eyed him. "Good day on the water?"

"Great. You should come out with me before the weather changes." His father had fished for years before he sold Dusty the boat and his quota for lobster. More and more these days, quotas were going to outsiders and not always by choice. Dusty considered himself lucky to be able to buy his father's business, when not so many years ago, it had been a given that a son, not a stranger, would take over the business.

Pops smiled. "Can't say I haven't thought of going."

Pops took his time studying the carnage he and Adam and Cal had wrought the past two nights. The floors were stripped down to the subfloor and the icky wallpaper in the living room—did people really choose to have roses on their walls?—had been pulled off in strips. His house was an open-concept with the kitchen and dining room one big room and the living room opening off both. The three bedrooms and the bathroom were clustered at the other end of the house. They hadn't touched those yet.

"You've got a lot of work in front of you."

"Yeah." He sank onto an arm of his black leather couch, the sum of what he hoped to accomplish weighing down on him.

Pops came over and put his hand on Dusty's shoulder. "I'm proud of you, Dusty. I know neither you nor Teressa are ready to live together yet, but I think it was important to let her know she can move here if she wants to. It would be a big adjustment for you, and it couldn't have been easy to offer her your home."

They both knew that was the understatement of the year. "I can't believe I'm going to be a dad."

Pops's face lit up. "Can't say I'm disappointed. I've been waiting on a grandchild for a long time now. I never thought you'd be the first, though."

Dusty laughed. "Me, neither."

"Having a child, that's nothing short of a miracle. You'll see."

"And having three kids?" Might as well get that elephant off his chest.

"I brought up three kids single-handedly, and even if I do say it myself, I think I did a damned fine job. You'll do fine, too. The thing about having kids? You only get to live the experience a day at a time. When you're feeling overwhelmed, remember that. All you have to do is get through the day."

"And then you get to do it all over again the next day." Pops's advice wasn't helping.

"See? There you go, getting ahead of yourself. Just concentrate on today."

Pops wandered around the living room and looked out the window. "Cal says he's busy with the Tolster job. He can only help you part-time."

"I can't let him do all that work for free, and I can only afford him part-time. Adam's been a big help so far, and I plan to work evenings."

"Your mate, Josh, he's handy with a hammer. He built his own house."

"He did a good job, too. But I'm working on a budget, Pops. I guess I could remortgage the house once I get a few more things done, but I was hoping to keep the building expenses under control." He looked at his hands, a tight knot in his chest. "I'm going to have a child to support." The knot twisted into a sharp pain. He couldn't breathe.

"That's what I came by to talk to you about." Pops pulled the ottoman in front of Dusty and sat. "I've got more money than I need after selling the café to Teressa and Sylvie and Adam."

Dusty reared back. "No way. That's your money. You need it."

"Not all of it. I planned to put aside a healthy sum for each of you to inherit. I gave the family home to Sylvie, so why can't I give you money? You need it. I don't. I always said better to give with a warm hand than a cold heart. This way I get to enjoy watching you spend it."

"I don't know, Pops. I just… I never figured…" Goddamn it, he was not going to start blubbering in front of his father.

"I know you didn't. That's what makes giving you money all the more enjoyable. I talked to Muriel at the bank. She's going to transfer fifty thousand into your account tomorrow. Maybe you can hire one or two carpenters to work during the day while you're fishing. Buy a few appliances. Whatever. It's yours to do with as you see fit."

They both stood, and Dusty felt his father's strong arms around him. A father's hug—*his* father's hugs were a wonderful thing. Would he be as good of a father as his own dad was? He had a lot to learn and a long way to go, but at least his family had his back. Could be, things wouldn't be so bad.

TERESSA HELD HER arm protectively over her stomach as her mother's words drilled into her.

"Can you not keep your legs closed to anyone? What are you, the village whore?" Her mother's face flared fiery red, and she screeched loud enough that Teressa worried the children would hear, and if they could, would they understand the foul words that were coming out of their grandmother's mouth? She'd known breaking the news to her mother was going to be bad, but she hadn't anticipated the depth of Linda's bitter disappointment.

"That's uncalled for," Teressa responded.

"Is it? What's uncalled for is having a slut for a daughter."

Teressa flinched, but refused to let her tears take over. Had she really thought something good might come out of her pregnancy? That for once in her life, she'd be happy? Or if not happy, content? Dusty had almost made her believe it was within her reach. But then she'd known Dusty had a glib tongue. What she'd do to feel his arms around her right now. She'd considered asking him to come over and support her while she told her mother about the pregnancy, but at the last moment decided against involving him. It had been a good call.

"Where do you think you're going to live? You can't stay here. It's too small. The money I could have made renting this place out."

"That's not fair. I pay rent."

Her mother snorted. "A portion of what it's worth. You'll have to move in with us. It's the only solution."

And eat crow for the rest of her life?

"We're moving in with Dusty." Oh, God, where had that come from? Now that she'd told her mother, she couldn't take it back. Dusty had looked so relieved when she'd turned down his offer to move into his house.

"You can't think a decent man like Dusty is going to put up with you for long. He's not stupid, Teressa. No man wants used goods, and someone else's children to boot."

Teressa sagged. Hadn't the very same thought plagued her continuously? What happened when Dusty woke up to the fact that this wasn't one of his wild romps? That she and her children weren't going to disappear? But she'd be damned if she'd admit her fears to her mother. The woman would feast on them like a starving vulture.

"I guess that's something Dusty and I will have to discuss."

Her mother's voice peaked into an even sharper screech. "I won't have my child and grandchildren treated like charity cases. It's bad enough everyone knows you're a slut. You'll move in with us. That's the end of it."

"I'd rather live in a shelter than live with you."

Linda's hand connected with Teressa's face at the same time the outside door opened. Tears that Teressa had held in check spilled over when she saw the horror stamped on Dusty's face as he stood in the doorway. She hadn't wanted him to bear witness to any of the ugliness her mother directed at her. The woman had just straight-out called her own daughter a slut. Which was totally unfair.

Everyone froze. Linda looked horror-struck at being caught in a violent act. Teressa could hear Dusty's heavy breathing. He sounded like a bull about to charge.

"What the hell is this?" he asked through clenched teeth.

"Linda thinks the children and I should move in with her and Dad."

He narrowed his eyes as he continued to stare at her mother. "Not going to happen. She's moving in with me."

"Why would you want someone like her to live with you?" A sly look crossed Linda's face. "Oh, of course. Because everyone knows my daughter puts out."

"Mother! Stop." She was going to die from embarrassment on the spot. Her own mother talking about her like that. Did Dusty think the same thing? What if Linda was right? What if she had no worth? Maybe she should admit defeat now rather than wait for the inevitable crash to happen. That Dusty would someday think the same thing was devastating.

A vein pulsed in Dusty's jaw. He opened his mouth to speak, but closed it as if he didn't trust what would come out. Finally he swallowed and tried again. "Your daughter is ten times the woman you are." He opened the door. "We're finished here."

Teressa choked back her tears. No one had ever defended her before, not even her own father.

"You can't kick me out of my own place," Linda protested.

"If Teressa's paying rent, I can."

A look of triumph stretched the skin tight on Linda's face. "There's no formal rental agreement. She has no rights."

"It's okay, Dusty." She tugged on his arm. "I'll handle this."

He finally looked her full in the face, and his anger blasted over her. "It's not okay. Go pack whatever you and the kids need for a couple of days. You're moving to my place tonight."

He turned to Linda. "We'll be back tomorrow to get everything else.

"Come on, Teressa." He took her by the arm and led her down the hallway. "Let me help."

Teressa's heart broke, and broke again when they stumbled into the children's room to find Sarah hugging her baby brother. Tears rolled down Sarah's cheeks and Brendon watched her with round, frightened eyes. She felt Dusty hesitate before he continued onto the bed where both children cuddled. If she had been in his shoes, she honestly couldn't say that she wouldn't have turned and run out the door.

She sat and gathered her babies into her arms, rocking them back and forth. She knew they both needed a minute to overcome the rush of relief they probably felt at seeing that she was okay. This was not the first time she and her mother had come to blows.

She felt broken inside. If she moved too fast or breathed too hard, she'd shatter. Not only because her mother hated her, but also because Dusty had witnessed Linda's disdain for her. What if he thought the same thing, that she didn't deserve respect? "Mama, are you hurt?" Brendon patted her cheek where her mother had hit her. She should have gone to the washroom first to check if Linda had left any marks.

She hugged her son closer. "I'm okay, baby. Your grandmother was upset. She didn't mean anything."

"If you point me in the direction of your suitcases, I'll start packing things," Dusty said in a low voice, as if afraid to upset the delicate balance in the room.

She blushed, amazed she could find something else to be embarrassed about. "We don't have any. There's a couple of cloth bags in the hall closet, and there are garbage bags." She smiled wanly. "We never go anywhere."

She could tell by the way the vein in his jaw

jumped that he was clenching his teeth again. "Garbage bags it is."

"Are we really moving to Dusty's house?" The fear on Sarah's face was replaced by curiosity. Brendon crawled up on her lap, his thumb in his mouth.

"Yes." As if a window had opened, her spirits lightened a bit.

"What's it like there?"

A mess. She sighed and ran her hand through her son's sleep-mussed hair. "It's bigger than this place. I'm not sure, but you may each get your own bedroom. Maybe not right away, because the house needs to be fixed."

Sarah stood up on the bed. "I can help him fix it. I got my hammer and saw."

"Perfect. Okay, we have to figure out what you need for tonight and tomorrow, and then we'll go to Dusty's."

"I hope I like it there." Sarah climbed down off the bed and headed for the shelves that held her toys.

"Me, too." Brendon drooled, a beatific smile lighting up his face.

Teressa held her baby to her chest and kissed the top of his head. "Me, too," she whispered.

An hour later, her hands shaking on the steering wheel of her old minivan, Teressa and the children followed Dusty's truck. She was leaving home.

Really leaving. She wasn't sure what she felt. Excited? Maybe. Definitely scared. What if Dusty decided he didn't really want them? Nice went only so far, and then there was reality. He had to be as scared as she was right now.

There had always been a push and pull between her and Linda, and yes, from now on she was Linda, not Mother. Linda was headstrong, wanted things done her way, and she... Dear God, was she really like her mother?

She'd complained nonstop the whole time Sylvie had been remodeling the café a few months ago, not that it had made any difference. At least she'd been big enough to admit to Sylvie that she'd been wrong, something Linda would never do. People loved coming to the café now. They'd liked it before, but now they loved it, because Sylvie had painted the constantly changing wall mural on the back wall that chronicled their lives, and installed Wi-Fi and comfy chairs surrounded by stacks of books and newspapers. Sylvie nourished their minds and Teressa nourished their bodies with good food. So maybe there was still a chance that she hadn't grown as rigid in her opinions as her mother.

She'd had to toughen up quickly when she'd gotten pregnant with Sarah. Lots of women had children by the time they were twenty-two, but she hadn't been prepared for suddenly being cut out of the small social scene in the village. Although having Sarah had helped compensate for almost everything she'd lost.

She glanced in the rearview mirror and noticed Brendon's eyes were closed. *Please let him stay asleep.* Sarah looked wide-awake, her gaze glued to Teressa's reflection in the mirror, as if afraid that if she took her eyes off her mother she might disappear.

"Hey, honey bun. Are you okay?"

"Grammy hit you," she whispered, her eyes round with disbelief.

How to put a positive spin on that? She'd hoped Sarah and Brendon had somehow missed that bit. "Sometimes when people are angry they say or do things they don't mean."

"Why are we going to Dusty's house?"

Great question. Her daughter was nothing short of brilliant. "Because Dusty's a good friend, and he wants us to live with him for a while." All true. She'd wanted to delay the news of having another baby sister or brother until her first trimester was over.

"Is he going to be our daddy now?"

Teressa groaned. How did life get so complicated? "Corey's your father, Sarah."

Sarah pushed against the back of the seat in front of her. "I like Dusty better."

So did Teressa. She hadn't heard from Corey for

two years since he'd gone out west to work. His parents were dead, and he only had one brother, who moved around a lot, as well. She had no idea how to locate either one. Corey wasn't a bad person, but neither had he been interested in being a dad. A few months after Sarah was born, he left and had come back only a couple of times to say hello. As for any financial support, it was hard to tap someone's pocketbook when you didn't know where to find them. Corey had been a fun guy, and he loved the good times and the parties.

Much like Dusty.

She blinked back tears. She was setting herself up for another fall, wasn't she? Only this time she had two—make that three—kids to drag down with her. She should turn the car around and go…anywhere but Dusty's. She clicked on the turn signal and pulled into his driveway. Maybe tomorrow she'd find somewhere else to live. Except she knew as well as Dusty that the only homes available to rent were drafty summer houses that were impossible to heat. She was backed into a corner with no way out. God, she hated her life.

DUSTY CLIMBED OUT of his truck and welcomed the cold as he waited for Teressa. He'd never in his life wanted to hit a woman before, but he was ashamed to admit he'd come close tonight. What kind of mother talked to her daughter that way? It burned a hole in his gut wondering how long Teressa had been putting up with that crap.

Collina was a small village, and if Teressa had ever been promiscuous, he'd never heard about it. And he'd always paid attention when the gossip involved her. He had no patience for the women-are-sluts, guys-are-studs bullshit. People were people, and normal people needed sex.

He leaned against the truck fender and crossed his ankles. Okay, so he hadn't liked it when she went out with Corey, but he'd been dating… He frowned and tried to recall who he'd been dating at the time. Patricia? Sherry? Point was, he wasn't a saint. But when she got pregnant… Yeah. Whole different ballgame. As far as he knew, Teressa had only had two boyfriends, and Stan, Brendon's father, had been more a bad idea than a boyfriend.

The point was Mrs. Wilder had no business talking to her daughter that way. Teressa was a good mom and a good woman. Earlier tonight, when her mother had bad-mouthed her, Dusty had watched something die in Teressa's eyes. She seemed to shrink right in front of him. That was so wrong. She worked hard to keep her little family together and to make a success of the café. He knew she'd always wanted to be a chef somewhere fancy, but he rarely heard her complain about being head cook at his family's café.

He'd been so proud of her a couple of months

ago, about the same time their child had been conceived, when she'd managed to come up with the funds to buy a third share of the café. Adam had decided to buy in to the deal as the second partner, but then Sylvie realized she needed to hold on to a part of the café that had been originally bought for their mother, and became the silent third partner. Dusty smirked. Silent, as in not working there daily. She was pretty damned vocal about her vision for the future of the café.

He straightened away from the truck and pulled up a smile as Teressa drove into the yard. She was going to have a fit when she saw the shape his house was in. He should have gone inside and tried to straighten stuff up.

"Want me to get Brendon?" he asked when she got out of the car.

"Could you carry Sarah instead? It's dark out here and she's heavier."

"Sorry. I'll get an outside light hooked up tomorrow." Right after he renovated the entire house.

He leaned down into the car. "Hey, Sarah. How about a piggyback to the house?"

She looked at him suspiciously. "What's a piggyback?"

"I'll show you. You get out of the car, and I get down like this. Now, you put your arms around my neck, and up we go." He grabbed her legs and pulled them around his waist. Sarah squealed as he stood, and she grabbed a handful of his hair.

"Look at me, Mommy."

Teressa pulled out of the backseat with a sleeping Brendon in her arms. She gave her daughter a weary smile. "You have to let go of Dusty's hair, honey, but hold tight to his neck."

Sarah released her death grip on his head to clamp a tiny hand right on his larynx. Dusty tried to breath, but his throat was blocked. He galloped to the house, anxious to get her off his back.

He put her down as soon as he reached the back stoop, took her hand and went inside, switching on the kitchen light. Teressa followed on his heels. They stood, silent, surveying the gutted house. The cold, gutted house. He'd been so excited that Pops had given him money to work with that he'd forgotten to start a fire before going to Teressa's to tell her the good news.

"I know it's a mess," he began. Sarah let go of his hand and slipped behind her mother. Teressa looked everywhere but at him, tears brimming in her eyes.

"We're going to fix it up," he said in a loud voice. "I've hired Josh to work on the house instead of coming out on the boat with me. Cal said he'd help when he could, and Adam will, too. And me, of course. And you." He sent a silent plea to Teressa. "It's going to be okay. I promise."

"Of course it is," Teressa said in a too bright

voice. "Where are the bedrooms? Sarah and Brendon need to be in bed."

He cleared his throat, feeling like a total loser. "Um…the bedrooms are crammed full of stuff right now. But I've got a king-size bed, and there's lots of room for you and the kids."

Teressa's mouth hung open. "I'll sleep out here," he said and waved vaguely around the living room. "Just let me change the sheets on my bed." And pick up the dirty clothes he'd left on the floor after his shower. And, hell, that magazine Andy had given him as a joke for his birthday last month.

He left them standing in the middle of the living room, looking like shell-shocked refugees. What was he supposed to have done? He couldn't leave them at Teressa's mom's, and the closest hotel open at this time of the year was sixty kilometers away.

You could have taken them home. Although his father had given the old family house to Sylvie, he still thought of the house as home. Sylvie was living with Adam in his tiny house next door to the family home, because they planned to start renovating the old house soon, if they hadn't already.

The truth was he needed to take care of Teressa and the kids himself. Which was stupid and selfish and proved he hadn't a clue what he was doing.

Sarah stood in the bedroom doorway, clutching her doll to her chest.

"Where's your mother?"

"In the bathroom, crying."

Hell. "Brendon?"

"He's sleeping on the couch." She stepped into the room. "You're a bigger slob than Brendon."

"I can change." He tucked the edge of the bottom sheet under the mattress corner.

"How come Grammy hit Mommy?"

Because she was an evil witch. Dusty punched the pillow before he put it back on the bed. "I don't know. I don't know your grammy very well, but it's wrong to hit people."

"You hit that man at the bonfire."

The annual bonfire, a couple months ago. He couldn't remember if he'd hit the SOB who'd been sniffing around Teressa that night or not. He'd been so drunk he doubted he'd done any damage, and he'd been too embarrassed afterward to ask. He'd gotten the idea that he and Teressa were going to the bonfire together. Sort of like a couple. But she'd turned up with that tourist who'd been hanging around her, and when one of his buddies had passed Dusty the rum, he'd gotten a glow on.

No wonder Teressa wasn't thrilled at the prospect of marrying him. At thirty-two, he still acted like a kid. He had to grow up fast.

"Are those your pajamas?" He threw the comforter over the clean bed.

"Yes."

"Okay, climb in bed. I'll get your brother."

"What about Mommy?" she asked after crawling under the blankets. She looked so tiny in the middle of his bed.

"I'll get her after you guys are settled."

Two minutes later he carried Brendon to the bed and tucked the sleeping boy in beside his sister. "Is he supposed to go to the washroom or something?" The last thing he needed was kid pee on his expensive mattress.

"No, silly. He wears diapers at night."

"Right. Okay. So, lights. Want them off or on?"

"Off, but leave the door open."

He switched off the light and edged toward the door. "I'll get your mom now."

"Dusty?"

"Yeah?"

"You're supposed to kiss us good-night."

He felt a weird snick inside, almost as if something was clicking into place. He strode back to the bed, dropped a kiss on Sarah's forehead, then leaned over her and kissed Brendon. "Good night, funny-face," he said from the doorway.

Sarah giggled. "That's not my name."

Dusty smiled in the dark. "It is now."

His smile slipped as he faced the closed bathroom door. He stared at it for a couple of minutes like the dumb idiot he was, then turned and walked back to the living room. Teressa had once told him she'd never caught a break in her life, and now here she was, stuck with him, a place she'd never wanted to be. He needed a beer.

He went to the kitchen, grabbed a beer and popped the lid. He didn't know what to say to Teressa to make her feel better. *Your mother's a bitch, forget about her? Everything's going to be okay?* Was it? He and Teressa squabbled on a regular basis, and that was with not nearly as much at stake. He had feelings for her, but were they enough to sustain them through having a child together?

He took a swig of beer. And yeah, he resented that she had children with two other guys. She'd have been smarter if she'd hung out with him. Except he'd been busy with…Suzy? Julie? He was such a shit. How could he be mad at Teressa for doing exactly what he'd been doing at the time? He put his beer on the counter and called Sylvie to let her know what had happened and ask for a favor. When he hung up, he went back to the bathroom. He had to at least try to make Teressa feel better.

He knocked softly on the door. "You okay?"

"Um, yes, of course." He heard her run the water in the sink.

"We need to talk, Teressa."

"I'll be out in a minute."

He stared at the door, waiting for her to say something else. Something smart-ass, like she usually did. After a couple of minutes he went back to his beer in the kitchen. He was out of his depth, and he wished someone would give him a checklist. *Crying woman locked in bathroom—break down door. Check.* All that would do was wake up the kids.

He tensed when he heard the bathroom door open and close. It took a few minutes, but Teressa finally walked into the kitchen. Shuffled into the kitchen. Hell. He stuffed his hands in his pockets to stop from hauling her into his arms. Her eyes and nose were red from crying.

He and Teressa may have had their differences from time to time, but underneath all the stuff that went on between them, they were good friends. Teressa was a fighter, but her mother's attack must have knocked her for sixty. And then, to come here to this mess.

"It'll get better. I promise."

She hugged herself. "Sure."

"We'll go to town tomorrow and pick up a few things. You have to start making a list of what we need. I mean, I know what building materials, but we'll get a new stove and fridge, too. What else?"

She took a weary look around the kitchen. "What's wrong with that stove? We don't need to buy new. You can't afford it, and neither can I."

"The oven doesn't work. What else do you need?"

She stuffed her hands into the sleeves of her faded pink dressing gown and hunched her shoulders. Damn it. He hadn't meant to snap at her. He'd been meaning to get the oven fixed for months, but what did he need an oven for when he had a microwave?

"Hey." He stepped into her space and waited until she looked at him. "It's killing me, you acting like this. I need you to be fighting mad."

"You hate when I argue with you."

"Yeah. No. I don't know. I like you just the way you are. Or the way you are most of the time. Spicy." He raised his eyebrows up and down.

She glanced longingly at his beer. "Wish I could have one of those."

He slapped a notepad and pen on the island in front of her. "Grocery list. We'll pick up some food tomorrow, too. We'll have to leave here by two."

"I can't. I'm working."

"Adam said he'd cover for you, and Sylvie will babysit the kids. I need you to go to town with me, Teressa. There's some business we need to take care of."

"Like what?"

Oh, no. If he got into that, they'd be up all night arguing. Best to spring it on her at the last minute. "Stuff." He finished his beer and put the empty on the counter. "If it'll make it easier for you, I'll quit drinking beer."

A gleam sparked in her eyes. "You? Quit drinking? Now I've heard everything."

"No biggie."

She hooted with derision. Personally, he thought she was overreacting, but he let it go.

"Want to bet?" she challenged him.

He may not have liked the direction of the conversation, but at least Teressa was back in fighting form. This was familiar ground for them. They were always challenging each other over silly things.

"Absolutely. A hundred bucks says I can quit drinking anytime I want."

"I don't have a hundred dollars."

His smile grew wider. "What have you got?"

"Get your mind out of the gutter." He loved watching her face turn a rosy pink as she punched him on the arm. She knew him too well. "I'll let you pick out the name for the baby."

"Really?" He frowned. "That's a big responsibility."

"I didn't say I'd agree to use it."

"What about the last name?"

"What about it?"

"I'd like my child to have my last name."

She shook her head. "That won't work. Both Sarah and Brendon have Wilder as their last name. It'll be too confusing if their brother or sister has a different one."

"That sucks. I just assumed when I had kids they'd have my name." It surprised him how much it bothered him.

A yawn caught him by surprise. Because he had to start work so early in the morning, he was usually in bed by now. "We'll talk about the name thing again. I'm too tired to argue with you right now. I've got to grab my clothes and sleeping bag out of the bedroom. I'll try not to wake you in the morning."

"Dusty?"

He stopped and turned back to her. "Yeah?"

"Thanks. For everything. I know you must be freaking out about...well, everything. If this—" she swept her hand as if to include the room "—doesn't work out, I'll find somewhere else to live."

For the first time since he'd walked into her house tonight, panic tiptoed up his spine. They both knew there was nowhere else for her to live in Collina, except with her parents, and if he had any say in the matter, that wasn't going to happen. He'd move out and let them have the house if he had to. But he knew if he told her that, she was contrary enough to pack up and leave that night.

But truthfully, the prospect of her—and Sarah and Brendon—staying was just as scary. It was a helluva situation they'd dug themselves into.

"Pops says you only get to live your life a day at a time. How about we concentrate on getting through tomorrow?"

"It's a place to start," she agreed.

He hated the sad smile on her face, and to stop himself from hugging her, he busied himself picking up a pair of dirty socks he'd kicked off by the door earlier. They both could use a hug, but she looked so fragile right now, he didn't dare touch her. Last time he'd done that, she'd gotten pregnant.

CHAPTER FOUR

THE NEXT EVENING, Teressa straightened in the passenger seat of Dusty's truck and rubbed sleep from her eyes. She'd hardly slept a wink last night, her brain working overtime, much like a rat in a cage, trying to find a means of escape. She was grateful to Dusty for helping her, but she'd have preferred to rescue herself. Look what misery had come from depending on her parents. Her mother didn't let an opportunity go by to remind her how much she'd helped her daughter. Teressa flat-out refused to be dependent on anyone ever again.

It was bad enough that at the moment she really had no alternative but to stay with Dusty. If he started in with the recriminations, she didn't know what she'd do. It wasn't as if she could run away from home. She didn't have a home.

It helped knowing Dusty was a good man. They'd been friends for years and had always had this "thing" between them. Maybe if she hadn't gotten pregnant with Sarah their relationship could have grown into something more. Brendon pretty much eliminated any possibility of that happening.

But before she'd gotten pregnant with Sarah, she hadn't planned on sticking around Collina, so even if she hadn't had the kids, she and Dusty wouldn't have happened. He belonged here, and he knew that, and that was one of the things she'd always liked about him. He knew exactly who he was.

And now she was living with her old friend and hated being so dependent on him. Dusty's opinion meant more to her than almost anyone else's in the village. She didn't want him to think of her as a loser, although after that scene with Linda last night it was a little late to hope for anything close to respect from him.

She frowned when she realized they were in the parking lot of a bank, not the shopping mall as they'd planned. "How long will you be inside?" There was a Tim Hortons coffee shop across the street. Maybe she had time to pick up a couple of beverages.

Dusty released his seat belt. "I need you to come with me."

She stilled. "Why?" Uh-oh. If his sigh was anything to go by, she wasn't going to like his answer, and the last thing they needed was more stuff to fight about.

He draped his hands over the steering wheel and stared out the windshield. "We need to open a joint bank account. It's the easiest way for us to pay the bills."

She turned the idea over. "No."

"It's just so there's money for food and…stuff. Whatever you need."

She burrowed down in her seat.

"Look." He finally turned to look at her. "I've got extra money right now to spend on the things we need for the house. You shouldn't have to pay for repairs on my house, but you'll probably be picking stuff up from time to time. And we have to buy food. I'm sure I eat the lion's share of that. I'm just being practical. Don't make this harder than it has to be."

She clenched her teeth, willing away the ball of emotion stuck in her throat. She had no idea how to handle his casual generosity. Didn't know if she wanted to handle it. "I've always taken care of myself."

She felt the comforting weight of his hand on her head before he ran his fingers down through her hair. "I know you have. You're amazing, how you always hold it together. But for now, this is the most practical way to cover our living costs. You can put money into the account whenever you want, okay?"

"I can't do it. Sorry." It was bad enough she had to move into his house like some kind of homeless woman. Her pride was still smarting from the shift of being independent to relying on Dusty's good-will for a roof over her and her babies' heads. Her stomach had been queasy all day, and she didn't think she could entirely blame that on morning sickness.

"Don't take it personally, okay? I need to pay my own way. It's bad enough I'm taking advantage of our friendship and living with you."

He rolled his hand into a fist and tapped it on the steering wheel. "Pretty hard not to take that personally. I'm not good enough for you?"

She covered his hand with hers. "I don't mean to hurt you, but I'm not budging on this. I need to maintain some control over my life. I'm not taking money from you."

He gave a curt nod and backed out of the parking spot. "Have it your way.

"Remember the winter we were all into sliding on old man MacEachern's hill, and I broke my Ziffy-Whomper sled?" he asked after driving a couple of blocks. "And even though you really wanted to be in the final race, you loaned me yours?"

Teressa smiled. "You won, too. I didn't have a chance. I was too much of a lightweight."

"You might have won. My point is, you let me use your sled, and I accepted your help."

"It's not the same. We were kids."

"Okay, two years ago. Remember Tania-with-an-*i?*"

Teressa rolled her eyes. "Who could forget her?"

"I went out with her once, and she thought…I

don't know. That I was going to marry her. And you walked into the café with Sarah and Brendon and shoved Brendon into my arms and said something like, *'Here's your daddy.'*" He laughed. "I never saw Tania-with-an-*i* again."

Teressa scowled out the window. Was she another Tania-with-an-*i,* hanging on to Dusty when he wanted to be free?

"You don't remember?" Dusty glanced at her.

"I remember."

"What's wrong?"

"You *dated* me once, too."

"Come on. There's no comparison. You're Teressa."

"What's that mean?"

"Well, you're…you're a friend, for one thing."

What every woman who took one look at Dusty and his muscles and blue eyes and blond hair wanted to be—a friend.

Dusty was doing what came naturally to him, being a good guy. How long before he started to resent her and the children? Started? Boy was she in la-la land. He had to have resented her the minute he found out she was pregnant.

"My point is," he persisted, "friends help friends."

"I got your point, Dusty. I'm not taking your money. But thank you," she added after a minute.

They drove the rest of the way to the mall in silence and went straight to the appliance section of a large department store. She headed to the back of the display, where they kept last years' models, but Dusty caught her hand in his and tugged her toward the front. "I like the flat-tops," he said.

"They're more expensive."

"The old ones are harder to keep clean. Pick one of these." He pointed to a line of midrange stoves.

Hmm. She ran her fingertips over the smooth ceramic top, tapped out a tune on the digital keypad. Against her will, a little thrill ran through her. She'd never owned a brand-new anything before. Deciding to get serious, she took her time examining each one and questioning the salesclerk. After the first ten minutes, Dusty wandered over to the flat-screen televisions, but she refused to make a decision without him at least looking at what she thought was the best buy. They ended up buying a stove, a refrigerator, a dryer and a bunk-bed set. He'd just bought a new washer and dishwasher in the summer. Against her protests—What did he need a second flat screen TV for? He had a gigantic one at home—he bought a smaller flat screen. She justified the purchases as things Dusty needed or wanted for his house anyway. Except for the bunk beds, but every house could use a set, right? And if she moved out, she'd buy them from him. Not that she mentioned her plan.

"I'm starving." Dusty rubbed his stomach as they exited the store.

"I could eat. The question is where?" She looked around the food court attached to the mall. Nothing appealed to her.

"There's a microbrewery over on Staples that's supposed to serve good pub food."

She raised an eyebrow, but didn't say anything.

He frowned at her and stuffed his hands in his jacket pockets. "Right. No drinking. I forgot. Okay," he said after a minute, "how about the new Thai restaurant on the waterfront? You like Thai food?"

She loved Thai food, but all the restaurants on the waterfront were expensive. She hunched her shoulders. "I'm not in the mood for an upscale dining experience tonight."

He sent her a sideways glance. "Don't suppose you'd let me take my friend out to dinner?"

Her stomach cramped with tension. Living with Dusty wasn't going to work. She didn't want to be taken care of. If she had to be in a relationship, she wanted to be an equal partner.

"Pizza it is, then," he said when she remained silent.

"I'm not trying to be difficult," she said as they pulled out of the parking lot.

"Right." By his tense reply she could tell he was fed up. Who could blame him? He'd been a goddamn prince.

"Would you feel comfortable if a woman paid all your expenses and let you move into her house?"

He huffed out a laugh. "I wish."

"Really?"

He stopped at the red light and looked over at her. "I get your point. You don't want anything from me."

She lowered her chin. "That's not it, either."

"Then what the hell is your problem?" A car beeped behind them, and he drove through the intersection.

"My problem is I'll never be able to pay you back, because for the next twenty years or so, all my extra money will go to raising my children," she yelled. "And I can't stand things not being equal between us. I want to be my own woman, live in my own house and pay my own bills."

"Fine." He pulled into the restaurant parking lot and jerked on the emergency brake after turning off the truck. "You can start by paying for the pizza tonight, and I want an eighteen-inch." He climbed out and walked into the pizzeria, leaving her sitting alone in the dark.

She stared out the windshield. That went well. Not. She had to get a grip. She wasn't the only one making a huge adjustment. Dusty's life had been turned upside down, as well. Truth was he was taking the harder hit of the two. She had to lighten up, and she had to start thinking of him. She slipped out of the truck. After they ate, she knew exactly what she needed to do.

"I hope you didn't order anchovies." She slipped into the booth across the table from him.

"Pepperoni, green peppers, mushrooms and black olives," he said.

She grinned. "You remembered."

"No, that was for me. What did you want?"

"Ha-ha." She opened the menu. "I might order a salad, too. I haven't eaten anything green today."

"You threw out the last of Adam's pea soup?"

"Oh, gag. Don't remind me." Adam had discovered pea soup, and in his enthusiasm had made far more than any living soul could consume in a lifetime. Every time she turned around, pea soup kept showing up as the lunch special. "Truth is, I did throw it out."

"No way. He thinks it got eaten. He even said he thought he should make another batch."

Teressa laughed. "I know. I didn't want to tell him I raided the freezer and chucked the last twenty gallons out, but I may have to if he insists on making more."

Dusty leaned back in his seat. "You two work together well, don't you?"

The waitress brought the water and coffee Dusty had ordered, and Teressa ordered a garden salad.

"Yes, we do," she answered when the waitress left. "I like Adam a lot. Your sister is a lucky woman."

"Yeah." He looked out the window as if the cars driving by were far more interesting than anything she had to say. No surprise he found her a boring dinner date. She spent most of her time divided between barking out orders in the café kitchen and playing with her kids.

"I have one more store I need to go to before we do the grocery shopping."

"Sure. Anything you need."

The food arrived, and they busied themselves with filling their plates and eating the first piece of pizza without talking. The longer Dusty remained silent, the more Teressa fidgeted. It had always been so easy to talk to him before. She'd never have imagined they'd run out of things to talk about.

Desperately, she searched for something they could discuss. "We need to figure out the bedrooms. I guess we can put the kids together for a while longer, and I'll take the smallest bedroom. My bed should fit into it."

His face closed down even more. "If that's what you want."

"I need to get the kids settled as soon as possible," she explained. "They need to have their toys and books and things around them."

"We can clean out one of the bedrooms tonight and set it up for them," he offered.

"We'll put all the stuff from that room into the

small bedroom. I'll sleep on the couch in the living room, and you can have your bed back."

When he got a stubborn look on his face, she put up her hand. "You're fishing, Dusty. You need your sleep."

"You're working at the café and looking after your children. You need yours."

"Fine." She picked a green pepper off her pizza. "When you get up, I'll crawl into your bed and catch another few hours of sleep." She shivered, thinking of how delicious it would feel to crawl into Dusty's still-warm bed.

"We'll get that second bedroom cleaned out as soon as we can. Most of the stuff is from the kitchen and living room because we were going to tackle those rooms first."

"I still think that's a good idea. We need a common living area."

He took another piece of pizza. "Starting tomorrow Josh is going to be working on the house during the day. I thought he should begin with the flooring, but if you need him to work on something else, just let him know when he arrives."

"I think the flooring is as good a place as any to start." She bit her tongue. She made his place sound like a total disaster area. Which it was, but still… "I need to find a babysitter for the kids after school."

She watched as Dusty's eyes followed a waitress

who was carrying a tray full of glasses of beer. Right. Not hard to tell what his priorities were.

"I'm sorry." He turned to her. "What did you say?"

"I need a babysitter for the children after school," she snapped. "Linda used to pick them up from school and watch them until I finished work."

"I usually get in around four, but I'm going to be pretty busy working on the house."

Tears ambushed her for the hundredth time that day. She didn't remember feeling this emotional when she was pregnant with Sarah or Brendon, and heaven knew her life had been a mess then, too, but for different reasons. She wasn't turning into a drama queen, was she?

Feeling suddenly overwhelmed with the amount of details she had to sort out, she tossed her napkin on the table. "Let's go."

Dusty frowned. "But…we haven't finished eating."

"I want to go home."

He sucked in his lips and signaled the waitress. What was it about him that undermined her defenses? She was a reasonably nice person to most people, but with Dusty she'd never been able to hide her feelings.

He leaned across the table. "Did I do something wrong?"

"No," she wailed. "I'm sorry. Blame it on my unstable hormones."

"Oh." He sat back. "So, do those hormones flip around like that for the whole pregnancy?"

"Yes."

"Right." He sighed and looked toward the table that had ordered all the beer. "Carmen's home. She called the other day. She's looking for something to do while she's here. She'd be good with the kids."

Carmen Sheldrick. She'd always had a crush on Dusty. She was what? Twenty-five now? Tall, slender and firm of body likely. God, Teressa thought to herself. She was turning into a bitch. She had no right to be jealous.

"What's she doing home?"

"I dunno. Didn't she study something to do with working with kids? Early child…something or other. She told me, but I forget. You should give her a call." He pulled out his cell phone and started scrolling. "I've got her cell number somewhere."

Of course he did. Carmen would make sure he had her number. Teressa dug in her wallet for her only twenty and laid it on the table. When Dusty handed her his phone, she concentrated on what she'd say to Carmen, thankful that Dusty decided to go to the men's room at the same time.

"Dusty! I knew you'd call."

Teressa made a face at the phone. Did Carmen have to sound so smug? "Actually, it's Teressa Wilder."

She could almost hear Carmen shifting gears. "Oh. Dusty's name came up on the call display."

"That's because I'm using his phone." Carmen would have gotten there sooner or later, but Teressa wanted to get the call over with before Dusty returned. "I wanted to run something by you."

Carmen was delighted to look after Sarah and Brendon for the few weeks she planned to be home, but she warned Teressa as soon as she got a proper job in the city she'd be leaving. She was not quite as enthusiastic when she learned Teressa was living at Dusty's.

What Dusty and Carmen got up to was none of Teressa's business. Or was it? Certainly, no one would fault her for complaining if Dusty started flirting with another woman. Strange. She'd never felt territorial about Dusty before, probably because there hadn't been much point. She'd been stuck in baby-land, and he'd always looked as if he was enjoying the full benefits of bachelorhood.

Everyone would soon know the only reason they were together was because she was pregnant. And if she wasn't pregnant, they wouldn't be together, right? Or would they? Things had certainly heated up between them in the past couple of months, and they'd been enjoying each other's company more frequently, almost as if they were a couple. It would have been interesting to see where their relationship would have gone if she hadn't gotten pregnant.

Hoping to outrun her stupid thoughts, she stood and strode to the door to wait for Dusty. A minute later, he appeared by their table and frowned as he looked around the room for her. Her breath caught when his gaze landed on her, and his face lit up. She might be pregnant and twenty-eight and a little saggy, but there was still something between them. She'd hang on to that thought for now.

Although it went against her common sense to spend good money on lingerie for herself, she was determined to do something to please Dusty. Their relationship couldn't all be about her. She had to give a little, too.

DUSTY WAS SURPRISED when Teressa insisted on visiting a lingerie store after the grocery shopping. They stashed the groceries in an insulated box in the back of his truck. Often when he was in town, he ended up staying the night and needed to lock things up.

He almost told Teressa they should skip the lingerie shopping because she looked so tired, but he couldn't resist the thought of her wearing bits of lace under her usual shirts and jeans. He'd noticed that her beautiful breasts already looked a tad fuller. Her stomach was still flat, but it wouldn't be long before she started to show. Because his baby was growing inside her. A wave of emotion he couldn't identify—panic?—gripped him by the throat. He wasn't used to dealing with…stuff. Feelings. Sure, sometimes he felt sad. Mostly happy, though, because face it, he had a pretty good life. He loved his work and loved his family, and if there were times when he felt a little lonely, well, that was what friends were for, right?

Life had been pretty much on an even keel for him for a long time until a few months ago when Pops's heart attack had rocked his world. Then Sylvie moved home with a whole load of baggage that made him and Cal and Pops face the truth about his mom's death. Adam showed up at the same time that Teressa started dating a guy who'd been hanging around on vacation. Man, he'd hated that guy. He shouldn't have gotten so drunk, though, and tried to punch out the guy's lights. Especially in front of the kids. He'd never handled her dating other guys too well, but hadn't looked too hard for the reason why the thought of her with another man bothered him.

And now, this. More change. Scary change. But okay, too, in a way, because it was with Teressa, and despite all the stuff going on, he believed he and Tee would find a way to make everything work. Maybe not in a traditional way, but they respected each other enough that good things could happen. They just had to find a way that worked for them.

"So." He cleared his throat. "Do I get to go with you to the store?"

"No. Yes. Do you want to?"

He glanced at her sideways and smiled. "What do you think?"

"Don't."

"What?"

"Flirt with me."

"I love flirting with you." His smile spread.

"Dusty!"

"What?" He pulled into a parking spot, killed the engine and draped his arm along the back of the seat. He was tired of tiptoeing around his attraction to her. He couldn't stop thinking about kissing her the other night, and he wanted to kiss her again. Now. And later. And do other things, too.

"You promised we'd take things slowly."

He slipped his hand from the back of the seat into the hair at the back of her neck. "We're going into a store to buy you sexy underwear. I'm just trying to get us in the mood."

"This is a bad idea."

He shifted closer until his mouth hovered next to hers. "It's a great idea. One of my best." She smelled good enough to eat. Spicy, like cinnamon.

"Dusty?"

"Hmm?" He dropped a kiss on her jawline, followed it to her ear and found the sensitive spot below her ear he knew drove her crazy. He smiled to himself when he heard her hiss out a breath.

"Just one kiss, Tee, and then I'll behave myself." He slipped his hand inside her open jacket. She shifted sideways until her breast brushed against his hand. Not needing any more encouragement, he took the full weight of her breast in his hand and flicked his thumb over her nipple.

Teressa slid her hands around his neck and pulled his mouth to hers. She kissed him as though she'd been waiting for him forever. He moaned into her mouth and dropped his hands to her hips to pick her up and put her in his lap. He cursed when his elbow hit the steering wheel, reminding him where they were.

"Holy mackerel, Teressa." He pulled away from her, and then went back for a quick taste. "Where did that come from?"

She buried her face in the folds of his jacket.

"You okay?"

"A little embarrassed," she said into his chest.

"Of what?"

"Of attacking you."

He huffed out a laugh. "I've got a hard-on that's probably not going away until I...whatever. I got the dibs on being embarrassed around here."

She peeked up at him. "You're not upset?"

"You can attack me anytime you want. I'm good with that." He grinned. "I am curious, though. You're kind of running hot and cold." He sat up straighter. "That's hormones, too?"

"Yup."

"You get horny when you're pregnant?"

When Teressa pulled away from him and sat on her side of the cab, his arms felt empty. "I wouldn't put it quite like that."

"How would you put it, 'cause it felt like you were really into me for a minute."

She straightened the front of her jacket, flipped her hair over her shoulder and finger-combed the long strands into place. "I get…urges. Strong urges."

His grin spread across his face. "Really? I've heard of women eating lots of ice cream and stuff, but I've never heard about pregnant women feeling hot."

"Stop it." She swatted his arm. Guess the wave of hormones had crested. "It's not a joke. It's embarrassing. And FYI, if you tell anyone about this, I'll never forgive you."

"On one condition." He knew he should wipe the stupid grin off his face, but he was having too much fun.

"What?" she asked suspiciously.

"Let me know when those hormones of yours get the upper hand. I'd be more than happy to help you out."

"Everything's a game to you, isn't it?" She jerked open the door.

He immediately sobered. As usual, he'd pushed too far. "Sorry. I was just…trying to have a bit of fun."

She looked at his crotch. "Are you decent enough to come into the store?"

He climbed out of the truck and adjusted the front of his jeans before pulling his coat closed. "I'm as decent as I'm going to get."

And that was probably the crux of his and Teressa's problems right there. He wasn't good enough for Teressa and her children. She needed someone serious about life who would take care of her. He could barely take care of himself.

He followed her into the mall, blinking at the bright lights when they entered. He hated shopping, but it hadn't been too bad tonight with Teressa. Strange, he'd never looked at it that way before, but he almost always felt good when he was with her. Not so much when she was mad at him, which happened more than he liked. So maybe he should smarten up and stop tormenting her. Make an effort to be more considerate.

"If you're uncomfortable with me going in with you, I can meet you later." There. See? He could play nice. He was dying to go into the lingerie store with Teressa, although she probably wouldn't let him watch her try on any outfits or model anything for him.

"I'm not uncomfortable, but you might be. It's a very…feminine place."

"I've been in there before. I don't mind it."

Teressa sent him a sour look. Crap. Would he ever learn to keep his mouth closed?

"Just once," he added. And winced.

"Do what you want." Teressa flounced into the store, leaving him on his own.

What he wanted was to down three cold beers in a row, but he was almost certain that wasn't what she'd meant. For sure he didn't feel like going in the store now, which probably meant that was what he should do. Or maybe not. A guy hanging around a lingerie store probably made women nervous. Or something.

He sat on a bench outside the store, crossed his arms and closed his eyes. He should have told Teressa his favorite color was black—when it came to lingerie, that was. Imagining her wearing nothing but a couple of scraps of black lace was not a good idea. Not in public. He couldn't believe she'd agreed to go along with his suggestion.

He shifted on the bench. Was she interested in pursuing the physical part of their relationship? Or… This was the kind of stuff that drove him nuts. In a lot of ways, he didn't understand her, but in other ways he totally got her. Women generally mystified him, but the stakes always felt higher when it came to not understanding Teressa.

He'd been so ambushed by everything that had happened in the past forty-eight hours, he hadn't had a second to think about how *he* felt about the changes happening in his life. If he was being honest, he had to admit he didn't look forward to going home to a crowded house at the end of a long hard day of working on the water. With so many people helping with the renos on the house it felt as though his life had been ripped wide open for everyone to look at and discuss.

Not that he had anything to hide. As a matter of fact, his life seemed to be so…ordinary there wasn't much to talk about. When had he slowed down? Used to be if anyone was looking for excitement they'd give him a call, because he always had something on the go. But somehow the entire summer had passed without him even going out on a date, let alone chasing after some harebrained idea. Whatever happened to buying a small seaplane or, even better, one of those islands for sale farther up in the bay? And now it was too late. He was going to be a father and had responsibilities and couldn't afford anything like that.

He hunched over on the bench, feeling as though someone had punched him in the gut. He was scared shitless, and he hadn't even realized it until now. He needed…needed—

"You look green around the gills, sailor." Teressa stood in front of him. "Guess what I'm wearing." She wiggled her eyebrows up and down.

He took a calming breath and hooked a finger

through her belt loop and pulled her close enough to stand between his legs. "Euclid."

"What?"

"Our baby. If it's a boy, let's call it Euclid."

She giggled. "No."

His tense muscles relaxed, and he grinned. He didn't hear her giggle often enough. "Euclid doesn't work for you, huh?"

Her brown eyes sparked at him. "No. Sorry. Let's go."

"You going to show me what you're wearing?"

"Not a chance, sailor."

He hadn't thought so. Didn't mean he couldn't imagine what she looked like in her new lingerie, though.

Teressa slipped her hand in his as they walked out of the mall, her bag of lingerie swinging in her other hand. "Every woman should buy something sexy for themselves once in a while. You wouldn't believe how great it makes me feel, knowing what I'm wearing underneath. Thanks, Dusty." She raised up on her tiptoes and kissed him on the cheek when they reached the truck. "I'd forgotten how much fun you can be."

He pointed the truck in the direction of home, feeling a hundred percent better than he had in the mall. He just had to keep reminding himself *who* he was having a baby with. He couldn't imagine a time when he wouldn't want to be with Teressa.

Well, okay he could. Like when she was mad at him or in an ornery mood. But generally, he really liked hanging out with her.

"When are you going to put on a fashion show for me?" She'd acted like a young, carefree girl in the mall, and it made him realize for all her responsibilities and grown-up ways, Teressa was still a young woman.

"Never."

"Seriously?"

She shrugged her shoulders. "I don't know. If I parade around in front of you in my new underwear, you're going to get all hot and bothered."

"I do know how to control myself."

She looked at him from the corner of her eye, as if she was uncertain of herself, or of them. "We're supposed to be taking things slow, remember?"

He grabbed her hand and squeezed it. "We will. I promise. I'm just yanking your chain."

He settled in for the hour-long drive home as Teressa closed her eyes and nodded off to sleep. He usually hated driving home in the dark, but with Teressa beside him, it kind of felt cozy in the truck. And it hadn't escaped his notice that he'd gone from extremely freaked out in the mall to having fun with her teasing him. When they were good together, they were really good.

Too bad there were so many obstacles in their way of having a normal relationship. Him being one of the bigger obstacles, he supposed. Although Teressa was a handful at times. And then, of course, there were the kids. His good mood dimmed, and he switched the radio to his favorite music station that played the golden oldies. The good old days. What had someone said to him once? *These are the good old days.* It was a strange way of looking at life, but he kind of liked the idea.

AN HOUR LATER, Teressa stretched and opened her eyes when Dusty pulled into Adam's yard. She'd left her minivan at Adam and Sylvie's because she had the car seat and Sarah's booster seat, and it was easier if she drove Sarah and Brendon home.

She climbed down from the truck and turned to Dusty sitting behind the steering wheel. He looked exhausted. "You might as well go home. I'll bring the kids. Don't forget about the groceries."

"Good enough." He backed out only after Adam opened the door of his tiny house.

Teressa told Adam and Sylvie they'd bought groceries and things for the house, but kept shopping for lingerie to herself. She smiled as she gently snugged Brendon into his car seat. That was her and Dusty's secret. She'd had no idea wearing sexy underwear would make her feel so…desirable.

She'd struggled half the way home from the city with a boatload of should-haves. She should have put that money toward the kids' winter jackets.

Should have resisted the sudden desire to indulge. Should have been satisfied with what she had. But she couldn't remember the last time she'd done something for herself, and it was suddenly important that she prove to herself that she was worth spending a few dollars on, too. Besides, what she'd spent tonight wasn't even the price of one child's jacket, let alone two.

She frowned when she pulled into the dark yard. Dusty still hadn't repaired the outside light. Of course, they *had* gone to town right after work. She stared at the house, hoping Dusty would come out to help her.

With a resigned sigh, she woke Sarah and kept her by her side as she struggled to get Brendon out of his car seat. Once Brendon was asleep, he was down for the night. Tears pricked the backs of her eyes as she gathered forty pounds of dead weight and finally stood up with Brendon in her arms. What was wrong with her? She'd hauled half-asleep kids to the house hundreds of times before, and it had never made her feel weepy. Just because Dusty hadn't come out to help didn't mean she got to feel sorry for herself. He was probably busy putting the groceries away and hadn't heard her pull up.

She staggered through the dark yard with the two children and finally made it inside the house. Bags of groceries covered the kitchen counter. "Dusty?"

When he didn't answer she shepherded Sarah

and Brendon into the bedroom and tucked them into Dusty's big bed. What had happened to him?

She went back out to the kitchen and almost cried when she looked at the amount of groceries that needed to be put away. What had they been thinking to buy so much? She had no idea how she was going to pay for her and the kids' share of all that food. On top of that, she'd splurged good money on lingerie. Although she had to admit, wearing the lilac lace set made her feel wonderful. It was such a fine line between putting the needs of others first and depriving yourself of the small things that gave you joy. She'd never been good at keeping a balance, mostly because Linda had always been looking over her shoulder. *Do you really need that new sweater when Sarah needs new gym shoes?* The truth was, sometimes she did, and this was one of those times.

A snore from the vicinity of the couch drew her into the living room. Dusty lay sprawled on the couch sound asleep. He was still wearing the clothes he'd worn that day. His thick eyelashes feathered against his cheeks. God, he looked beautiful. He had a full, generous bottom lip, and she licked her own lips remembering how soft it had felt against hers. The Carson chin reminded her how stubborn he could be at times, and those damned high cheekbones that she loved were part of the reason women always stole a second glance at him, along with his muscled shoulders and tight butt.

"Dusty." She shook his shoulder.

"Yeah?" He batted the air with his hand, as in *go away*.

"I need help with the groceries," she whispered.

"I'll get 'em tomorrow."

"Tomorrow's no good. We have to put them away tonight."

He rolled on his side, turning his back to her. "Put 'em away, then."

She sat back on her haunches and blinked away her tears when he started snoring again. She wasn't being anal. You couldn't leave meat and vegetables out all night, even if it was cool in the house. And mornings were crazy. Dusty was already gone when they got up, which left her alone with two children to get ready for the day. The groceries had to be put away tonight, and it looked as if she was on her own.

So what else was new? She struggled to her feet and returned to the kitchen and started stashing the food into cupboards and the refrigerator. She was tired and knew she was overreacting. The problem was she'd expected more. She had to be careful in the future not to set herself up for disappointment like she had tonight.

Dusty may be a great guy, fun and generous, and even considerate at times, but he had no idea how to act like an adult. And she really, really did not want another child to take care of. She needed more. She needed a *real* man.

She was stuck. Again. For years she'd had to live under her parents' rule, and it looked as though the same thing was happening with Dusty. She could stay, as long as everything was done his way, on his time. She slammed the cupboard door shut. Would she ever own her own place, be her own person, have control over her own life? Ever?

Depending on Dusty was a bitter pill to swallow. In some ways it was much worse than living with her parents. Dusty was her contemporary, and her present living situation played right into the image of "poor Teressa." Damn it. She'd worked hard for so many years so people would see her as successful, because if other people thought that, maybe she'd believe her life wasn't a total failure. Sometimes it felt the harder she tried, the more success eluded her. Pride was such a bitch.

CHAPTER FIVE

EARLY THE NEXT morning Dusty stopped in the middle of pouring his first cup of coffee when he noticed Teressa leaning against the kitchen door frame. She looked cute wearing her fuzzy pink bathrobe. He'd never thought of Teressa as cute before. He saw her as sleek and strong and…forget going down that road.

"Coffee?" He held up the pot.

"Please." She slid into a chair at the table and pulled another chair closer to put her feet up on.

"You're up early. Sorry if I woke you."

She accepted the cup of coffee from him and took a sip. She closed her eyes, took another sip and put the mug down on the table. Dusty smiled to himself. She looked cuddly and still half-asleep.

"You didn't wake me," she said in a husky voice.

"Good." He waited for her to say something else, but when she continued her routine of taking a sip, closing her eyes and taking another sip, he sat and turned his chair so he could look out the window that faced east. Nothing he liked better than watching the sun come up.

After a couple of minutes of silence, he relaxed and drank his coffee, watching the sun crest the horizon. The sky turned a clear blue with only a scattering of light clouds. It was going to be a good day on the water, weather-wise, anyway. So far it had been a good season for lobster, one of his best. It was almost time to haul his traps, but he thought he could push the season another couple of weeks if the weather held. He sure could use the extra coin.

When he finished his coffee, he packed his lunch, which consisted of left-over pizza from last night. Then he turned on one of the front burners on the stove and cracked two eggs into a frying pan.

"Need help?"

"Huh?" He'd almost forgotten Teressa was there. "Thanks. I've got it. I've been doing this routine for so long if someone tried to help, I'd screw it up. Want an egg? Toast?"

"Just coffee's good for now. I'm always slow to wake up."

"I didn't know that about you." If he had to guess, he'd have assumed Teressa was a jump-out-of-bed-and-get-going type of person. He liked to shuffle through the first hour of his day. It was nice that Teressa did, too.

He ate his breakfast, went off to the bathroom to finish getting cleaned up and returned to the kitchen. He smiled when he saw Teressa still sitting, her now empty coffee mug cradled to her chest.

"Want another coffee?" He grabbed his stainless steel travel mug and filled it.

"I do, but I won't. I should probably cut out caffeine all together, but I allow myself one cup in the morning."

He packed up all his stuff and dragged his jacket and boots on. "I've got to go."

She nodded, a faint smile on her lips. "Be careful out there."

"I always am. See ya." He started out the door, but turned back and crossed the kitchen to where she sat and dropped a kiss on her mouth. "Sorry about not helping with the groceries last night. I passed out. Thanks for putting them away. See you tonight."

Dusty didn't feel the cold as keenly as he usually did first thing in the morning. He felt as if he had a little glow inside him, a warm spot like…contentment. It was nice, starting his day with Teressa, partly because for once there were no demands being made on either of them. If it were just him and Teressa, without kids and a baby on the way, living with her might really appeal to him. Somehow, they had to make time for the two of them.

TERESSA WATCHED OVER Sylvie's shoulder as her friend added to the constantly changing mural that covered the back wall of the café. When Sylvie had first arrived home after living away for ten years, she'd painted a mural of the village to brighten up the café, which she'd transformed from a hole-in-the-wall into a place where people enjoyed spending time—and their money.

Teressa hadn't had much say in the changes at the time because Pops still owned the café, but she'd been happy with them all the same. People often parked themselves on the comfy old couch or matching armchair and picked up a book from the stacks Sylvie had randomly piled around the restaurant. She'd even installed a couple of laptops with Wi-Fi, and a corner of books and toys for children. Sarah and Brendon often played there while waiting for her to finish for the day.

"How long do you think it'll take Beanie to notice your newest addition?" She watched her friend magically transform the bare-bones sketch of Dusty's house into a bright, light-filled home with a few strokes of her brush. Beanie, the local plumber, was the one who'd started the game of "what's new in the mural." Soon after completing the painting, Sylvie realized the Hacheys' boat was missing from the local fishing wharf she'd drawn, and quietly added it so they didn't feel offended. Since then, Sylvie had inadvertently become the village's chronicler, and people spent a fair amount of time studying the mural.

Everyone in the village knew she and Sarah and Brendon had moved in with Dusty, but seeing them together in the mural somehow fixed it in people's minds and made the move more real. Personally, Teressa thought Sylvie was being a little too hasty, but a strangely warm feeling threaded through her as she had an odd thought: If things were equal between her and Dusty, if she wasn't homeless and pregnant, how would she feel about moving in with him? Excited?

"Never mind Beanie. I want to see Dusty's face when he sees this. He's always whining that his house doesn't look very nice. Duh." Sylvie grinned over her shoulder. "I told him I paint it as I sees it. I have to say, though, once he makes up his mind to do something, he gives it one hundred percent."

Smiling to herself, Teressa pulled out a chair and sat. They'd decided to close the café at four starting in November as there were precious few visitors at this time of year and most of the locals preferred having supper at home with it turning dark out so early. Normally, she'd hurry home after work, but Carmen had stopped by the café earlier with Sarah and Brendon to ask if she could take them to the beach. The weather had turned unseasonably warm, and she thought they could hunt for sea glass. With the beach only half a block away, Teressa suggested bringing the children back to the café when they were finished.

She'd toyed with the idea of making supper for herself and the children at the café to avoid the chaos at Dusty's house. In the past three days, they'd finished installing the flooring in the main part of the house. With Anita's help, she'd cleared out one of the smaller bedrooms and set up the new bunk beds for the kids. She'd even managed to unpack some of their clothes and toys. Dusty had moved back into his bedroom at her insistence, and she now slept on the couch in the living room.

Dusty had offered that she could sleep in his bed, either alone or with him. He pointed out that it was a king-size bed, and they could both sleep comfortably without bumping into each other. Ha! As if they could share a bed and keep their hands off each other. The first morning, she'd crawled into his bed to catch a few more hours of sleep after he'd left for work, but the sheets still held his body heat and his scent, and the combination had...stimulated her hormones. What little sleep she'd managed to get had left her sweat-soaked and wanting.

The past two mornings she'd gotten up at the same time as he had and they'd shared an almost silent cup of coffee as they watched the sun come up, cracking open a brand-new day. It was the only time during the day that they could be together without anyone asking them for something. No carpenters, no children, no customers. She'd never seen the restful side of Dusty before, and it made her realize it was possible that sometimes she judged him too harshly. She didn't know him as well as she'd thought, and she was pleasantly surprised to find herself enjoying discovering new things that she liked about her old friend.

Since the first morning, Dusty kissed her on his way out the door every morning with a "See you later." Like, she supposed, a husband would kiss his wife. She hadn't been able to stop thinking about those brief kisses. Sometimes the memory made her smile, other times it made her wonder…who did he think he was? Her husband? But the thought wasn't as irritating as it should have been.

"What are you thinking about?" Sylvie put her tube of paint on the table alongside her paintbrush. "You've got a goofy look on your face."

"Nothing," she snapped. She hated goofy. With relief, she spun round when the door of the café opened.

"Anita!" Geez, tone it down, Goofy Girl. She sounded as if she hadn't seen Cal's wife for ages. Anita had stopped by the café that morning on her way to town to ask if Teressa wanted her to pick up some paint chips while she was there.

Anita was beautiful. Period. She looked and dressed like a model, and she made Teressa feel like the country bumpkin she was. Not that Anita did it intentionally—she was bred-in-the-bone class. Cal was a pretty cool guy, but Teressa still wondered what Anita was doing with him after two years of being together.

"I don't believe I've ever seen you wear jeans before," Teressa observed. "Why does everything look so good on you? What's your secret?"

ANITA FINGERED THE ironed crease down the front of her jeans. Cal had had a fit the first time and only time she'd ironed his jeans. Apparently it just wasn't done. But she couldn't not iron her own pair. Wearing jeans was one of her pathetic attempts at trying to fit in. She probably looked as stiff wearing them as the fabric felt against her legs.

"No secret that I'm aware of," she said. "But I think I have the body type that a lot of clothes are designed for these days. That helps, I suppose."

Sylvie spared her a smile before dabbling yellow paint on her mural. Her sister-in-law was turning on the lights in Dusty's house, just as she had in her depiction of Adam's house a few months ago. Anita watched, fascinated. The small paintbrush looked like an extension of Sylvie's hand.

What would it be like to be so amazingly skilled at something? Not only did both Sylvie and Teressa excel at what they did, they exuded a confidence that made Anita want to emulate them. She was turning thirty in a few weeks, and she wasn't good at anything, except hosting formal dinner parties and looking decorative while keeping her mouth shut so she wouldn't embarrass her father. Thank God Cal had come into her life when he had. He'd shown her she didn't have to live in that box if she didn't want to, and she didn't.

"Wonder what your old man would say if he saw you now," Teressa said.

"Teressa!" Sylvie reprimanded.

Teressa glared at Sylvie. "It burns my ass the way her father didn't attend his only daughter's wedding." She turned her glare on Anita. "You've been living here for two years, and he hasn't once come to see you. I'm sorry. I don't mean to upset you, but I don't think people should tiptoe around about what a crappy father he is. Sorry," she added again.

Anita blushed, amazed to realize she was embarrassed for her father, the man who practically wrote the book on etiquette. Teressa wasn't saying anything she herself hadn't thought a hundred times before, but no one had ever stated it so honestly, not even Cal. She waited to feel resentment toward Teressa, but was surprised to find relief. She liked that Teressa cared enough about her to get mad.

Having grown up with a succession of housekeepers when she was on vacation from the expensive boarding schools her father insisted she attend, she didn't have many people in her life who cared about her. There had always been paid professionals to attend to her needs, but never anyone who cared just because. Until Cal. And now his family and friends.

"It's probably better he doesn't visit," Anita assured her. "He can be very critical." When she'd turned eighteen and begged to go to university, she discovered what a formidable opponent her father could be. He agreed to pay her fees at a local university, if she stayed home and acted as his hostess, a role she'd been groomed to fill. She didn't qualify for a student loan because her father made too much money. Not trained for any work beyond a minimum-wage job, she took the coward's way out and agreed to her father's terms. She wasn't strong like Teressa and Sylvie who knew what they wanted and stood their ground. But she wanted to be.

Sylvie studied her. "Your mom's dead, right?"

"Yes." Until recently, Sylvie had lived in Toronto, and she and her sister-in-law hadn't had much opportunity to become acquainted.

"Mine, too. I imagine Cal told you about that. How did yours die?"

Anita swallowed the lump that always blocked her throat when people asked her about her mother. According to her father, Anita had killed her mother.

"She died giving birth to me."

Sylvie rubbed her hand over Anita's shoulder and gave it a reassuring squeeze.

"How sad," Teressa said. "Are you and Cal planning to have kids?"

She avoided their interested stares. "He wants to wait." *Forever.* She needed to prove to him that she was strong enough to have children, both physically and emotionally.

"I planned to pick out a few paint chips for you to look at when I was in town today, but opted to bring the full charts. I thought it might be more fun that way." She handed the file folder to Teressa, who slid it on the table beside her and stood. *Please drop the baby talk.* Her heart broke every time she thought of the beautiful babies she and Cal might never have.

"First you've got to test drive a piece of coffee cake I made from a new recipe. I used maple syrup instead of sugar, and I'm not sure of the texture," Teressa said.

Resigned, Anita sat at the table as Teressa disappeared into the kitchen. Anita had lost a lot of weight after the miscarriage, and although she'd gained back a few pounds, it felt as if the entire village was conspiring to fatten her up. Once she realized their concern, she'd made a concentrated effort to gain a few pounds because she didn't want to worry anyone. She didn't have much of a sweet tooth, but Teressa was an excellent cook, and the cake was sure to taste delicious.

"Have you been up to Dusty's house lately?" Sylvie asked quietly.

"Yesterday. He wanted to know which bathroom fixtures looked best."

Sylvie dropped her brush into a jar of water. "What did Teressa think?"

"I'm not sure. Dusty said she didn't care one way or the other. He seemed confused," she added.

Sylvie gave her a tight smile. "I think we have to do an intervention with Teressa. She should be making more decisions about the house. I thought she'd love doing that, you know?"

"Who'd love doing what?" Teressa asked, emerging from the kitchen with a loaded tray.

Anita edged back from the table. All she'd wanted to do was drop off some paint chips and spend a few minutes chatting about inconsequential things, like the weather. That was the problem with stepping outside her comfort zone—things came up she wasn't prepared to deal with. But she wanted these two women to be her friends, and if that meant extending herself beyond her normal, polite boundaries, so be it.

She fixed a smile on her face. "We thought you'd love picking out colors for the house."

Sylvie shoved the file of paint chips in front of Teressa. "What color do you want for the kitchen?"

Teressa ignored the file as she placed a full dessert plate in front of each of them. "I haven't thought about it."

"Well, think about it now." Sylvie flipped the file folder open.

Without looking at it, Teressa turned to Anita. "What do you think?"

"Umm…." She stabbed a small piece of cake with her fork and ate it. "The cake's delicious."

"I meant what color do you think we should paint the kitchen?"

"Good dodge, Anita." Sylvie glared at Teressa. "It's your kitchen, not hers. What color do you want?"

Anita put down her fork as Teressa got a mutinous look on her face. Maybe she should leave. She'd never been good at handling conflict. She pushed back from the table.

Sylvie narrowed her eyes at her. "Don't even think about it. If you leave me alone with her, I might have to kill her, and it'll be on your head."

Anita opened her mouth to make a polite protest, but giggled instead. Giggling, according to her father, was an unforgivable social gaffe that rivaled farting or burping. Both women stared at her before they started giggling at the same time. Pleased, Anita grinned and had another bite of cake.

Teressa pulled the file in front of her and flipped through several pages before stopping at the golds and yellows. "What do you think of this color?" She pointed at a dark gold.

Anita tried not to grimace. She glanced at Sylvie

for the go-ahead to offer her opinion. "Gold is a lovely idea for the living room. What about this one?" She pointed to a much lighter tone.

Teressa smirked. "I was thinking of the kitchen, but okay."

"I'm so sorry," Anita apologized.

"She's yanking your chain." Sylvie laughed.

She'd suspected as much, although understanding people's sense of humor had never been her strong suit. When she wasn't certain she was reading the situation clearly, she defaulted to her polite mode.

Cal hated it when she did that and often pushed her to speak her mind. It was the exact opposite of what she'd been taught, which was to listen carefully and give the person what you thought they wanted to hear. Speak your own mind? That took a boldness and certainty she'd yet to cultivate, but she was willing to try.

"Dusty said something about oak doors for the kitchen cabinets," Sylvie continued. "Gold or yellow would be too close to the same color. You have to pick something that contrasts. Right, Anita?"

"Since when did you become the expert?" Teressa flipped through more sheets of color.

"Gee, I don't know. Since I first picked up a paintbrush and started fooling around with paint?"

Anita glanced at Teressa, expecting her to be angry, but Sylvie's words seemed to roll off her like water off a duck's back. How did they do that? Anita would have been crushed if Sylvie talked to her that way.

"I don't care. Let's paint it all white. Can't go wrong that way." Teressa flipped the folder closed and shoved it away from her.

Anita pulled the folder back and opened it to the white/beige page. "You're right. I think beige would work well in the kitchen. And there are so many different shades and tones to choose from."

Teressa looked at Sylvie and laughed. "She actually sounds excited."

"Of course I'm excited, and you should be, too," Anita agreed. "It's your home."

"It's Dusty's home. We're just… I don't know. Visiting?"

Anita leaned forward and covered Teressa's hand with hers. "I know exactly what you mean. I felt the same way when I first moved in with Cal. The Carson family is so much a part of Collina." She turned to Sylvie. "Forgive me. I'm not being rude, but you and your brothers—you're so certain of who you are and where you belong. It can be a little overwhelming."

Sylvie picked up her brush again and wiped it clean with a rag. "Teressa's known us forever. She's practically part of the family."

"But she's not," Anita pointed out. "Yet."

Teressa sighed. "So what you're saying is I have

to make a space for myself. Invest part of myself in the house. Even if it's not my home."

"Exactly." Anita beamed, pleased she understood. "Decorating can be fun."

Teressa pulled the file of paint chips in front of her again. "I suppose it's not fair to leave all the decisions to Dusty." She closed her eyes. "Trying to visualize here. Red's probably not a good color for the bathroom?"

"No," Anita agreed gently.

"Bedroom?"

"No red."

Teressa's lips twitched as she pointed at one of the beige hues, her eyes still closed. "Am I getting close?"

Anita tried not to laugh and encourage Teressa's silliness. Because there was something, a feeling, just out of sight, as she goofed around. If Anita didn't know better, she'd think Teressa was afraid, which was ridiculous because she was one of the most fearless women she knew. Wasn't she?

"You know, I think that color may actually work."

Teressa's eyes flew open. "Which one?"

"This one, and see how it has the faintest hint of yellow? That will reflect the gold of the living room."

"Okay." Teressa flipped over several sheets until she came to the blue/green page. "Bedrooms. Sure I can't have red for Dusty's?"

"Well, he did say something about painting it purple, and that's close to red, I suppose."

"Purple?" Teressa sputtered. "No way. You can't paint a bedroom purple. It would look like a bordello. Isn't that just like a man."

Anita grinned. "I'm just yanking your chain."

Sylvie stopped painting and turned around. Oh, dear. Sylvie and Teressa were staring at her as if she was the worst kind of idiot in the world. What had she been thinking to try to make a joke? She was hopeless at light repartee.

Sylvie started laughing first. Teressa joined in a second later with her lovely, deep laugh. A giggle bubbled out of Anita, and suddenly she was laughing so hard, the muscles in her face hurt.

She was wearing jeans, and she'd made a joke that her friends were laughing at. She could do this. She could change and grow into someone Cal could fall in love with again.

When she'd finally admitted to Cal that she'd had a miscarriage, their marriage had been damaged almost beyond repair. She hadn't even told him she was pregnant to begin with. They hadn't been trying for a child, because Cal had said he wanted to wait another two years. She'd been paralyzed with fear that Cal would leave her when he found out she was pregnant. Her father often withdrew his attention when she went against his wishes and isolated her emotionally. So she shut down and didn't tell

Cal about the pregnancy or the miscarriage. When Cal begged her to tell him what was going on, and she finally confessed, his reaction had been the opposite of what she'd expected. Instead of pushing her away, he'd hovered over her, as if he were her guardian angel and no harm could come to her as long as he was by her side.

Two years ago, she could have tolerated his overprotective behavior, but she'd changed. She wanted to have what Sylvie and Teressa had, a man who loved her not because she was weak and needed him, but because she was strong, and he needed her as much as she needed him. She wanted them to have a normal life, to have children, be involved with the community and have close friends and family. All the things that had been missing in her life before she met Cal.

DUSTY PULLED INTO his driveway and parked behind Teressa's minivan. It probably wasn't a good thing that he was less than thrilled she was home. The past couple of days she and the kids had hung out at the café after hours doing whatever. He'd come home to an almost empty house, and man, he hated to admit it, but everything had been so much easier without any of them underfoot.

All he wanted to do right now was have a shower and crash for an hour or two. He'd been working sixteen-hour days the past week, and the house was starting to shape up. They had a long way to go yet, but it was no longer the bare shell of a house he'd brought Teressa and the kids to a week ago.

The house was the only thing that had improved, though. The best part of his day was first thing in the morning when he and Teressa had their coffee before he left to go fishing. Thank God she wasn't a morning person. He liked that they had their coffee together and watched the sun come up and didn't talk. That was okay, wasn't it? Not talking? She seemed as happy as he was with the silence.

Because if they talked, they'd have to discuss not only the progress on the house, which he was sick of thinking about, but also their relationship. Their problems. He got a headache thinking about everything they needed to hash out.

Instead, he spent most of his time wondering what she had on under her fuzzy pink housecoat that covered her from her chin down to her toes. A couple of times it had gaped open, and he'd caught the flash of a shapely white thigh before she flicked it closed again. Whatever kind of nightie she wore, it was short and skimpy.

He rested his head on the steering wheel. Man, he'd love to walk into the house and have her throw her arms around his neck and plant a big, fat, juicy kiss on him. Or even a little kiss. They'd had fun flirting with each other before she moved in, but now it felt as if she was almost afraid to make eye contact. Never mind full-body contact.

He kept telling himself it was early days yet. Teressa and the kids needed more time to settle, and he did, too. He just had to be patient. Things were bound to work out some day. Right?

"Hey, Josh. How'd it go today?" he called from the open truck window when Josh exited the house.

His first mate closed the house door behind him and tromped down the porch steps. "I'd rather be on the water in weather like this."

"Yeah. Sorry about that. It's made a big difference having you work on the house, though."

He missed having Josh on the boat, because he was in good shape and smart enough that Dusty didn't have to tell him every little thing to do, like he did with Andy, his other helper. Josh could think for himself and had some experience with carpentry, which was why Dusty had asked him to work on the house. He couldn't be in two places at once and needed someone reliable to fill in for him.

"I could run the boat, too, you know. And you could stay home and work on the house."

"No!" Dusty cleared his throat, embarrassed that he'd almost shouted the word. "No," he continued in a calmer voice. "Too many things can go wrong on the water. You know that. I feel better captaining my own boat."

It had been hard enough last Sunday when he'd

tried to get some work done on the house with Teressa and the kids underfoot. Sarah had followed him around like a lost puppy. He'd had to invent a reason to go down to the boat for an hour just to get a decent breath of air. And do some fast talking to get out of taking the kids with him. It wasn't that he didn't like spending time with them, but give a guy a break.

Josh grinned. "I bet you do. Well, have fun, boss. I'm off to the legion for a few cold ones. I'll think of you as that ice-cold beer is sliding down my throat." He laughed as he made his way to his truck.

He loved living in Collina, couldn't imagine living anywhere else. But sometimes everyone knowing his business got a little old. Dusty sighed, got out of the truck and strode up to the house, but stopped outside the door. Teressa was yelling at one of the kids. Brendon, probably. He could hear the boy's piercing whine that usually preceded a full-out crying jag. He didn't remember crying like that as a kid. Then again, he didn't remember *any* kid crying that hard. Ever.

Wasn't this rich? Here he was, standing on his own doorstep, afraid to go inside. Maybe he was approaching the whole situation wrong. There had to be some way he could make everything better. He needed to look at their situation the same way he did when his boat motor acted up. Take it apart, change a couple of filters and put it back together again.

A mouthwatering smell greeted him when he finally stepped inside the house. Teressa had been outdoing herself lately with the suppers she cooked for them. She glanced at him from the kitchen, a harried look on her face. "Sorry about the noise. I blew up at Brendon. Sorry."

Dusty shoved his lunchbox on the counter. "I heard." He had to be just about the most selfish person alive. As tired as he felt, she looked far more exhausted.

She needed her own bed, her own bedroom. What was it she'd asked for? Fifteen minutes to herself. She hadn't had five minutes since she and the kids had moved in. See? Dissect the problem. Teressa was tired, and she needed some time and space to herself.

He walked around the half-finished island and moved close to her. "What's for supper? Smells delicious." He crowded her up against the counter and slid his hands around her waist. "You smell delicious."

"Dusty." She pushed against his shoulder when he nibbled on her earlobe.

"How long before supper?"

"Thirty minutes or so." The tension leaked out of his body as she leaned into him. She felt so good, her curves melding into his angles.

"Here's what we're going to do." Reluctantly, he stepped away from her. "You're going to take a bath. Or go for a walk. Or hide in my room and stare at the wall. I'm going to hang out with the kids. We'll set the table. Put the timer on that thing." He nodded at the stove. "I'll call you when it's ready."

"Really?" She blinked several times, and he saw a tear before she wiped it away.

"Go before I change my mind."

"Thank you."

He glanced at his watch. "Time's a ticking."

She smiled, suddenly looking years younger. "Thanks. Brendon, Sarah, I'm taking a bath. You need anything, ask Dusty. And help him set the table. Both of you," she called over her shoulder as she sped down the hall toward the bathroom after she set the oven timer.

Dusty washed his hands at the kitchen sink in lieu of his usual shower. That wasn't so hard, was it?

"Dusty?" Sarah pulled on the hem of his T-shirt.

He grabbed a towel and dried his hands as he looked down at the little girl. Man, she had a head of hair on her. Teressa should keep it cut short. The kid's curls were all over the place. "Yeah?"

"Brendon's still crying."

Huh. Funny how he'd managed to block that out for a while. "Where is he?"

"Under his bed."

"Why?" He headed toward the kid's bedroom.

"'Cause he's hiding from you."

Dusty skidded to a stop. "Excuse me?"

"He thinks you're scary." She smiled, revealing a missing front tooth. When had she lost that? "I don't."

Dusty took a second look at the tiny girl before he entered the bedroom. Was she *flirting* with him? He was almost certain she'd blinked her eyelashes at him right after she smiled. He knelt and looked under the lower bunk bed. Brendon lay on his stomach, sniffling back tears. "Hey, buddy." Dusty tried a smile. "Wanna come out from there?"

Brendon stuck his thumb in his mouth. "No."

"You like it under there?"

"Yes."

"Okay." Dusty stood and looked around the room. It was too small for two kids, but would have to do for now. He'd looked at the basement last night and wondered how much it would cost to build a bathroom, another bedroom and a family room down there if he did most of the work himself.

"I promised your mom we'd set the table," he said to Sarah, who stood by the bedroom door, watching him. "Let's go do it."

Sarah followed him out of the room. "Are you going to leave Brendon under the bed?"

"He said he likes it there. Here." He handed her four forks.

She stared up at him. "You're weird."

Dusty snorted. "And you're not?"

"I'm not weird," she said in a small voice that sounded suspiciously like a prelude to crying.

"Oh, hey." Dusty squatted down. "I was teasing you. You're not weird. You're my princess." He tweaked her nose and stood, relieved to see her face light up.

"Am I really?"

"Yup. Really." He grabbed four plates, crowded the glasses on top of the plates and put them on the table. Sarah followed him to the table. "Wanna put everything where it belongs, Princess?"

"Okay," she giggled. She continued to stare up at him.

"I meant now, Sarah. I'll get the rest of the stuff."

He picked out the rest of cutlery and napkins and helped Sarah arrange everything on the table. He half listened to her long, convoluted story about a dog and a piece of candy. This wasn't so bad. Teressa was happy for the moment, Sarah certainly sounded happy and Brendon...? Maybe he just liked lying under his bed and wasn't really afraid of him.

"So, we can get one, right?" Sarah beamed up at him.

He eased back a step. "You're doing that thing with your eyelashes. Blinking them."

"So can we?" She grinned at him, fluffed her hair over her shoulder. Sarah, the six-year-old femme fatale.

He opened the oven and inhaled deeply as he slid the casserole out. "Get what?"

Sarah curled her arm around his leg and leaned against him. "A puppy."

He shoved the casserole on the counter before he dropped it. Wow, she was good. He'd have to pay closer attention if he planned to avoid trouble down the road. Like promising to get a puppy because he hadn't been listening to what she was saying.

"No animals, Sarah. You and Brendon are enough."

She hit his leg. "I hate you."

"Guess that means you're not a princess, then, 'cause princesses aren't allowed to hate anyone. And don't hit me. I don't like it." Teressa would probably kill him if she heard him talking to her daughter that way.

When Sarah's bottom lip started trembling, he figured the safest bet was to pretend she wasn't about to cry and carry on with getting supper on the table. He rolled the baked potatoes out of the oven and chucked one on each plate.

"I'm going to get your mother." He escaped out of the kitchen before the dam broke. He called to

Teressa through the locked bathroom door that supper was on the table, dashed into his bedroom and sank down on the edge of his bed. He didn't know how Teressa did it. How did she take care of her kids every day, work full-time and remain sane? No wonder she got grumpy sometimes.

When he heard Teressa come out of the bathroom, he returned to the kitchen. Sarah was sitting at the table. She smiled at him and continued trying to saw her potato into smaller pieces. He guessed she was hungrier than she was upset. He put a spoonful of fish casserole on her plate, and scooped several onto his.

"Want me to cut your potato for you?" Dusty asked Sarah.

"Yes, please."

After cutting up her potato, Dusty sat and shoveled in a mouthful of casserole. He groaned and ate another forkful before attacking his own potato.

"Does it taste good?" Teressa breezed into the kitchen, glowing. Dusty became momentarily distracted by the amount of cleavage she was showing, having left several buttons undone at the top of her blouse. Her lips curved into that secret smile of hers when she caught his gaze.

"Beautiful," he said.

When Teressa and Sarah giggled, the tension from his day evaporated. "Food tastes good, not beautiful, silly," Sarah said.

Dusty winked at her. "The food tastes good, too."

Teressa sat and looked around the table. "Where's Brendon?"

"Under his bed, hiding." Dusty savored another mouthful of fish. "Are these scallops from the freezer?"

"Why is he hiding?"

Aw, hell. He knew things had been going too smoothly. He put down his fork. "He didn't want to come out. You know, I used to pull that cr—stuff all the time when I was a kid. It's nothing."

Teressa narrowed her eyes at him. "What happened when you hid under your bed?"

"Cal would pull me out by the scruff of my neck, kick my…behind and drag me to the table."

"And your father?"

Dusty rested his head in his hands. He'd never hid under his bed, but he'd climbed a lot of trees and hid in their branches. Pops would come out with a chair and sit under the tree and just talk. About his day. Sometimes about his childhood. Sometimes even about Dusty's mother. After a half hour or so, he'd ask Dusty if he was ready to go inside, and he always was, because whatever had upset him didn't seem to matter as much anymore, because Pops loved him and would always be there for him, no matter what.

Brendon, poor little sucker, might as well not have a father for all the face time he got with Stan.

He got to his feet. "I'll talk to him again."

He entered the kids' bedroom, grabbed a couple of pillows from the bed and lay down, putting one pillow under his head. "Want a pillow?" He pushed it under the bed.

"Okay."

The kid sounded so damned forlorn and tiny. "What did you do today?"

"Nothing."

"You hung out with Carmen, right?"

"Yes."

"You like her?"

"Yes."

"I saw a pod of whales today." Whale sightings in the Bay of Fundy weren't all that uncommon, but it was something to talk about. He started telling Brendon what he knew about the whales, which turned out to be a lot more than he realized. At one point he realized the time between his sentences was getting longer and longer, and he was having a hard time remembering what he wanted to say.

It wasn't so bad lying on the floor of the dark room. At least it was quiet, except for the occasional sniffle from Brendon. He closed his eyes and drifted away.

TERESSA STOOD IN the doorway of the bedroom, her knuckles jammed in her mouth, as if she could cork the emotions that threatened to spill out. After the drone of Dusty's voice had stopped, Teressa had given them another few minutes before checking up on them. Dusty was stretched out on the floor beside the bunk bed, sound asleep. Brendon sat beside Dusty, holding one of his huge, work-roughened hands. It was probably the first time in his life he'd held a working man's hand.

Brendon smiled up at her. "He's got lots of boo-boos."

She blinked back a tear. Dusty had always been a hard worker, and now he was almost killing himself to make his house into a home for her. She had to try harder to make things easier for him. And gosh, wouldn't she love to stretch out beside him and rest her head on his chest. But she didn't need fireworks right now. She needed peace and quiet so she could think the way through all the changes coming at her. Fireworks were what got her in this mess to start with.

"Come," she whispered and held out her hand to Brendon. "You need supper, and he needs to sleep."

Brendon got up and put his hand in hers. "I'm going to be a whale when I grow up. Dusty says he's got a pet whale, and it comes and plays with his boat sometimes."

"You can't be a whale because you're my little boy." She tickled him before helping him into his chair at the table. "But you can be a marine biologist and study whales."

"Or a fisherman, just like Dusty."

Just like Dusty. She'd been so busy catching up to her life, had she really taken the time to consider the consequences of her decisions? Dusty was a good man in many ways, but he could also be irresponsible and even selfish sometimes. Did she want her son to grow up to be *just like Dusty?* Did she have a choice?

Until now, it had just been her and the kids. Her mother had had an influence on them, but now that she thought about it, Linda had never encouraged them to dream. While Dusty was full of dreams.

She wasn't sure how she felt about giving up some of the control she had over the children's lives, or about the amount of influence Dusty suddenly seemed to have on Sarah and Brendon. She did know there wasn't much she could do about it at the moment, but she'd keep a closer eye on the situation. She needed to talk to Dusty and make him aware of how impressionable young children were.

CHAPTER SIX

AN HOUR LATER, Teressa put her hands on the small of her back and leaned backward, hoping to work out the kinks. It had been ages since she'd seen Sarah and Brendon so fired up. She'd had to read them three different books before they calmed down enough to go to sleep. Not trusting herself to touch Dusty, she'd let Sarah do the honors of waking him up so they could climb into bed. He'd looked so big and…well, yummy stretched out on the floor. With a grunt, he'd wandered off to the bathroom or bedroom while she tucked the children in.

She hoped he'd gone to bed, because Dusty Carson looked sexy without trying. And when he got that hot look in his eyes…heat rushed through her. Yeah, she should avoid him tonight.

"Any supper left? I'm starving," he asked from behind her.

She spun around, her face red from the lascivious thoughts that had been churning through her head. "Lots. Let me heat it up for you."

"S'okay. I can do it." He took the casserole dish

out of the refrigerator, ladled some onto a plate, shoved it in the microwave and slammed the door shut.

She stood uncertainly in the middle of the kitchen, wanting to stay, but knowing she shouldn't. Was this what her relationship with Dusty had come to? Everything so prickly between them that she avoided him as much as possible? That had never been her intention.

"Thanks for giving me a break tonight. You can't imagine how wonderful it was to soak in the bath without the kids knocking on the door every few minutes."

His gaze dropped from her eyes to her chest, then back up again. "I've been working hard at not imagining exactly that." He gave her a tight smile. "Glad you enjoyed it. I guess I blew it with Brendon again. Sorry. I didn't intend to fall asleep."

She relaxed against the island. "You did something right, because he says he wants to be just like you when he grows up."

Dusty looked stunned. The microwave beeped behind him, but he ignored it. "Why?"

"Because he doesn't have a strong male role model, and until he finds one, he latches on to whoever's around."

"Ah. So don't take it personally, is that it?" He turned and took the plate out of the microwave. His shoulders looked tight with tension.

Interesting. Was Dusty starting to become invested in her children? So far he'd treated them like a minor—and sometimes not so minor—inconvenience. "Brendon hasn't been around a lot of men," she said carefully. "When he acts like he's afraid of you, it's just him not understanding. You're a big man, Dusty, and you have a big voice. He's not used to that."

"So what you're saying is I get in his way." Holding his full plate in one hand, he forked in a mouthful of food.

Dusty sounded like a child himself. Why couldn't he act like an adult and show some compassion for Brendon? Except hadn't he done exactly that when he'd laid down and talked to him? "I thought it was sweet of you to talk to him. Thank you."

"Yeah, I did great, falling asleep on the job."

She tilted her head and studied him. All the Carsons were so confident, it had never occurred to her that Dusty would feel unsure of himself around the children. But he didn't have any experience with kids as far as she knew, so it made sense. Maybe she could work on being more considerate, too. "When I went into the room to see what was going on, Brendon was sitting beside you, holding your hand."

He frowned at his plate. "I don't get kids. I'm as afraid of them as they are of me."

When she laughed, he threw her a sheepish

look. "I could have sworn Sarah was flirting with me today."

She smiled and fluttered her eyelashes at him. "You big strong men do bring out our feminine wiles."

"Really?" He shoved his half-finished supper on the counter behind him then ambled toward her. "I happen to be very interested in your feminine wiles." He rested his hands on the counter on either side of her, caging her in. Her heart tap-danced out a warning as she inhaled his scent. He smelled salty like the ocean and masculine, too. Was it wrong to want to taste his skin? She scrunched her hands into fists to stop herself from pulling him closer.

Her breathing quickened, and she cursed her sensitive skin, heat prickling across the surface. "We need ground rules," she croaked.

"I hate rules." He dipped his head and flicked his tongue over her bottom lip. "So do you," he murmured against her mouth.

Heat slowly uncoiled in her belly. He was right, she hated rules. Unless she was the one making them, but she was tired of being the one who always applied the brakes. Well, not always or she wouldn't be pregnant. For just a few minutes, she wanted to indulge. She slid her arms up around his shoulders and tunneled her fingers into his hair. He whispered his mouth over hers, moved over to her earlobe and gently tugged on it with his teeth before nuzzling in under her ear.

She leaned into him and sighed, nipped at his jaw, then stood on tiptoe to reach his mouth, but he turned his head away from her and kissed a slow path down her neck to her cleavage. All very nice, but Dusty kissed her as if she was made of glass, and he had all the time in the world. She wanted passion.

He pulled back and grinned at her. "Esmeralda."

She pulled herself out of the sexual haze that engulfed her. "What?"

"If we have a girl, I think we should call her Esmeralda."

She was ready to rip his clothes off and he was thinking names—stupid names—for the baby. Obviously, he wasn't nearly as turned on as she was.

"Really? You'd want your daughter going through life with a name like that?"

His grin disappeared. "It was a joke."

"The whole damned pregnancy is a lark to you, isn't it? It's not real. That kind of attitude is exactly what worries me."

"What? That I make a joke once in a while?"

No, that he wasn't attracted to her as much as she was attracted to him. It was the only strong part of their relationship, or so she'd thought, but even that was a game to him. Because he'd never taken any woman in his life seriously. And he probably never would.

She dragged a hand across her eyes. "I'm talking about the fact that the full implications of having a child haven't really sunk in for you. Once they're born, they don't go away. Ever." Another time she'd tell him the good part, that your children were the most fascinating people in the world, and you'd do anything to keep them by your side.

His face paled. "Thank you for that update. God forbid I should actually be excited about having a kid. Excuse me, I need to take a shower."

Teressa covered her face with her hands as he left the room. Was it true? Was he excited about this baby? Because mostly he acted scared. They'd been so busy adjusting to all the curveballs coming at them, they needed to have a real heart-to-heart about how they felt.

A few minutes later, Dusty, smelling of soap and shampoo, came out of the bathroom and sauntered into the living room. "It's too early for bed," he said over his shoulder to her as he grabbed the remote. "And I need a break from working all the time. Do you mind?"

Other than hiding out in the bathroom or the kitchen, the only place for her to relax was in the living room with him. At least she'd cooled off some. Fingers crossed, he had, too. Maybe they could have that heart-to-heart now.

"Of course not." She rounded the sofa and perched on the arm. She stared at the flickering images on the TV, trying to gauge if things had returned to normal between them or if they were still awkward. "I meant to mention how much I like the new cushion flooring in the kitchen."

She watched his face for a change of expression as he lowered the volume. "Josh said it was easy to install. We should clean out that second bedroom tomorrow night. You need a better bed than this couch to sleep on. If you want, I can start tonight."

"I'm okay, Dusty. Thanks," she added.

He turned his attention back to the TV. So, back to normal, then. Good.

"I picked out colors for all the rooms today."

He sighed and turned down the sound on the TV again.

She should let the poor man relax for an hour without bothering him. Heaven knows he deserved some peace and quiet.

"That's good." He fingered the remote. "Whoever goes to town next should pick up the paint. I've got a list on the telephone table by the door. Write the names of the colors on that."

"I could probably help paint the rooms," she offered. "I'll ask Anita to watch the kids. She wore jeans today," she added.

"Who?"

"Anita."

"So?"

"So have you ever seen Anita wear anything casual before?"

"I dunno. Guess not."

"And she made a joke."

"We're still talking about Anita, right?"

Teressa slid down onto the couch, grabbed one of the throw pillows and hugged it. "Are you being a smart-ass?"

"I just don't understand why we're talking about her."

"Because I'm trying to tell you something."

He raised his eyebrows. "Which is?"

"Anita is making an effort to fit in. We should support her. That's why I'm going to ask her, not Sylvie, to look after the kids."

"Go ahead, but Cal won't let her. Whenever anyone mentions asking Anita to do anything he blows up."

"Yeah, I noticed. What's up with that?"

"I don't know. He doesn't want to talk about it."

"And that's it? You just…don't talk?"

"Talking's overrated."

She laughed. "Spoken like a man. I'm going to ask her to babysit anyway. Ow!" She doubled over and rubbed her side.

Dusty scooted over to her side. "What's wrong?"

"Nothing. Just a stitch, I think. I had a couple of twinges earlier today."

His face turned fish-belly white. "Twinges? Like…there?" He stared at her stomach.

"No. In my side. It's nothing. Don't worry."

"That's it. You're sleeping in my bed until we can fix up a bedroom for you. I'll sleep here." He pointed a finger at her. "Don't bother arguing with me. Give me your feet. I read pregnant women like foot massages."

"You're awfully bossy." But she uncurled her legs and rested her feet in his lap.

"Seems like that's the only way I can get anyone to listen to me these days." He picked up her foot and pressed his thumb along her arch.

She groaned and closed her eyes. "God, that feels good. You always give the best foot massages."

When he didn't say anything, she cracked open one eye to catch him smirking. "What?"

A mischievous glint kindled in his blue eyes. "Just thinking of other hidden talents I wouldn't mind showing you."

Another groan escaped her, but it had little to do with the foot massage. She couldn't remember exactly *why* she'd decided it was a good idea for them not to have sex, just that she had. With a groan, she pulled her feet out of his lap and sat up.

"Was that a good groan or a bad one?"

"Depends on how you look at it." She sighed. They had to talk about the sex thing because it was like having a tiger on the loose in their living room.

"Maybe I was wrong saying that we shouldn't… you know."

"Um…you're going to have to clue me in, 'cause there's been a lot of rules lately. It's hard to keep them all straight."

She hoped he didn't hear the tears in her laugh. Sometimes he was so adorable. Why couldn't they be young and free and starting out with a clean slate? Not that she didn't want her children, but she seriously doubted Dusty did. "Forget it. I was wishing for the moon."

Without her realizing it, he'd slid next to her again. He put an arm around her shoulders and pulled her close until her head rested on his chest. The sure, constant beating of his heart soothed her. "Sometimes I think wishing is half the work of getting what you want."

If that was true, she wished she could stay snuggled up against him for hours. She needed the physical contact and the strength he gave her just by putting his arms around her.

He kissed the top of her head. "Sometimes I think you're right. About the no-sex thing. It's not that I don't want to have sex with you, 'cause believe me, I do. But things are pretty complicated between us, and it's better if we wait until…I don't know when. Until we're ready to take that step, I guess."

So he'd known all along what she'd been thinking. She leaned back so she could watch his face. "You're a lot smarter than you let on."

"Me? Nah. Cal's the brains of the family."

"And Sylvie's the talented one. Where does that leave you?"

His smile turned brittle. "I'll get back to you on that one."

She slid her hand over his, where it rested on his thigh. "You're the heart. You're plenty smart, but you're also kind and generous. Everyone in this village knows if they need help who to ask."

It was true. When Andy's Jeep had broken down in the middle of the night and in the middle of nowhere, he'd called Dusty to tow him home. And when Josh's father didn't have enough wood to last him the winter to heat his house, Dusty helped Josh cut a few extra cords for the elderly man. Everyone knew who to hit up for a small loan. She'd never heard of him refusing to give ten or twenty dollars even when he knew he'd never see that money again.

And now he'd opened his house to her in the same generous way. She loved him for being so kindhearted, but there was nothing she hated more than being dependent on anyone. Especially someone as important to her as her old friend. She'd been so caught up in making things work—in picking out paint colors for God's sake—that she'd lost sight of the truth. She was nothing more than a charity case to Dusty. The thought made her heart hurt. How could they ever be equal?

The hard truth was, it was impossible for her to expect to be independent right now, so she'd do what she could to make things easier for him in exchange for his generosity. She'd work harder—at everything.

"Dusty?"

"Yeah."

"How are you feeling about my pregnancy? There have been so many practical things to take care of, we haven't talked about it."

He turned off the TV. "You want the truth?"

Another twinge shot through her, but she held herself still. "Yes."

"Bewildered, mostly. And maybe a little excited, like I said. But kind of scared, too. As you pointed out, the kid's here to stay. I don't think I've ever experienced anything so…permanent and irreversible in my life. Except, maybe, my mom dying."

She heard the sadness in his voice. Strange to mention his mother's death now. He never talked about her.

"We don't have to live together. We have alternatives. Right now, yeah, because there's nowhere else to go." How she hated admitting her helplessness. "But sooner or later, probably in the spring, a house will go up for sale. You don't have to take care of us. I've been doing it for years. And we can share fifty-fifty custody of Esmeralda. What I'm trying to say is you don't have to give up your life for us. We'll be fine." The words had come out hard and low, and she ached all over from saying them. What she'd said was true, but it felt wrong to her.

He tossed the remote on the coffee table. "You don't want to live with me. I get it. That's fine. I'll move out—"

She put her hand on his arm. His muscles were hard from tension. "That's not what I mean. I hate depending on you as much as you hate taking care of all three of us. All I'm saying is you're free. If you want to be." She held her breath and her tears. She hadn't realized it would be so hard to say that to him.

"Free." He huffed out a breath as if she'd knocked the wind out of him. She braced herself when he opened his mouth to say something, but nothing came out. After a minute, he seemed to pull himself together. "You know, if you'd asked me a few days ago how I'd react to that, I'd have said I'd be packing my bags and out of here in a flash." He sent her a puzzling look as he picked up her hand and held it in his. "I don't know how I feel now. Mixed up, I guess. Let's just get through the next few months and see where they take us, okay?"

Teressa let out her pent-up breath. Dusty wasn't the only one who'd started to change. She hadn't wanted him to go. Not yet, anyway.

She relaxed back into the sofa and snuggled up beside him as she picked up the remote and turned on the TV. It was a relief to get all that out in the open and talk about how they were feeling. She loved that she could still talk to Dusty about anything. They'd always been good together like that. Now, they'd taken another baby step in their relationship. They were nowhere near declaring their undying love for each other, but neither one was pushing to run out the door. It didn't sound like much, but it felt good. For the first time, Teressa wondered if they actually had a chance to build a life together.

"THANK GOD YOU'RE HOME." Carmen stood in Dusty's doorway, hugging herself against the cold day.

"What's wrong?" Dusty's stomach dive-bombed, and he stalled in the act of grabbing his gear and the bag of fresh haddock he'd caught for Teressa from the back of his truck. All day he'd worried about the twinges Teressa had had last night and what they meant.

Things had changed between them last night. His tension had eased, and all because she said he was free to leave, but he wasn't sure what *free* meant anymore. The idea didn't sound as appealing to him as it used to. If there was something seriously wrong with Teressa or with her pregnancy, he knew he wouldn't handle it well. Wasn't that exactly what he'd been trying to avoid all his life? Never, ever let yourself become too involved, because people could disappear on you. Hell, even Pops had almost checked out. Against his will, yeah, but his heart attack was a harsh reminder that things never stayed the same.

Carmen flapped her hand at him. "Nothing serious. I can't get the fire started, and the house is cold."

He grabbed his stuff and followed her into the chilly kitchen. "Where's Teressa? I thought she was getting off early today."

He'd hurried home as soon as he got in, determined to clean out the second bedroom for Teressa. His back had ached all day from sleeping on the couch. No wonder she was getting muscle spasms.

"She went to town with Anita to buy paint, but she forgot to put wood in the fire before she left, and I'm clueless about stuff like that. You need a backup heating system, Dusty."

Sarah skipped into the kitchen and assumed her usual position, wrapped around his leg. Great. He limped over to the refrigerator, dragging Sarah with him and stuffed the fish inside.

"You stink." She wrinkled her little pug nose. "I'm cold. What are we having for supper? I hate fish."

Carmen snickered. "Time for me to go. Have fun."

"Wait a minute. Don't you usually work until four-thirty?"

A guilty look passed over her face. "Yeah, but you're home now, so…"

"But I have work to do. I can't work and watch the kids at the same time."

"Sure you can. Teressa does it all the time."

"No, I can't," he said through clenched teeth.

Carmen grimaced. "Give me a break. I've got to get ready for a hot date and drive all the way to Lancaster before seven. Come on," she wailed. "You'd do the same thing if you were in my shoes."

She was right. He'd disappointed his friends and family numerous times, all in the pursuit of happiness. More like selfishness. How many times had he said he'd be home for supper, but ended up running into a friend and going for a few drinks instead? Or promised to help Pops put in the winter wood, then put the chore off until the first snowfall because he was so busy doing whatever. It was a miracle he had any friends left or that his family even talked to him.

"Go." He hunched his shoulders as he watched her grab her jacket and slip out the door. "Have a good time," he mumbled. Sarah clung more tightly to his leg. He absently patted her head. "Where's Brendon?" he asked.

As if waiting for his cue, Brendon poked his head around the corner, great gobs of goop running out of his nose while he sucked his thumb. He looked as if he was one blink away from crying.

Dusty closed his eyes to block out the view. "Sarah?"

She beamed up at him. "Yes?"

"You have to let go of my leg so I can go down to the basement and start the fire."

Her bottom lip trembled. "What am I going to do?"

"When?"

"When you're gone."

He reached down and unpeeled her arms from his leg as a lightbulb went off in his head. "Watch TV," he said.

"We're not allowed to watch during the day."

He strode into the living room and turned on the TV, then passed the remote to her. "You are now. Brendon, wipe your nose," he said over his shoulder as he headed for the basement stairs.

He started a fire in the furnace and stood staring at the flames longer than necessary. Carmen was probably right. Now that he had kids—and, man, he still couldn't process that thought without his neck muscles cranking into tight knots— he needed to keep the house warm all the time. He used to feed the fire before going out fishing, then bank it, and when he got home, if the house wasn't warm, it wasn't freezing, either. He was going to need more wood and another heat source, both of which translated into more money. It wouldn't be long before he'd burn through the entire fifty grand Pops had dropped on him.

He threw a few logs into the fire and slammed the door shut. The things he could have bought with that fifty grand.

When he went upstairs, to his surprise the kids were glued to the TV. Sarah didn't attach herself to his leg like a leech, and Brendon didn't even look his way, let alone start crying.

"I'm taking a shower," he yelled to them as he headed to the bathroom. TV was the best damned thing ever invented.

Curiosity got the better of him when he finished cleaning up, and he wandered into the living room to see what had captured the kids' attention. "What are you watching?" He sat on the couch beside Sarah.

"Cowboys." Sarah grinned at him.

"*Bonanza*. Right. I used to watch that when I was a kid. Didn't know they still ran that show."

When Brendon studied him over his shoulder from where he was lying on the floor, Dusty chuckled to himself. He never thought he'd see the day when someone couldn't imagine *him* as a kid.

Well, he wasn't a kid. He was a responsible adult, taking care of the children and trying to figure out what to eat for supper. Carmen was supposed to have taken care of that, too.

He wandered into the kitchen and gravitated to the refrigerator out of habit. A list stuck to the refrigerator door with a magnet caught his attention, and he pulled it off and started reading the detailed instructions Teressa had written. No wonder Carmen had left.

It was cool that Teressa had somehow found time to prepare their supper for them before she left, but not so great that the kids were such picky eaters. Brendon had to have his carrots mashed, without butter, but with salt, and Sarah did not eat peas. Ever.

Whatever. He tossed the list on the counter, turned on the oven and put the shepherd's pie in. Teressa must have remembered how much he loved shepherd's pie. He could find a lot of things to complain about, but she'd been outdoing herself with the suppers she'd been cooking for them. And that after a full day of working in the café's kitchen. He'd have to remember to thank her.

He went into the second bedroom and started hauling furniture and boxes of stuff from Teressa's apartment down to the basement. Maybe they could throw away some of the junk they weren't using. He stopped a couple of times to check on Sarah and Brendon, who were now watching some doctor yakking on about diets. The show looked fairly harmless.

Once he had the room almost clear, he washed his hands and turned off the TV. It was a lot later than he'd thought. Both kids stared at him with hollow looks. "Supper," he said.

When Brendon started whining, Dusty pointed his finger at him and barked, "Don't." Which seemed to work for all of two minutes before the kid started again.

Sarah followed him into the kitchen. "He has to pee," she said. "I'm not hungry." She sounded as whiny as Brendon.

"You'll feel better when you eat. Want to set the table while I take Brendon to the bathroom?"

"No." She flounced out of the room, went back to the living room and turned on the TV again.

"Turn it off, Sarah, and set the table." He turned to Brendon. "Come on, sport. I'll set you up to pee."

"Standing up," Brendon said grouchily. "You promised."

Dusty stopped midstride. "You're right. I did promise to teach you how to pee standing up. I'm sorry. If I forget about stuff like that again, you have to tell me. Come on." He headed for the door.

"Where?" Brendon's little face wrinkled in surprise.

Dusty grinned. "It's always more fun peeing

outside. Wait until the snow comes. I'll teach you how to write your name in snow." He ushered the tiny boy outside. "Do you know how to spell your name?"

"No," he giggled.

Dusty laughed. "Well, when you do, I'll teach you."

"What are you guys doing?" Sarah called from the house.

"Peeing," Brendon called to his sister from the edge of the side yard.

"I want to, too."

Like he'd let a six-year-old girl watch him take a leak. Bad enough if someone was driving by they might see them. But he hadn't wanted to take Brendon too far from the house. "Not a good idea, Sarah. Stay in the house." He showed Brendon the mechanics of getting into position and letting it go, and was about to caution him on the most important part, safely tucking Mr. Jolly away, when Sarah skipped over to them, pulled down her pants and attempted to pee standing up.

For God's sake.

Dusty barely got himself zipped up when Brendon started wailing. Dusty winced. The kid had caught his wiener in his zipper. He squatted down in front of Brendon to see if he could help when headlights suddenly illuminated the yard. Dusty,

Brendon and Sarah all froze as the blinding light pinned them in place.

Dusty fell back on his ass as Teressa drove into the yard.

CHAPTER SEVEN

TERESSA MADE HERSELF walk slowly as she moved across the yard to her babies. She wanted to race across the yard and tear them away from Dusty. Which was so unfair. She knew he would never, ever hurt her children. "What's going on?"

Brendon burst into tears before she could reach him, and Sarah hobbled over to her mother with her pants still around her ankles and threw herself at her, wailing like the devil himself was after her. Dusty sat on his butt, looking as if he wanted to murder someone. She knew the feeling.

Teressa squatted down and wrapped one arm around each of her children as she glared at Dusty. "Using the yard as a bathroom? Really? Is this what you call responsible behavior?"

Dusty took his time to stand up. He dusted himself off before looking at her, his face carefully arranged in a neutral expression. "You're absolutely right. I'm not parent material."

With a sinking heart, Teressa watched him stalk into the house. What had she done? Why had she criticized him in front of the children? Why criticize him at all?

"Pull up your pants, Sarah. What were you doing out here?"

Sarah pulled her thumb out of her mouth. Teressa hadn't seen her suck her thumb for over a year now, and she couldn't even blame Dusty for the backward step. The fault lay entirely on her shoulders. She should have found out what was going on before she opened her big mouth.

She'd love to pretend she didn't know why she'd lost her temper, but it had been building since she'd moved into Dusty's house. Even their talk last night hadn't helped as much as she'd hoped. There was still so much uncertainty in their future. If she had any other place to move to, now would be a good time to pack up and go, because the longer she stayed, the more she depended on Dusty, and the more entwined their lives became, the more desperate she grew. By moving in with him, she'd lost the small amount of control she had over her life, and every day felt like a struggle—a battle, really—to gain back the ground she'd lost.

And the worst part? Some days she wanted to let Dusty take care of her. He would if she asked, because that's the kind of man he was. And she was a screaming bitch who was afraid to appreciate the good things that did come her way. She knew she was going to disappoint him eventually, might as well get it over with sooner than later. Hadn't she disappointed her mother over and over again, so why would it be any different with Dusty?

Brendon slipped his hand into hers. "Dusty was teaching me how to pee standing up. My wee-wee got stuck in the zipper, but Dusty fixed it."

That almost made sense. "And you, Sarah?"

"I wanted to pee standing up, too."

"And Dusty said that was okay?"

"No." Sarah's bottom lip trembled. "He told me to stay in the house."

"You didn't listen to him."

"No, but he's stupid. I don't have to listen to him."

Teressa frowned at her daughter. "Why would you say a thing like that?"

Sarah glared at her defiantly. "Because you're always saying he is."

Teressa reeled back as if Sarah had hit her. She often muttered under her breath, complaining about Dusty leaving his work boots in front of the door where she tripped over them. Or a wet towel on the bathroom floor. Dirty jeans, socks, tools. Dusty was a slob, and it drove her crazy. And she liked having something to bitch about at the end of the day. She was tired when she got home and faced so much chaos when she walked through that door that it felt good to blow off steam. But not at Dusty's expense.

Dusty probably felt the same way after work. But he never called her a bitch or stupid, did he?

"Mommy, I'm cold," Brendon whimpered.

"Sorry."

When they entered the house, she looked with dismay at the shepherd's pie sitting on the top of the stove and the plates piled on the table. "You haven't eaten supper yet."

"I'm hungry." Brendon climbed up on a chair.

"Me, too." Sarah grabbed a plate and put it on the table.

Teressa shucked off her coat and started serving the food to them. "Wash your hands at the sink. I don't understand. Didn't Carmen get your supper?"

Sarah dried her hands on her pants and climbed up to the table. She stuffed a forkful of creamy potato into her mouth. "Nope."

Teressa sat at the table. "What did she do?"

"Carmen went," Brendon volunteered from the sink. "Dusty made the fire go and let us watch TV and made a bedroom for you."

And heated up supper and tried to teach her son how to pee standing up. A male ritual, likely. She leaned forward and laid her head down on the table. Here she'd been preaching to him about Brendon needing a male role model, and Dusty had been doing that just by being himself.

She wasn't crazy about the kids watching TV, but when Dusty made up his mind to complete a job, she knew nothing got in his way. Apparently, the job du jour was cleaning out the bedroom. For her.

She blinked back tears. She didn't like herself very much at the moment. She was always telling Dusty to grow up, but she had some growing up to do, too. She might as well admit if Dusty left her and the kids, she'd be in trouble. She hadn't given much thought—any thought, really—to how much he anchored her. She always dumped her worries on him because she trusted he'd always be her friend. She'd talked his ear off before she'd approached Adam about going in with her to buy the café. And when she needed a sounding board on whether to put Brendon in day care or let her mother take care of him, Dusty had made her write the pros and cons down and argued them with her.

She'd lied to herself—she depended on Dusty. Always had. She just hadn't *depended* depended on him. But she had taken their friendship for granted.

She turned when Dusty came up from the basement, jumped out of her chair and threw herself into his arms. They both staggered backward.

"Bedroom. Now." She grabbed his arm and dragged him down the hallway to his bedroom. The minute they were inside the room, she pushed him against the wall and kissed him. Dusty made a weird, strangling sound in his throat, but she persisted until his body softened against hers, and he cupped her behind and lifted her against him.

She didn't hold back, exploring his beautiful, velvet mouth with her tongue. He tasted so good, she could eat him up.

"Jesus, Teressa. You're going to be the death of me," he gasped, coming up for air. He let her body slide down his until she stood on her own two feet.

"I'm an idiot and a bitch and a shrew."

"Shut up." He took her jaw in his hand and forced her to look at him. "You're talking about a good friend of mine." He grinned. "Kiss me like that again, and I might forgive you."

Instead she burrowed her face into his chest, trying to hold her tears at bay. "I'm so lucky to have you. I apologize for everything."

She breathed more easily when she felt his laugh rumble through his chest. "That's supposed to be my line, I think."

"Seriously." She pulled back to look at him. "I apologize for taking my bad mood out on you. I do that a lot, and I think it's because no matter what I say or do, I can count on you to be there for me. I'll try harder to think before I open my mouth. Promise."

"It must have looked pretty strange, all of us in the yard, taking a piss." He frowned. "The kids get away on me sometimes. I can't control them."

"Welcome to parenting."

"Yeah, but you always know what you're doing, and Sarah and Brendon listen to you."

"On a good day. Not even a good day. A good hour. Kids test limits. That's what they do. And if you're consistent, that's how they know they can trust you."

"I kind of get it, but…not. I worry I'm going to mess up and hurt them. They're so little, so…tender." He settled his hands on her hips. "How about another kiss to boost my battered ego before we go back out there?" He grinned. "FYI, I *really* like it when you attack me. I could get into that."

"You could, huh? I'll take that into consideration." She spread her hands over his chest, allowing herself to revel in the feel of his solid muscles under his T-shirt.

He seized the initiative this time and covered her mouth with his, his tongue sliding over hers, taking control. He tasted like licorice, and she flashed on the bag of licorice nibs on the front console of his truck. She loved the sweet, spicy taste. He turned them until her back was against the wall, then brought his body full length against hers and pushed with his hips. Automatically, she pushed back, his arousal jutting into her belly. Her pregnant belly.

As if reading her mind, he pulled back and placed his large, warm hand over her stomach. He rested his forehead against hers. "I feel the tiniest, little…"

She covered his hand with hers. "It's okay to say it, Dusty. You feel a bulge, right?"

"Yeah."

She smiled at the look of wonder in his eyes. "It's going to get a lot bigger."

His lips curved upward. "So are your breasts."

She laughed. "So are my hips and ass."

His stomach growled, and she poked him in the side with her elbow, relieved to move on. "That's why you came up from the basement, isn't it? You couldn't resist my shepherd's pie."

He caught her finger in his hand and kissed the tip. "Guilty as charged. Have you finished having your way with me, Ms. Wilder, or do you still require my services?"

"You're free to go."

His smile dimmed. Bad choice of words because he wasn't free, and they both knew whether they stayed together or not, they were bound for life because of the child they'd made. He kissed the tip of her nose, and then ambled down the hallway in front of her. Oh, for another hour alone with him. In the bedroom. Just the two of them.

But she'd have to be someone else for that to happen. Someone without two children and another one on the way. Dusty had been a good sport about tonight because that was what Dusty did. He kept the peace. And there was no doubt he wanted to have sex with her. But they both knew the morning after would be hell. He wasn't ready to have two kids climb over him in bed to snuggle with their mommy. There was a good chance he may never be. Heavens, she'd been a parent for six years, and there were days when she could barely handle being a mom. And they were *her* kids, not Dusty's. He didn't have to love them, and she'd never settle for less than the best for them.

But imagine if Dusty did fall in love with Sarah and Brendon. And with her. She'd never indulged in that particular fantasy, and she was surprised to realize she liked the scenario in her head more than she thought she would. If she and Dusty could work past their individual hang-ups, they could have a chance as a couple. Not one of those they-got-married-because-they-had-to couples, but like soul mates. All the ingredients were there, they just had to put it together, and they needed time for that. But her pregnancy put a limit on the time they had to figure things out.

DUSTY STOOD WAITING at the checkout of his favorite tool store. Man, he loved this place. Everything he'd ever wanted was here. He'd come in to town to pick up a couple new filters for his boat motor and some rope. Then he found the table saw he'd always wanted, but had never been able to convince himself he should buy. Somehow, today, he didn't have that problem. Having Pops's healthy check in his bank account had made the decision to buy it so easy. And he was also buying the new stereo for his truck he'd been looking at for a whole year. He'd meant to buy it months ago, but had never gotten around to it. He cursed under his breath when a twinge of guilt shot through him. He deserved this stuff. He needed it.

When the man standing behind him started telling his buddy about the great deal on chain saws the store had on for one day only, Dusty looked around and spied the front-end display of Husqvarna chain saws. No way. They had them on sale for four hundred and seventy-five dollars, a fantastic price.

He left his cart in line and hurried over to pick up a saw from the display. He hefted the saw in his hands, liking the weight of it. This wasn't one of those toylike electric saws. This was the real thing. He already had a perfectly good chain saw. It was a few years old, but still running well. He didn't *need* this one. He didn't need the stereo, either. Not really. Didn't mean he shouldn't get it, though.

He hesitated as he felt another guilty twinge. There were a lot better things he could be spending his money on. He'd noticed the kids' winter coats looked worn out, although Teressa would probably never let him buy them new coats, anyway.

What the hell. He hurried back just as the checkout line moved forward so it was his turn. He could always bring some of the stuff back for a refund if he changed his mind when he got home. He snorted. As if that would happen.

By the time he'd paid and loaded his booty into the truck, he wasn't as excited as he thought he'd be about his purchases. But it was stupid to feel guilty about spending money when Teressa wouldn't let him help her, anyway. As she'd pointed out, it was *his* money, not hers.

SEVERAL DAYS LATER, Dusty nodded to a table of men sitting close to the door as he entered the café. Normally, he'd stop and chat with everyone, but Stan, Brendon's father, was part of the group. He hadn't liked Stan all that much before he'd gotten Teressa pregnant, and he sure as hell didn't like him any better now.

Stan had been a jock in high school, but so had Dusty. When Stan was a teenager, he was drafted by the Ottawa Senators and the whole village celebrated. Collina was going to have their very own superstar hockey player. But Stan had been taken out in the first season because of a knee injury, and he limped home, literally, to replay his glory year over and over in the legion for free drinks. Like his father, Stan slipped into alcoholism. Now, he worked as a deckhand on the Peters' fishing boat, lived with his parents and still spent a lot of time drinking at the legion, although not many people were willing to buy him a beer anymore to hear his worn-out tales of glory.

It was a sad story, and in a way, Dusty felt sorry for him. Stan had worked hard for years to make the National Hockey League, and his dream had been taken away from him almost before his professional career got off the ground. It would be hard to want something so much and know you were never going to be good enough to get it. But Brendon shouldn't have to suffer because of Stan's disappointments.

Dusty liked to think he was a better man than Stan, but he knew that wasn't necessarily true. Up until a year ago, Dusty had coasted through life with hardly a care in the world. At least when he got a woman pregnant, he took responsibility for his actions. Stan had never spent any time with his own kid and had refused to pay child support until Teressa took him to court. He spent a lot of energy thinking up reasons why he couldn't pay and managed to escape his financial responsibilities about half the time.

A couple of years ago when Dusty had tried to talk to Stan man-to-man about how much Teressa needed the money, Stan told him to take a hike, and that if he was so concerned about Teressa, Dusty could send her a monthly check. They'd barely spoken to each other since then.

Dusty knew he'd never renege on making sure

Esmeralda had everything she needed, but it embarrassed him that he still struggled with the added responsibility of Brendon and Sarah. They were just little kids, and he knew they deserved to be loved the same as he knew he'd love his own child. Too bad love wasn't something that could be forced. The best he could do for now was concentrate on liking Teressa's children.

If Adam hadn't begged him to come down to the café tonight, Dusty would have turned around and walked out the minute he saw Stan. He didn't want to deal with him right now. Instead, he strode past the crowded table and into the kitchen.

His dark mood lifted the second he saw his soon-to-be brother-in-law, who was over six feet of solid muscle, wore a red bandana over his hair and, as usual, looked as though he was ready to rumble. Strange that was the impression Adam gave people, because the dude was just about the gentlest person Dusty knew. *Now.* Adam's past, however, wasn't something he cared to share with many people, and Dusty didn't want to know the details.

Adam and Teressa were business partners, both owning a third of the café. When Adam had first moved to Collina a few months ago, Dusty had kept a close eye on him, thinking—and yeah, okay, maybe worrying a bit—that he and Teressa were going to hook up. Man, did he get that wrong. Adam was going to marry Dusty's sister, Sylvie, in several weeks. He knew his sister was superbusy preparing for an art show in Toronto, but what was she thinking, making the dude completely responsible for their wedding?

"Hey." Adam looked up from scrubbing the sink. "I've got brownies."

Dusty pulled the chair away from the desk, swung it backward and straddled it. "How come you have the café open tonight? I thought you closed at four?"

Adam chucked the scrub pad into the sink and yanked off his bandana. "When the guys asked if they could come in for coffee, I couldn't think of a good reason to say no."

Dusty scowled at Adam's hopeful expression. "Whatever you're asking, the answer is no."

"You don't even know what you're saying no to."

"Doesn't matter. I haven't got a spare second for anything."

"I promised Sylvie I'd take care of the wedding, and I know dick-all about them. And—" he raised his voice "—as my best man, it's your duty to help. Don't forget I'm helping you with your house."

"Once."

"And I babysat your kids."

Dusty opened his mouth to say they weren't his kids, but snapped it closed. He liked shooting the breeze with Adam and didn't want to change the tone of the conversation. If he mentioned the kids, he'd open the door to a discussion he didn't want to get into tonight.

Plus the man must be desperate if he was asking *him* to help with the wedding. And it was *his* little sister's wedding they were talking about. He supposed Adam had helped here and there with renovating Dusty's house, even though he was busy with working at the café and handling his own renovations. Bottom line, he liked Adam and was happy he and Sylvie were getting married. It had been a good day all around when Sylvie made up her mind to move home. He didn't like to make a big deal about it, but he was crazy proud of his sister.

"Bring on the brownies. But, I gotta warn you, I haven't a clue about weddings, either."

Adam grinned and pulled a plate of brownies from the refrigerator. "I knew I could count on you, bro."

Bro. As in brother. That was cool with him. He'd liked Adam from the minute he met him. He bit into a brownie while Adam grabbed a notepad and sat by the desk. "What do we do first?" Adam looked at him expectantly.

"Well..." Dusty tried to imagine what he'd want if he and Teressa got married. He'd want the ceremony to take place somewhere he loved, like his boat. And she'd wear a really hot dress with lots of cleavage. And they'd buy kegs of beer and get a band, and… He blew out a lung full of air. Sounded like a recipe for divorce.

"Where do you want to get married?"

Adam's forehead wrinkled. "I haven't thought about it."

"Think about it now." He reached for a second brownie as Cal pushed through the swinging door. "The other wedding planner. Thank God you're here. Adam insists on wearing a baby-blue tux. I told him that's so sixties."

Cal hesitated by the door. "Jesus. Can I leave now?"

"He made brownies."

"There's beer, but Dusty's not drinking, so I made coffee," Adam offered.

"I can have a beer," Dusty objected.

"I thought you and Teressa had some kind of bet about you not drinking," Cal said as he sat down on the stool by the chopping table.

"Yeah. Sort of."

Cal raised his eyebrows. "What's the payoff? It must be good for you to quit."

"I get to name our child."

When Cal and Adam hooted with laughter, Dusty relaxed and grinned. Man, it felt good to hang out with them.

"In your dreams, little brother. You might as well have a beer. No way in hell Teressa's going to let you name that kid. I bet she already has the name picked out."

Dusty frowned. Maybe he should start taking this naming the baby more seriously. Everyone else seemed to.

"How many people are you inviting to your wedding?" he asked Adam to take the heat off himself.

"Me? No one. Well, you guys, but you're Sylvie's family. So, yeah, no one."

They were quiet for a moment as Dusty cursed himself for asking the question. He forgot how messed up Adam's family was.

"How's your mom doing?" Cal asked.

"Same old, same old. She won't be coming to the wedding. At least that scumbag who was beating on her is still in jail, but she's not ready to try rehab."

Dusty studied the toes of his work boots. It must be tough having a mom who was a junkie. Having lost his own mother, he knew how it felt to be overwhelmed with emotion and not know what to do with it. It could mess a person up. At least he'd had Pops to rely on. Adam's father had been an enforcer for a biker gang, and although Adam rarely talked about his dad, it didn't take a lot of imagination to figure out what kind of parent he'd been when he was alive.

Sarah and Brendon had no idea how lucky they were to have Teressa for their mom. She was one hundred percent there for them. It wouldn't hurt him to pay a bit more attention to them, either. If he was going to be their male role model, he'd better start acting like he cared. It would be weird if they started calling him *Dad,* though. He didn't feel qualified to be anyone's father. Would he feel differently with his own child?

He dragged his attention back to the wedding. "You could have the reception here," he said. "Or some people rent the legion. Or hey, how about the Waterside Inn? That's a great old place."

"They do weddings?" Adam looked hopeful.

"Sure. Rita Price told me they do the whole thing, if you want them to. She got married there last year."

Adam's face lit up. "That's exactly what I need. Then all I have to do is make a list of people to invite."

"Sylvie should help with that," Cal said.

"She's painting like crazy, and when she's like that, forget it. She barely remembers who I am, let alone who to ask to a wedding. How about Anita? She knows everyone."

Cal stood. "No."

Silence filled the room. "You're acting a little crazy about her lately, Cal," Dusty finally said.

Cal glared at his brother. "Butt out."

"Teressa said she was wearing jeans the other day," Dusty said to see what Cal's reaction would be. He still didn't get what the big deal was about her wearing jeans. But he did know enough not to tell Cal that Teressa planned to ask Anita to baby-sit the kids so they could paint some rooms this weekend.

A soft smile lit Cal's face. "Yeah, she showed me."

"She's looking good these days." Adam said. "She's gained weight."

"Yeah, and I don't want her getting worn-out again."

"What was wrong with her?" Dusty asked. He'd asked before and had been told to mind his own business. He thought family was his business, and he liked Anita, even though she was a little too perfect for his liking. After two years, he still didn't know if she was stuck-up or shy.

"Nothing," Cal barked, his face closing up, then cursed himself for overreacting.

Dusty didn't understand. No one did. Two years ago he'd persuaded Anita to leave her life behind and live with him in Collina. But not before he'd tried to fit into the frightening world her father had built for himself and his daughter. Cal had not been welcome there. At all. He'd fallen so deeply in love with Anita he couldn't imagine living without her. He still felt that way.

So, he'd enticed her here, and damned near killed himself building a house for her good enough to replace the mansion she'd left behind. He worked hard to make sure she had everything she needed or wanted, even though she kept telling him he was all she needed, and she had more money than he'd ever see in a lifetime. Not that he'd touch a cent of it, even if it came from her mother's side of the family. He'd thought things had been going great. And then, suddenly, they weren't.

"It's not good to keep things bottled up, Cal," Dusty said. "If you two have problems, you should talk to her about it."

Cal waited for Dusty's punch line, but realized he was being serious. Huh. Maybe Teressa getting pregnant would turn out to be a good thing.

Anita had had a miscarriage, and she didn't want him to tell anyone. Hell, she hadn't wanted to tell *him*. He'd lost her for a while, thought her shutting down was a prelude to leaving him. Finally, he got her to confess what was wrong, that she'd lost a baby and had been afraid to tell him, because, selfishly, he hadn't wanted children for another couple of years. Since her confession, he could barely stand to let her out of his sight, let alone let people make demands on her. She was so fragile and easily broken. He'd taken her away from the life she knew, and it was up to him to protect her. Even knowing he was overreacting, he couldn't help himself.

Cal reminded himself that Dusty was trying to

help. "We talk. It's getting better. Every marriage has its rough spots, you know."

"Don't talk to me about rough spots. I know all about them. Speaking of which, I promised Teressa I wouldn't be gone for more than an hour. I've gotta go."

Cal was tempted to tease his brother about being kept on a short leash, but he kept his mouth shut. He was proud of how well Dusty was adjusting to being a father. Lucky man. There was a good chance he may never be as lucky.

"I HAVE TO GO, TOO," Adam said. "I'll call the inn in the morning, but I'll probably have a lot more questions after that. And I still need a list of Sylvie's guests to invite to the wedding."

Adam switched off the lights as they moved from the kitchen into the dining area. "Closing time, boys," he said to the table of men.

"How much do we owe you, Adam?" They all stood at the same time.

Dusty shoved his hands into the pockets of his old leather jacket and ignored the way Stan was eyeing him. Knowing Stan, he probably had some smart-ass comment to make about Teressa.

"It's on the house. Have a good night." Adam held the door open.

Dusty tensed up when Stan wandered over to him rather than following his friends out the door.

"I hear you knocked up Teressa. She's a wild one, isn't she?"

The group of men stopped and swung around to watch. Cal stepped closer and put his hand on Dusty's arm, but Dusty shrugged him off. "Think you can afford your child-care payment this month, Stan?"

Stan's face turned red. "Don't forget, Brendon's my kid, and I can have him anytime I want." He pushed past the other men to go outside.

Dusty blew out a breath. "I can never keep my goddamn mouth shut," he murmured through clenched teeth.

Cal squeezed his shoulder. "I'd have slugged him. You did good, Dusty."

Dusty looked at his big brother. "Yeah?"

"Absolutely. I'm proud of you. Now go home to your family."

Home to his family. A couple of months ago that had meant something entirely different. Now it meant going home to Teressa, and, yeah, okay, things weren't entirely copacetic between them, but they weren't all bad. Matter of fact, some parts were very, very good. Like the way she'd kissed him earlier in the week.

A HALF HOUR LATER, Teressa looked at him with exasperation. "You did what?" She obviously didn't share Cal's opinion of how he'd handled Stan.

"I didn't hit him," Dusty pointed out.

She bit her bottom lip, no doubt biting back a few choice words about how stupid he was. Tough. He didn't regret poking at the man's pride. "No one's talking about you that way and getting away with it."

Teressa blushed. "What did he say?"

"Nothing you want to hear."

"I can handle that dickless wonder. I don't need your help."

"I noticed. Most of the time you treat me like a kid you have to take care of, not a partner. I can't believe I'm saying this, but you're driving me nuts the way you always have an incredible meal cooked for supper, as if I've suddenly forgotten how to feed myself. Not that I don't appreciate the meals—I do. The point is, you don't have to cook for me, especially every night. My clothes barely hit the floor before you've washed and dried them and put them away. And God forbid I should stand up for you, because we all know you fight your own battles. I don't even know what I'm doing here, except getting in your way."

"It's your house, you idiot."

"If it wasn't, I sure as hell wouldn't be here, because you don't need anyone. I'm going out again." He grabbed his jacket from where he'd hung it on the back of a kitchen chair. "I'm a man, Teressa. I don't need you to look after me, and if you gave me a chance you might find out *I* can look after *you* and our kids for a change."

Our kids. Where the hell had that come from? Now Brendon and Sarah were his responsibility, too? He barged outside and jammed his hands in the pockets as he looked up at the sky. Fishtail clouds floated in front of the half moon. It would probably rain tomorrow. Or snow. The warm front had moved out a couple of days ago. He shivered and started walking down his driveway.

The damned thing was he knew Teressa was right. He shouldn't have mouthed off to Stan, because he'd given the turd a reason to hit back at Teressa. Dusty often suspected he himself hurt the kids' feelings, and he wasn't even trying. Stan wasn't a sicko or anything, just thoughtless. Being inconsiderate was something Dusty recognized right away, because he was beginning to realize how careless he'd been of other people's needs. Thoughtlessness could hurt more than he'd imagined. He'd put his needs before everyone else's for years now.

He flipped up his collar and walked faster. He was acting like Brendon was his kid. He wasn't, but damn if the little fellow hadn't sunk his hooks into him. *Our* kids. He'd been so busy being careful around Teressa, Sarah and Brendon had snuck into his heart without him noticing, and they weren't even his kids. Had Stan told the truth? Did he have the right to take Brendon anytime he wanted? Surely, Teressa wouldn't let that happen. But could she prevent it if Stan had the law on his side?

He reached the end of his driveway and stopped, staring at the empty road in front of him. Why couldn't Teressa have full rights to the children? Well, except for his child. He planned to be there a hundred percent for Esmeralda.

He needed to know what kind of legal position he'd be in with Sarah and Brendon. If he and Teressa got married he wasn't going to spend his life accommodating Corey's or Stan's schedules, that was for damned sure. He needed to call his lawyer and find out what his rights were.

And he needed to go back to the house. He couldn't keep stomping out every time Teressa got mad at him. They'd never resolve anything if he kept disappearing on her.

Although, man, what he'd give to go down to the legion, hang out with his friends and not think about anything for a while. He missed his buddies, and he missed just hanging out, and not having to worry about picking up kids on time or dropping them off somewhere, keeping the house warm or making sure Teressa wasn't overdoing things. Watching out for touchy-feely feelings. Speaking of which, the longer he stayed outside, the more time she had to work herself into a snit. Might as well go back in and face the music.

When he went back into the house, Teressa was kneeling in front of the fireplace, staring into the black hole.

"Do you ever have a fire in this thing?" she asked without looking around.

He squatted down beside her. "Not for a few months. It always felt like too much work for just me. I'll get the kindling and a few sticks of wood if you want a fire, though."

"I'd like that. My mother never used her fireplace. Want me to make cocoa?"

"Sounds good." Not to his stomach, though. Cocoa on top of eating three brownies would be a record, even for him. But he knew an olive branch when he saw one and wouldn't dream of denying her the chance to make peace.

He grabbed the kindling and an armload of wood from where he'd stacked the winter supply in the basement. Fireplaces burned wood inefficiently, and if they were going to start using it more, he needed to order even more wood again.

"Remind me to call Ron Hachey and ask him to deliver more wood. I keep forgetting to, and sometimes he runs out," he said when he returned to the living room. He dumped the wood on the hearth and crumbled up paper to start the kindling.

"I can call him," Teressa said from the kitchen.

"Sure," he agreed after a minute. He and Ron were old buddies, both fishermen, and usually they had a good long chat when Dusty ran in to him, but they never phoned each other just to talk. It felt strange letting Teressa call him. He hadn't talked to Ron since he'd dumped a load of wood in the yard earlier in the summer, and he wouldn't have minded comparing notes on this year's lobster season. But he also needed to start fitting Teressa into his life if their relationship was going anywhere, and he supposed letting her call for more firewood came under that heading.

He placed a couple of logs on top of the blazing kindling and sprawled on the couch. Having a fire was kind of nice. "I've been looking in to buying something else in addition to the wood furnace to heat the house. Thanks." He accepted a full mug of cocoa from Teressa.

She sat beside him and blew on her hot cocoa. "Why?"

"'Cause if I'm late getting in from fishing or you get caught up at the café, it'd be nice to not have to worry about feeding the fire. I don't like you having to tend the fire when you get home, anyway. You do too much as it is."

"That's sweet of you, but honestly? I love wood heat. It would be nice to have a backup system, though. I hear heat pumps work really well, but they're expensive to buy. Once you get them, though, they don't use too much electricity."

"I'll check in to it." A weight settled on his

shoulders. Thank God his father had given him the fifty grand.

"If you can't afford it, it's not a problem. We can live without the heat pump." She narrowed her eyes. "But I can't imagine how you burned through the money your father gave you already."

"Ye—ah." He knew buying all that stuff was going to come back and bite him on the ass.

"I don't like the sound of that."

Dusty shoved his cocoa on the end table beside him. "I needed some stuff for my boat, okay? And I bought a new table saw so I could make more cupboards and stuff."

Teressa relaxed into the couch. "That sounds reasonable."

Damn it. She was guilting him into telling her everything. "And a new stereo for my truck," he admitted. "And a new chain saw," he added. Might as well get it all out at once.

She sniffed. "It's your money. Spend it any way you want." Disapproval came off her in waves.

He'd been thinking about getting a new stereo for his truck for at least three years. Standing at the cash register, he'd known in his gut it was a bad idea. But a surge of rebellion had hit him, and he'd gone ahead and bought the damned thing, anyway. And the table saw and the chain saw. Because he could.

"I'll take it all back. Will that make you happy?"

"Honestly? No." She smiled sadly at him. "I wish you could buy everything your heart desires, Dusty."

He hung his head, feeling the same way he had when he was twelve years old and had stolen Pops's pocket change. He was such a selfish idiot. "I messed up. I'm sorry. I'll take all that sh—stuff back."

"It's up to you."

They sat on the couch side by side and stared straight ahead. The fire had almost gone out, but neither felt motivated to put more wood on it.

"I hate this kind of stuff," Dusty finally admitted.

"Me, too. I either feel like a killjoy or guilty for doing something stupid."

"You never do anything wrong."

One of Teressa's eyebrows rose. "How about forget you're pregnant?"

Dusty laughed. "Yeah, right."

She bumped his shoulder with hers. "Remember Roxy?"

"Roxanne Sears. Sure do. First girl I got to second base with." He quickly doused his smile when Teressa drilled a you're-an-idiot look his way.

"She came home to visit the spring I was pregnant with Sarah," Teressa continued. "When she came over to my place with a bottle of wine, I drank three glasses before I remembered I wasn't supposed to have alcohol."

Dusty picked up her hand. "And you probably never forgave yourself."

"Yeah."

"Yet Sarah seems fine to me. Except for how clingy she is."

"You're her first love, Dusty. Treat her gently."

"I try. But I've got to tell you, little girls are a complete mystery to me. She scares the crap out of me. Corey doesn't know what he's missing, not seeing Sarah grow up. How about your dad? Does Sarah spend any time with him?"

She slid her fingers through his. "Never without my mother."

"You're going to have to call her, you know."

The minute Teressa snatched her hand away, he missed her touch. "No, I don't, but maybe I should call my dad."

"Brendon needs a haircut, anyway."

"My father has cut almost everyone's hair in this village, but not his grandchildren's. Crazy, isn't it?"

"Why not?"

"My mother forbade it. She's the queen of denial. She likes to pretend he's not really the local barber. She never forgave him for getting laid off of his government job."

"But there were a lot of layoffs at the time. That

was when all those government cutbacks happened, wasn't it?"

"Yeah. Still his fault, according to my mother."

"Your father's a nice man. It's too bad Sarah and Brendon don't know him better."

"You're right. I'll take Brendon to get his hair cut this week."

"Good girl." He glanced at her from under his lashes. For once she looked relaxed and almost happy.

"This is nice," he said.

She leaned into his side. "It is. I love talking to you about things that are bothering me. You always help me see the right thing to do."

He cleared his throat. "I was thinking about something you said the other day. About the names I pick for the baby. What do you think of Emma?"

CHAPTER EIGHT

"Emma," she repeated, her voice husky. "I love it."

Dusty smiled. "So do I. I still haven't come up with a boy's name, but it'll come to me."

"Thank you." She leaned over and kissed his cheek.

"For what?"

"For taking the naming of our baby seriously."

"I take everything about our baby seriously."

"Even if you didn't plan on having children?"

He looked at her, surprised. "I always planned to get married and have kids, just not…"

"Just not with me. It's okay. We might as well be honest with each other. I never planned to stick around Collina, and yet, here I am."

"I was going to say just not yet. I don't think it's unreasonable to hope to marry someone who loves you."

"It's not." Her heart sank. If she loved Dusty life would be so much easier. What if she let herself fall in love with him? She suspected she might be able to if she could let go of the tightness, the need for control inside her. But what if she disappointed him or if he decided she wasn't the one for him? Face it, Dusty didn't need her, and he certainly didn't need Brendon and Sarah. She'd not only lose her best friend, and she didn't have that many, but she'd also lose the man she'd fallen in love with. Was she brave enough to open that door? Because it felt as though they were stuck, and one of them had to do something.

"Kiss me." Teressa's hands trembled as she reached for him. She shouldn't be encouraging Dusty when he'd just proven how unreliable he could be by spending all that money. But she wanted him. Badly. She couldn't remember a time when she hadn't wanted him. Just as she couldn't remember not feeling conflicted about that desire.

Sometimes she had a hard time making a case for not getting involved with him. He was such a great guy—until he wasn't. Like spending all that money on things he didn't need while she was pinching pennies. Kind of all beside the point because Dusty hadn't committed himself to them. His own child, yes, but her and Sarah and Brendon? He could go either way, and that wasn't good enough. She needed someone she could rely on one hundred percent.

Did she have unrealistic expectations? She didn't really expect Dusty to be perfect, but she did need him to be reliable.

His soft lips brushed over hers, and her nipples

hardened instantly. She dipped the tip of her tongue into his mouth, loving his taste and the feel of his large warm hands on her. Without letting herself think, she arched up into his hand and sighed when he cupped her breast.

"I've always loved your breasts," he whispered.

She groaned, heat pooling between her legs.

"You like that?" He pressed his face into her cleavage.

"Yes," she managed to respond.

"Me, too. Know what else I like?" He pushed her shirt up.

"No." The word popped out of her, her entire body strung tight with need.

"This." He flipped open the front clasp of her bra, shoved it out of his way and took her into his mouth.

"Oh, God, Dusty." She gripped his massive shoulders, felt the rock-hard muscles beneath her fingertips. She arched up into him again as he moved from one breast to the other. A line of heat darted from her breast straight to her belly. She wanted to get naked. Now. With him.

He moved from her breasts to her mouth and kissed her hard, his tongue plunging into her again and again, imitating what the rest of his body wanted. What they both wanted. She wound her arms more tightly around him, wanting to climb right in under his skin. And even that wouldn't get her close enough to him. She loved how his body felt pressed against her. Loved his smell, the rough scrape of his hands against her skin.

Suddenly, he jerked back and yanked her shirt down, then stood and turned to leave the room.

She reached out for him, her hands snapping greedily in the empty space between them. She wanted him back. Now. "Where are you going?"

And now she was whining. Begging and whining. What a turn-on that must be.

"I heard Brendon. I'm going to check on him."

Teressa didn't move a muscle. Dusty had heard Brendon when she hadn't. She'd always, *always* believed she had an almost supernatural communication with her children. They barely turned over in their sleep, and she woke up.

And yet, she'd been so consumed with desire, she hadn't heard her own son call out. But Dusty had. Not only that, but he'd also pulled himself away from her to check on her son, and she knew that hadn't been easy for him.

She pulled her bra and shirt into place and gripped the front edge of the couch with both hands, beating back the compulsion to run down the hallway to see if her little boy was okay. She couldn't recall ever letting someone else check on her children at night if she was capable of doing it herself.

Relax. Let him handle it. Think of something else

like how Dusty's comment earlier that she treated him like a child had dented her pride. By picking up after him and cooking, she'd wanted to pay him back in a small way for opening his house to them. Apparently, her effort to balance the scales had insulted him. She'd hoped not to have to explain to him why she was doing all those extra chores for him, because she knew Dusty well enough that he didn't expect a payback. He wouldn't understand she was doing it as much for herself as for him. It was her way of keeping things equal between them.

She strained forward, listening to the rumble of Dusty's voice as he spoke quietly to her son. Was Dusty connecting with her children? Did she dare hope he could actually grow into being their father some day?

She pressed her fingers into her eyes and leaned back. *Getting a little ahead of yourself, aren't you?* So he heard Brendon wake up. Dusty had probably seduced so many women in so many different places, keeping an ear open for trouble would be second nature to him. Lord knows, she'd heard enough wild rumors about him. She had to be careful not to expect too much, because she wanted so much, and Dusty...tomorrow he'd be as likely to disappear for a couple days to hang out with his buddies as come home to dinner on time.

She'd only moved into his house two weeks ago, and now she was daydreaming that they could be a happy couple? Had there even been a day in those two weeks when they hadn't fought, or wanted to fight, about something? And, okay, she was willing to admit she was part of the problem. She had to learn not be so controlling. Like she was doing right now, although it was killing her to stay in the living room and let someone else tend to Brendon. Why wasn't Brendon crying? He'd been so afraid of Dusty when they first moved in.

Dusty breezed into the room and slumped into the armchair, instead of sitting on the couch beside her. She waited a full minute for him to say something about Brendon, but he seemed preoccupied.

"How's Brendon?"

"Huh?" He looked toward her. "Oh, fine."

"What did he want?"

"A drink of water."

"Is he okay?"

"He's fine. Check on him if you want, but he's probably asleep again."

She nibbled on the cuticle of her index finger. "Did he ask where I was?"

With obvious effort, Dusty gave her his full attention. "No, he didn't. Is there something wrong?"

Other than she ached for him? Literally. And Brendon apparently didn't need his mother anymore? Dusty didn't need her, either. They'd been into some pretty heavy necking, and now he was completely preoccupied with something else, while she was still humming with the need to feel him pressed against her again. She was dying to ask him what he was thinking about, but how juvenile was that? Besides, he was probably lusting after that car stereo he had to return, not her.

"Nothing's wrong." She started feasting on the next cuticle. Oh, goody. A new bad habit. Dusty had returned to gazing at the air between them, his mind obviously elsewhere.

"Dusty?" she said after what felt like a half hour, but was probably only five minutes.

He swung his gaze toward her, his forehead wrinkled. "What?"

"I cooked your dinners and picked up after you and washed your clothes and all that stuff because I was trying to pay you back."

"For what?"

She spread her hands in front of her. "Everything. For taking us in. For fixing the house." She smiled. "For tucking Brendon into bed."

"Was that wrong? Me checking on Brendon? 'Cause I was just trying to save you a trip down the hallway. You're on your feet all day."

"No, it was great. He's never let anyone do that before if I'm around. Thank you."

His expression softened. "You can't ask me to get involved with the kids then freak out when I do. But I kind of get it, too. I don't feel good about Stan spending time with Brendon. I don't think he'd hurt Brendon or anything, but he doesn't seem like the kind of guy who'd be good around kids. What's the story on that? Does he have visiting rights?"

"He's allowed to have Brendon one day a month."

"There's nothing you can do about that?"

"He's Brendon's father. I was lucky to get the judge to agree to that small amount of time. The good news is he's never asked to spend time with Brendon." And she hoped he never would. She didn't completely trust him.

"I can't tell you how sorry I am I messed up. Maybe if I apologized to Stan, he'd forget about Brendon again."

Teressa felt the inevitable rush of tears. She knew Dusty would rather eat raw fish guts than apologize to Stan. "Thank you. I know how much you dislike Stan. Let's just leave it and hope he forgets about all of us."

"If that's what you want."

What she wanted was for Dusty to beat the stuffing out of Stan, then take him for a boat ride and come back alone. She also wanted to go over there and sit on Dusty's lap and feel his strong arms around her. She was tired of making decisions all by herself, of holding it together and fighting her own battles. It felt good to talk with Dusty about what they should do concerning Stan.

"I don't want you to think you owe me anything, Teressa. It doesn't feel right to me."

She swallowed the lump in her throat. "Because you'd do all this for anyone, wouldn't you?"

"Not exactly. Because it's you, and you and I—" It was Dusty's turn to clear his throat. "I'd do anything for you, Teressa."

Now she really was going to cry. It was one thing to lust after him; she always had and probably always would. But dear God, she wasn't falling in love with Dusty Carson, was she? That wasn't part of the plan. Falling in love meant giving up even more control, and she was barely hanging on by her fingertips as it was.

"WHOA. WHAT'S UP with you?" Tyler's eyes bugged out as he skidded to a stop halfway across the café kitchen and stared at Teressa the next day.

She allowed herself a small smile. "What do you mean?"

"You're…" He cocked his head to one side. "You're different."

She had to give the kid points. She certainly felt different. Desirable. Womanly. On fire. Dusty's kisses did that, stirred things up inside her. Made her want things she usually didn't allow herself to think about. What was the point of dreaming about being with a man when you knew he was never going to get serious? But maybe Dusty was serious about them as a couple. He'd certainly been acting like he was.

The clock on the wall caught her eye. "You're late."

"Yeah. See I missed the morning rush." He nodded toward the empty dining room.

"Very funny. I'm going to start docking your pay. You're always late, and you leave early."

"Aw, come on, Teressa. I leave because there's no one here after three. You know I'd stay if you needed me to."

Tyler wasn't a bad kid, so much as dumb. She turned her attention to chopping the pumpkin into wedges to make the daily soup, spicy pumpkin. "You should get a trade. You'll never be able to afford to move away from home with the wages you make here."

Tyler wrapped an apron around his lanky teenage body. "You could give me a raise."

She whacked the pumpkin into quarters. "No, I couldn't. Clean the washroom, okay?"

"Where's Adam?"

"Working on his wedding plans." Adam had told her yesterday afternoon he wouldn't be in until later because he had to finalize the marriage ceremony with the officiant. She wouldn't be surprised if he was still in bed with Sylvie instead. Sylvie liked to work late at night, and none of them had seen much of her the past few weeks. Adam was probably trying to get some quality time with her.

She could have used more quality time with Dusty. But Sarah and Brendon were always with them, demanding attention. She didn't mind, of course, but sometimes the children's dependence scared her. She used to think she could rely on her mother if anything happened to her. But Linda hadn't called or stopped by once since Teressa had moved out. She supposed her father would help, but she didn't know if he had the stamina it took to raise children. Linda had done the child-rearing in their family.

That pretty much left her with Dusty as backup. It disturbed her that she still had her doubts about whether he'd hang in there. She didn't doubt he loved Sarah and Brendon, or was well on his way to loving them.

She sliced the pumpkin into manageable pieces and pushed the innards into the compost bucket. She was being unfair to Dusty, letting her own fears color her judgment. She had to start trusting him to do the right thing and give him the benefit of the doubt. Otherwise their relationship would become static in a can-he, maybe-not cycle. If only their everyday relationship could be as perfect as the physical part.

Tyler pushed the swinging door between the kitchen and dining room open with his shoulder, kicking the mop bucket in front of him. "That guy's out there. Says he wants to talk to you."

She looked up from peeling the pumpkin. "What guy?" Tyler knew everyone in the village.

"Stan Ferris."

A wave of nausea erupted in her stomach. She carefully put the sharp knife she'd been using on the stainless steel workbench. "What does he want?"

"Told you. Wants to talk to you. I can say you're not here, Teressa."

"Why would you do that?" She squared her shoulders. She'd known this was coming. Stan wasn't the type of man who let things go. Her skin tightened with anger. "I can handle him, thanks."

She picked up the knife again, more for effect than any intention to use it, and marched into the empty dining room. Tyler followed on her heels. It was just like Stan to pick a time to talk to her when no one other than Tyler was around.

She kept the counter between them. Not because she was afraid of him, but she didn't trust herself not to slap him up the side of the head. "What do you want?"

Stan leered at her. "You're looking awfully good these days, Teressa. Got another bun in the oven, I hear."

"I'm busy. I don't have time to chat."

"Fine. My lawyer says I got a right to spend time with my own kid. I want Brendon today."

She staggered back a step, as if he'd punched her in the heart. "He's three years old, and you've never asked to spend time with him before. Why now?" She knew he was jealous of Dusty and was using Brendon to hurt him, but she didn't want to make anything easy for him.

"I don't have to have a reason."

"No, but you have to give me at least twenty-four hours' notice, I believe."

Stan got a stubborn look on his face. "If I don't get him today, I'll ask my lawyer if I can have him for a weekend visit instead of just today. Like you said, I haven't spent any time with him. The judge will probably let me have the kid for a couple of days to make up for lost time. My mother would like that better, anyway."

Teressa briefly thought of offering him money to leave Brendon alone, but she knew that would start a lifetime of bribes. And then she'd have to kill him. She tucked in her bottom lip to stem the tears crowding up her throat. "I need to phone my lawyer."

"Go ahead. I'll have a coffee while I wait," he said to Tyler.

Tyler tossed the dish towel he was holding over his shoulder. "Not from me you won't." Tyler followed Teressa into the kitchen. "I think you should phone Dusty."

"So he can come down here and beat up Stan? I

don't think so." She willed her hand to stop shaking long enough to dial the lawyer's number, although she already knew the answer to her question. Dusty had warned her to take care of this, and she hadn't. Brendon was going to have to spend the afternoon with Stan because of her negligence. She was a terrible mother. She didn't deserve her children.

She sucked back her tears and explained to the lawyer the situation. As she expected, he advised her to let Stan see his son for a few hours now instead of letting Stan appeal to the judge for an entire weekend visit. The lawyer pointed out, Stan would probably be happy enough to let Brendon go home after he'd made his point. And then they'd meet with the judge to review Stan's parental rights.

When she finished talking to the lawyer, she slipped into the chair by the desk, put her head down and cried.

"Teressa." Tyler put his hand on her shoulder. "Don't get mad at me, but I called Dusty on my cell. He and Adam are on their way. I don't trust Stan. He can get mean sometimes."

"You're fired," she said without picking up her head.

"I figured. But I don't care, because it was the right thing to do. Dusty's more Brendon's dad than that has-been out there."

She rubbed the pounding in her forehead. "I don't understand how my life got so complicated."

Tyler patted her. "It's not your fault you get pregnant every time you look at a guy."

"Thank you for that, Tyler. You're still fired, though." She stood and drew in a deep breath, searching for the courage to tell Stan he could have Brendon for the day. She forced her leaden feet to move toward the dining room. She was overreacting. Stan would probably take Brendon to his mother's. Mrs. Ferris had asked several times to visit with her grandson, and Teressa had agreed, but after the third time, the requests stopped. She couldn't pretend she hadn't been relieved. Although she didn't believe in blaming all a child's faults on the parent, Stan didn't get to be a self-absorbed... pumpkinhead all by himself. She didn't want her son to be exposed to the same influence. Although her own mother was super critical of Teressa, she had a soft spot when it came to her grandchildren, and Sarah and Brendon had escaped most of Linda's bitter criticism.

Making up names for Stan made her feel marginally better, and she pushed through the door, feeling as if she was marching into battle.

"You want him after day care for a couple of hours?"

Stan stood on the wrong side of the cash register. The swine. Thankfully, she hadn't unlocked it for the day yet. She stayed close to the kitchen door and wondered how it was possible that he'd once been the hometown hero every girl had lusted after, including her.

He swung around to face her. He was overweight and already had a beer belly as big as his father's. Life was probably not a garden of roses for him, because he'd reached the pinnacle of his life at twenty-two years old, and it had been downhill from there. He'd crawled home from playing hockey in the NHL and had given up. She shuddered. She'd been knocked down a couple of times, but she refused to believe the best of her life was behind her. Stan made it hard to feel sorry for him, because he thought everyone owed him.

"Nah. I'll take him now."

"This isn't take-out, Stan. You can't just order up a kid for the day."

Tyler slid through the door behind her.

Stan smirked. "I just did, didn't I?"

The doors to the restaurant burst open, and Adam and Dusty marched into the room, looking as if they wanted to rip someone apart. Stan cursed and shifted closer to her.

"What's going on, Teressa?" Dusty demanded.

Teressa looked across the counter, but didn't see her dear friend standing in front of her. She saw a man marked by anger and helplessness and hate. The man she'd been slowly falling in love with, who loved to laugh, was gone. Had she ever considered

what she'd taken away from Dusty by handing him
the responsibility of a child?

Tears flooded her eyes. "I'm sorry," she whispered.

Dusty reached forward, grabbed Stan by the collar of his jacket and yanked him across the counter,
cutlery and napkins, salt-and-pepper shakers and
receipt books scattering everywhere.

"I've been waiting to pound on you, Carson.
You think you're so goddamn smart." Stan's arms
flailed in the air as he attempted to free himself
from Dusty's hammerlock.

"Dusty." Adam stepped up beside him and did
no more than put his hand on Dusty's arm.

Dusty cursed and dropped Stan to the floor.

"I can get you for assault," Stan grumbled as he
dusted himself off.

"Really?" Dusty folded his arms, his glare gla-
cial.

Stan sneered as he eased toward the outside door.
"Brendon's my son. I'm spending the day with him,
and there's nothing you can do about it."

"If that kid so much as sheds one tear, I'll come
after you."

"And do what?" Stan clutched the door handle.

"Beat the crap out of you to start with."

"I'll have you arrested."

"So? If you hurt Brendon, I'll be happy to do

time in jail to teach you a lesson. You've been warned. Be good to Brendon."

Stan darted a look at Adam, who was doing his scary squeezing-his-hands-open-and-shut thing, but keeping quiet. "Where is he?" Stan directed his question to Teressa.

"At the day care."

When Stan slammed the door shut behind him, Teressa squatted down and mechanically started picking up forks and knives off the floor. She wanted to cry, not just for Brendon, but for all of them, because her messed-up life had just spilled over into everyone else's. Shame burned through her. This is what her mother had meant when she'd said Dusty was too good for her.

She looked up when she heard a rush of feet and saw Dusty race toward the bathroom. Feeling like an old woman, she stood up.

She'd made up her mind a long time ago to make the best of her situation. Didn't mean she'd stopped dreaming of leaving, though. She liked to think it didn't hurt to dream, but she was slowly realizing maybe it did. Instead of always wishing she was somewhere else, she should try being happy with living in Collina. Maybe she could trick herself into believing she loved her life.

She handed Tyler a handful of forks and pointed at the tables that needed to be set for the day. "Wash them first. I'll check on Dusty."

Adam made a sound as if to speak, but when she looked at him, he remained silent, his lips pressed tight together. Teressa smiled. "I'll be gentle with him. Promise."

Dusty was splashing water on his face when she walked into the washroom. When she caught his reflection in the mirror, her heart pinched tight. His eyes were red.

He looked up from the sink. "Not now, Teressa."

"I was hoping for a hug."

He tilted his head and regarded her in the mirror. Goodness knows what he saw—a woman going out of her mind? After a minute he nodded and turned and wrapped his arms around her. She sank into his embrace, savoring his warmth and the solid feel of him.

"You're not going to tell Brendon that he has to go with Stan for the day?"

"The day care won't let Brendon leave with anyone without my permission. I'll go up there in a minute. I just need this. You. I'm a terrible mother, Dusty. I should have called the lawyer like you said. If Stan hurts Brendon…"

"Shhh." He patted her back. "Brendon's going to be okay. Stan wouldn't dare lay a finger on that child now. Not after Adam and I made it clear what would happen if he did. Besides, Stan isn't evil, just selfish."

"That's why you came? To remind Stan someone besides me is taking care of Brendon?"

"Nah. I just want to beat the shit out of the idiot. Adam came along for a show of strength."

"Adam's the one who almost killed a man with his fists, yet you're the one ready to fight Stan."

Dusty pulled back to look down at her. "The man Adam beat up had abused his mother. I'd do the same for Brendon or Sarah or you. Sorry to be Neanderthal about it, but that's the way I am with family. You fight me, you fight my gang."

He pulled her back into his arms. "I take that back. I'm not sorry I feel protective toward you and the kids. But I am sorry I caused this mess to start with. I should have kept my mouth shut around that ass-hat."

"You're not responsible for Stan's actions, Dusty. I'm going to contact the lawyer and take care of the situation. We can't keep tiptoeing around Stan."

Dusty raised her chin up with his finger until their gazes met and locked. "We'll figure it out together."

Teressa closed her eyes against her tears as they both moved toward the door, Dusty's arm still around her shoulders. She loved having him by her side. Already couldn't imagine facing Stan and the lawyers and judge without his support. She finally had someone she could rely on.

"DID STAN BRING Brendon home yet?"

Dusty strolled down the street with Adam, his hands jammed in the pockets of his leather jacket. The cold, dirty gray afternoon matched his mood. He hunched his shoulders against the wind, wishing he'd thought to wear his toque.

"Don't know. Teressa said she'd phone if anything was wrong. Stan doesn't have to have Brendon back until six. It's only five."

"I feel bad leaving Teressa on her own so much at work. I told her I'll make it up to her after the wedding."

Thankful to have something else to think about besides Brendon, Dusty took the bait. "You and Sylvie aren't planning a honeymoon?"

"My life is a honeymoon, man. Doesn't get any better than this. I'll be gone for a few days when Sylvie has her show in Toronto, but that's all."

Dusty slowed his pace. He liked hiking and had jumped at Adam's offer to walk up the ridge behind the village to look for some kind of tree or branches or leaves to use for decoration for the wedding. He hadn't paid close attention to what it was they were looking for—he was just glad that he had something to occupy him for the next hour or so.

"You don't sound too happy about going to the city."

"Toronto isn't my favorite place, and I don't fit in with Sylvie's artsy friends."

"You're worried about Oliver." Or maybe about that biker gang Adam's father used to run with. Dusty had caught a glimpse of a couple of gang members when they'd swung through the village earlier in the summer. They looked like scary dudes. But then so did Adam, and he was a good man, no doubt about it. Some people wore their scars on the outside. Adam was one of them.

"No. Yeah. I don't know." Adam stopped. "You have to admit he's perfect for Sylvie."

"She chose you. No accounting for some people's taste." He play-punched Adam on the shoulder. "The path's up behind the barber shop. We should hurry. It won't stay light out for long.

"Seriously, Adam," Dusty continued as they turned onto the main street. "She picked the better man. Sylvie's crazy about you."

"All these compliments. If you don't stop, I'm gonna blush."

Dusty laughed. "I'd like to see… Son of a bitch." He picked up his pace as his heart jackhammered in his chest.

Adam followed on his heels. "What is it?"

"Stan's Mustang is parked outside the legion. You're not supposed to take kids in there, and he shouldn't be drinking when he has Brendon, anyway."

A curse exploded out of him when they came up

behind the car. He was going to murder Stan. With his bare hands. Slowly.

Brendon was kneeling in the car, crying, his face pressed up against the backseat window.

"Brendon." Dusty called out the name as if it were ripped from his gut. He rushed the car, fumbled with the door handle closest to Brendon and found it locked. "Goddamn it. I'll kill him." He punched the roof of the car.

Adam grabbed his arm. "Settle down. You're upsetting Brendon. Talk to the kid. Tell him everything's going to be all right."

Settle down? It wasn't Adam's kid inside the car, freezing and crying. Brendon wasn't even wearing a jacket or hat.

"Brendon." He knelt in front of the window and bit back another howl when he noticed Brendon had wet himself. How long had Stan left him in the car, and why hadn't anyone else seen him crying and stopped to help? This damned town. Everyone went home and closed the door when it started to get dark.

Brendon was still crying, but slowed from gulps to whimpers. Dusty leaned his head against the window, fighting back his own tears. *This. Was. Hell.* Why had no one warned him how vulnerable a little kid could make him feel? Ironic that a three-year-old boy, who struggled to like him,

could breech the barricades he'd spent his whole
life erecting.

He jumped to his feet and looked around. There,
under the old maple tree, lay a huge branch that
had come down in the storm last week. He grabbed
the branch, welcoming the solid weight of it in his
hand.

"Brendon, climb into the front seat and get down
on the floor. That's right. Put your hands over your
head."

Adam was shouting at someone on his phone.
He knew he only had a minute to break open the
window before Adam tried to stop him. But he'd
be damned if he was going into that legion to beg
Stan to come out to unlock the doors. Plus he didn't
dare be within yards of the man right now.

He hoisted the heavy branch to his shoulder like
a baseball bat and swung hard at the rear passenger window of the classic Mustang. The car was
Stan's pride and joy, his trophy for almost making
it in the big leagues. *Take that, you son of a bitch.*
Hundreds of cracks ran through the window, but
it held together, looking like a mosaic. He swung
again, satisfied when the window collapsed out into
the street.

He reached in and unlocked the front door. "This
way, Brendon. Come on. Careful of the glass." He
swept an armload into the street.

Brendon stuck his head up and looked at him,

his face still covered with tears. After a minute he crawled over to the driver's door. Dusty dropped the branch when Brendon got close enough for him to grab the small boy. He held the tiny, trembling body close to him and blinked back tears as he kissed the top of Brendon's head. "You okay?"

Brendon buried his head inside Dusty's jacket. "I peed my pants," he confessed in a shaky, tearstained voice.

Rage quaked inside Dusty. He felt as if he were breaking apart into a million pieces. He loved this kid, and it felt like a miracle to hold his small body against his. "No blame, little man. You were stuck in the car. I'm proud of you for being so brave. I'm just going to pass you to Adam for a minute."

Adam kept his arms by his side. "You should hold him."

"Take him. Now." He shoved Brendon into Adam's arms, picked up the branch and circled the car. Stan was never, ever going to threaten or hurt his family again. He smashed both headlights, the death grip of anger inside him loosening.

"Dusty. Don't," Adam called from a few feet away.

Dust attacked the windshield. It took him three swings before the window shattered. That's exactly how his heart felt, like a thousand jagged pieces. He used all his strength to bring the branch down on the hood of the car.

He heard people talking behind him, but his attention was channeled into destroying the car. It was either the car or Stan.

"Hey, hey, hey." Stan came running out of the legion. "What are you doing? That's my car, you asshole."

Dusty turned toward him, the branch held high over his shoulder. *The slimy snot-nosed snake.* Stan stopped whining midsentence. The crowd that had formed across the street went quiet. Dusty gripped the branch harder, his eyes drilling into Stan's. Anger vibrated through him.

"Dusty, my man." Adam spoke quietly from behind him. "He's not worth it."

Dusty blinked back a sudden rush of tears. *Goddamn it.* "I know." He tossed the branch on the ground and walked away. He hunched his shoulders and walked past his friends and his family on the sidewalk. Feeling as if he'd been flailed alive, his skin stripped away with no protection against the world and the flood of emotions that threatened to drown him, he thought he might walk right out of his life.

"I'm going to have you arrested for destroying my car, dick-wad," Stan shouted after him. "It's a classic. You're never going to be able to afford to replace it."

Dusty stopped, but didn't turn around. He didn't trust himself to go back and not kill Stan. He hunched his shoulders and walked past his friends and his family on the sidewalk. Not surprisingly, news had spread fast around town.

He'd screwed up big-time, in so many ways. He hadn't been watching where he was headed with Teressa and the kids. Probably because he hadn't known the endgame. He'd forgotten about the sheer nakedness of love. Hell, sometimes he wondered if he'd ever gotten over his mother's desertion. It had taken him years to shake off the feeling that he wasn't worth coming home for, and he'd sworn to never, ever open his heart like that again. And yet, here he was, all chewed up inside because a three-year-old kid peed his pants inside a locked car. *Damn it to hell.*

And the truth was he'd do it all over again, if necessary. No one hurt his family.

"You need witnesses," Adam said.

Stan laughed. "I got all kinds."

"I didn't see anything," Adam said. "Anyone else see what happened here?"

"I didn't," Pops said.

"Me, either," agreed Cal.

"All I see is a piece of shit," Sylvie called out in a loud voice.

"I work right across the street," Teressa's father said in his wobbly voice. "I'm sure I saw a branch fall out of the tree and land on the car. Branches came down in that storm last week."

Stan looked around wildly. "You all saw him."

"Prove it," Pops challenged him.

"It's not fair," Stan whined. He stopped when Pops stepped toward him.

"Show's over, folks," Pops said. "Time to go home."

Dusty started walking again. He wouldn't be going home tonight. Couldn't handle seeing the fear in Brendon's eyes or the recriminations Teressa was sure to lay on him. Couldn't handle the damned fear that twisted through his gut. He'd fallen in love with a family that didn't want him. He'd tried to convince himself and Teressa that Teressa wanted him, but she didn't. He just happened to be the father of her third child, that was all. He'd known all along that he wasn't good enough to be a husband and father, and frankly, he was tired of trying.

TERESSA STOOD OUTSIDE Dusty's hunting cabin and watched the smoke curl up into the ice-blue sky. She'd never thought of herself as a coward, but today she was showing her true colors. Dusty had holed up in his camp for two days after rescuing Brendon, and she needed him to come home. They all needed him back, because it wasn't home without him.

"Do you think he's here?" Sarah whispered.

"I don't know. Probably." He wasn't answering his phone, so she couldn't warn him they were coming.

Brendon slipped his hand into hers and held on tight. She'd talked to both Brendon and Sarah about what Dusty had done, why he'd demolished Stan's car, and how they felt about the whole thing. Sarah was old enough to understand that what Dusty had done was wrong, but he'd been trying to protect Brendon and that was all right with her. She just wanted him home. She didn't care what he'd done or why.

Brendon had grown even more quiet than his usual self since the incident. He'd never been a typical noisy little boy, whooping and hollering and roughhousing around the house, but now he was a ghost, hanging around the edges of the rooms. She'd tried everything, but nothing had brought him out of his shell. She needed Dusty to breathe life back into him again.

She understood how Brendon felt, because for the past two days, she'd had a hard time dragging herself out of bed in the morning and feeling enthusiastic about anything. She needed Dusty to breathe life into her, too. But she was also ticked off at him. You don't just quit a family. Either he was in or he wasn't, but he didn't get to play hot and cold with her kids or with her. They deserved better than that.

If she didn't go home with Dusty today, she'd survive. She didn't know how, but she would. But she was not letting him off easy. If he was done with them, he had to tell all three of them to their faces. That was the price he had to pay for his freedom.

Sarah rushed toward the door and pounded on it, calling Dusty's name before Teressa had completely gathered her wits for the confrontation. Then again, she doubted she'd ever be prepared to let Dusty go. And that surprised her. She hadn't realized she'd been holding on to him.

The door flew open and Dusty appeared, a startled look on his face. Brendon gave out a small whimper, but Sarah threw herself against him and wrapped her arms around one leg. He staggered back, a surprised laugh escaping him. "Hold on there, Princess." He ran his large hand over her head and knelt down to hug her, but all the while he watched Teressa.

Teressa swallowed a surge of tears and tore her gaze away from the sad look in his eyes.

"Mommy said you don't get to quit us unless you tell us first." Sarah patted Dusty's cheek. "You don't want to quit us, do you?"

Yup. One-hundred-percent coward. Her six-year-old daughter had more courage than she'd ever have. Or maybe Sarah had more faith in Dusty than she did.

"Sarah," she admonished her daughter. "I'm sorry." Not able to look Dusty in the eye, she kept her gaze trained over his right shoulder. "I had a speech prepared to give you, but I suppose Sarah gave you the gist of it. If you're not coming back, we need closure."

Instead of answering her, Dusty let go of Sarah and turned to Brendon. "Hey, there, little man."

Brendon took his thumb out of his mouth and, for the first time in two days, smiled. It wasn't big, but it was a smile. The hard knot of anxiety in Teressa's chest loosened enough for her to take a decent breath.

"Brendon, I'm really sorry for what I did. I didn't mean to scare you. It was wrong what I did."

"It was not. You saved him." Sarah leaned against his shoulder.

Dusty shook his head. "I shouldn't have gotten so mad, and I never should have beat on Stan's car. I understand if you're scared of me now." He looked up at Teressa. "That's why I came here. I didn't want to scare the kids any more than I already had."

"I peed standing up," Brendon announced.

Dusty stilled and turned his gaze back to Brendon, a big smile slowly stretching over his face. "All by yourself?"

Brendon nodded his head.

"You're the man. Slap the hand." He held up his hand, and with a giggle Brendon high-fived him.

Teressa used the back of her hand to wipe away her tears. Damn hormones.

"How about you and Brendon go inside for a minute while I talk to your mother. There might be some chocolate bars left over from Halloween in the kitchen."

Sarah rushed inside, then peeked back out and motioned for Brendon to join her. Brendon let go of Teressa's hand and followed his sister. Dusty closed the door behind them and leaned against it.

"I don't suppose it's going to be that easy," he said.

She shoved her hands in her pockets and studied her boots. "We're not toys you can take off the shelf, then put back when you get tired of playing with us."

"Come on, Teressa. I never took you or the kids lightly."

"Seems like the first opportunity that came along, you were out the door pretty damned fast."

"I'd terrorized Brendon. I really didn't think he wanted to be in the same room as me."

She looked straight at him. "That was the only reason you left?"

Dusty stared back at her for a minute, but dropped his gaze. "No one told me I could fall in love with a three-year-old kid. I didn't see it coming."

Oh, my. How long had she waited to hear him

say something, anything, about loving her children? He loved Brendon. The tightness in her chest eased and she smiled, inside and out. She wanted to wrap her arms around him and hold him. She hadn't expected him to be so honest or so sensitive to his feelings.

"You're scared?"

Dusty dragged a hand through his hair. "Yeah."

"And that's what you do. You run away from commitments. How's that working for you this time?"

"Not so good. It's different when it's a kid. They're so damned vulnerable. They can break your heart like that." He snapped his fingers.

"They can also love you unconditionally. That means, no matter what you do, how much you screw up, they'll probably still love you."

"So, think Brendon's scarred for life?"

"I think he'll be okay, but I wouldn't pick up a stick of wood around him anytime soon."

"I'm so sorry, Teressa. The kids seem kind of okay, but what about you?"

Oh, please let her say this without crying. "I don't like that you left us. But I missed you, and I want you to come home."

A crooked smile lifted a corner of his mouth. "You know what?"

"What?" she asked suspiciously.

"I missed you, too. I want to come home."

Teressa felt as if a ton of bricks had been lifted off her shoulders. "Really?"

His eyes softened. "Yeah, really. Would I be pushing my luck to ask for a kiss?"

She pursed her lips. "That depends. Are you planning on running away from home again?"

Dusty moved closer to her and slid his hands around her waist. "I'll make you a deal. Next time I run away, how about I take you with me?"

She leaned into him and sighed deeply. Despite her faith being shaken by Dusty disappearing from their lives, for even a brief period of time, she knew she was falling in love with him. She'd put her doubts on hold for now and hope for the best. "I like the sound of that." She stood on tiptoe and touched her mouth to his.

ANITA'S HEART PING-PONGED inside her chest when she heard Cal's truck pull into their driveway late Saturday afternoon. She should have told him she was babysitting Brendon and Sarah this evening, but she knew he'd say it was a bad idea, and she was tired of trying to convince him that she was all right. Instead, she'd opted to show him that she could handle being around children.

She was a nervous wreck.

Cal smiled when he saw her waiting for him at the back door. "Hey, honey-bunch."

He dropped a kiss on her cheek and shrugged

out of his jacket and hung it up in the closet. Last week, she and Teressa had discussed how different Cal and Dusty were from each other. Cal, for instance, always took his boots off at the door and hung up his jacket in the closet. Teressa said she was forever tripping over Dusty's work boots and picking up after him. Anita had noticed the same thing with Sarah and Brendon. Both had brought a few toys with them today, Sarah's organized in her knapsack, while Brendon's was stuffed under his arm when they arrived earlier. How could two children, brought up in the same household, be so different? Being an only child, siblings had always fascinated her.

"Did you have a good day?" She grabbed a beer out of the refrigerator and handed it to Cal at the same time he put his lunch box on the counter.

He raised his eyebrows at the beer before taking it. "It was okay. The Tolsters want to install a second bathroom on their main floor. We need another plumber in this village besides Beanie. He's good, but man, is he slow."

"Maybe he'll work faster if he knows he has more than one job. Teressa mentioned they were thinking of installing a bathroom in the basement."

Cal sipped his beer. "Probably not a bad idea with two kids and another one on the way. I almost feel sorry for my little brother. He's always got this startled look on his face these days. Like he doesn't know what hit him." He snickered.

"Um…Brendon and Sarah are here." She'd planned to segue into that with a little more finesse, but she couldn't risk Cal saying anything that might hurt their feelings if they overheard.

Cal's mouth tightened as he lowered the beer bottle. "What's going on?"

"I'm babysitting," she said as cheerfully as she could. "Teressa and Dusty are painting some rooms tonight, and Teressa asked if I'd look after the children for a few hours. I wasn't doing anything." As usual. "So I said yes."

"I thought we agreed that you wouldn't take on any projects until you felt stronger."

"Looking after children is not a project, Cal. And I feel fine. Really." She stood taller to emphasize her point.

He studied her for a minute. "How about emotionally? I mean…you know, being with kids?"

Her cheeks heated up. "I'm okay." She flipped open his lunch box and started to unpack the empty containers.

Cal came up behind her and slid his arms around her waist. "Really? Or are you telling me what you think I need to hear?"

She scrunched an empty plastic bag in her hands. The counselor had said it was important to be honest, but Anita wasn't certain that was good advice.

Except she'd almost lost Cal when she hadn't told him the truth a few months ago.

She leaned into him. "I felt a little weepy when Sarah gave me a kiss."

Cal nuzzled the sensitive spot behind her ear. "You're such a softy." He skimmed his hand over her stomach and up to her breast.

"Cal! The children."

He dropped his hands to her hips and pressed himself against her behind. "They're going home soon, right?"

She laughed and turned around to face him. It frightened her how much she loved her husband. "You're incorrigible. And incredibly sexy. But tonight, you'll have to wait."

"Are you guys smooching? Mommy and Dusty smooch when they think we're not watching." Sarah skipped into the room and climbed up on a chair by the table. "I'm hungry, Anita. Can we eat now?"

"Is that all the hello I get from my favorite girl?" Cal sat beside her and tickled her. She giggled and climbed from her chair to sit on his lap.

Anita's heart unfurled. She loved watching her big, strong husband act so gentle with children. He'd make a wonderful father someday.

Tears ripped into her, and she spun around to face the counter. She gave herself a second to get her emotions under control before opening the oven and taking out a casserole. Cal was probably right.

Taking care of Sarah and Brendon was too much for her just yet. She still felt too fragile emotionally to spend any amount of time around children. Except Teressa obviously thought she was capable of babysitting, because she'd asked her, not Sylvie, to take the children. Teressa had no idea how good Anita had felt when she'd asked.

"I hope you like macaroni and cheese."

"I do. So does Dusty. He smacks his lips when he eats it," Sarah said.

From the corner of her eye, Anita watched Brendon slip into the room. He stayed close to the door as if he wasn't sure of his welcome. Before she could encourage him, Cal grabbed the tiny boy and swung him around the room like he was flying. Brendon's face turned red, but instead of breaking out in tears, he started giggling, his sweet laugh clear and innocent. Brendon might be the quiet, shy one, but Anita suspected he had hidden talents that had yet to bloom. By the time Cal set him on a chair, they were all laughing.

"Again!" Brendon yelled.

Cal grabbed him again and swung him around, then set him down. "That's all for now, little man. You won't be able to eat."

"My turn." Sarah hopped down and held up her arms to Cal.

"Brendon, will you help me set the table?" Anita said.

The three-year-old nodded as Cal swung Sarah around the room.

Anita squatted down and gave him the forks and knives. "You're getting to be such a big boy. I bet you help your mommy a lot."

His eyes grew big and round, as if he was looking at an exotic creature. Anita smiled. "You smell good," he said.

Her smile grew wider. Definitely hidden talents. Teressa would have to keep her eye on this one. "So do you," she said. "You smell like sunshine and fresh air."

"I'm going to be a whale when I grow up. No." He shook his head. "I mean a fisherman. Like Dusty. Mommy says I can't be a whale. Dusty has a whale for a friend. He said he'd take me to see him one day, but he hasn't."

She knew it wasn't right to be envious of someone else's good fortune, but, oh, how she longed for a little boy, just like Brendon, who would tell her his deepest secrets. Did Dusty have any idea how lucky he was? She liked Dusty a lot. Who didn't? But sometimes she wondered if he was a little… careless with people. She made a mental note to remind him of his promise to Brendon.

"Can I come?" she asked impulsively.

"You have to ask Dusty."

She gave him the cutlery. "I will." It would give her the perfect excuse to remind Dusty of his promise.

Supper went much better than she'd dared hope. She smiled to herself, thinking of the all formal meals she'd attended and hosted in her life. She'd been more nervous about this simple supper than any business dinner her father had ever asked her to host.

She gazed lovingly at Cal. Her hero. He'd saved her from a life of rules and rigidity. She'd been engaged to marry her father's younger, and very ambitious, partner when she'd literally bumped into Cal on the street and spilled her armload of parcels on the sidewalk. Cal told her later he'd fallen in love with her on the spot. It hadn't occurred to her to even take a second look at him, her life was that different from his. One glance had taken in his worn jeans and work boots, and although he made a very attractive parcel, she didn't know anyone who owned work boots.

She paid closer attention when he sent her flowers the next day. And chocolates the next and followed them up with the first of many phone calls. He ignored her when she told him she was engaged, and it didn't take long before she was rushing home from work, anxious to hear his deep, rich voice gently teasing her over the phone. When he turned up on her doorstep with a packed picnic basket and a smile, she didn't think of turning him down. She moved in with him two weeks later. Not once had she regretted her hasty decision.

Her father lost interest in her when she left her job and her family to follow Cal to Collina. It didn't altogether surprise her that he'd seen her more as an asset than a daughter, because he'd often talked about people as if they were commodities. She just hadn't expected him to treat *her* that way. Now, two years later, she was still trying to understand how to fit into village life. She'd begun to think she never would, but lately, people had started reaching out to her, and she was ready to reach back.

Cal plugged in a movie for the children and sat down with them while Anita cleaned up after supper. This was the way it would be if they had children. They'd take turns helping with homework or on a weekend night, like this one, watch a movie with them or play a board game. She grimaced. More like a video game.

Her smile disappeared as she wiped the counter clean. Somehow she had to convince Cal it was time to try again.

When the door flew open, she was startled from her thoughts and staggered backward.

"Hey, there." Dusty grabbed her elbow to steady her. "You okay?"

"Yes, of course. You startled me."

"What's going on?" Cal asked from the arch that opened into the living room.

"I thought she was going to faint." Dusty frowned at her.

"No, I… You…" She closed her mouth. She could hardly accuse him of barging into her house. "He surprised me."

"You do look awfully white." Cal advanced into the room and took her elbow in his hand. "Maybe you should sit down."

She pulled away. "I'm fine," she snapped, then immediately regretted it as the room fell silent. Cal would never agree to her trying to get pregnant again if he thought of her as an invalid.

She pasted a bright smile on her face. "You're early," she said to Dusty. "Would you like a coffee?"

Dusty looked from her to Cal as if gauging the mood. "No. Thanks, though. Teressa says it's better to get the kids home and in bed before they fall asleep here. They sleep better that way, I guess."

"I think she's right. If you make sure your child goes to bed at the correct time every night, they not only sleep better, but often longer, as well." She stopped when she realized both men were staring at her. "I read about it. In a book."

"Right. Where are the kiddos?" Dusty craned his neck in the direction of the living room and whistled.

For heaven's sake, did he think they were animals? "I'll get their coats and things," Anita offered. Why did she have to jabber on about children's sleeping habits? Both Carson brothers thought she was weak *and* crazy. Dusty and Teressa would never let her babysit the children again. And Cal—Cal would say it was too soon to try for another baby.

She carried her armload of coats and hats and boots into the living room. Sarah was clinging to Dusty's leg and gazing up at him as though he was the sun, while he ignored her as he talked to Cal. Cal was frowning down at Brendon, who had fallen asleep on the couch.

"Here's Sarah's jacket." As she passed the bright red jacket to Dusty, she noticed the sleeves were starting to fray. She'd love to take Sarah shopping, but Teressa would never let her. She was fiercely protective of her children. And, Anita supposed, buying clothing for someone else's child could be seen as slightly insulting. Not that that was her intention.

Anita bit her tongue when Dusty took the jacket and absently passed it to Sarah. Anita kneeled down and slipped Brendon's limp arms into the sleeves of his jacket. It, too, looked worn around the cuffs. She zipped up Brendon's jacket and turned to Sarah.

"Need help with that?"

"Nope." Sarah did up her zipper and tugged on Dusty's denim-clad leg. He stopped talking and looked down. "What?"

"I want to go home."

Anita held her breath as Dusty sighed loud enough for the entire village to hear. He took a second or two, then squatted down and tapped Sarah's nose with his finger. "Wait 'til you see your and Brendon's room, Princess. You're going to love it."

Sarah jumped up and down. "Let's go home."

Dusty scooped up Brendon under his arm as if he were a football and took Sarah's hand. "Thanks, Anita." He leaned forward and kissed her cheek. "The kids behave themselves?"

He looked surprised when she turned her head in time to kiss his cheek, as well. "We had fun. And I have a request."

"Name it, it's yours."

"Brendon told me you were going to take him out on your boat to see a whale? I'd love to come, if it's not too much of an imposition."

"Sounds good to me. I'll let you know when we go. Should be soon."

She stood back, satisfied that she'd reminded him of his promise to Brendon.

"When are you taking your traps out?" Cal followed him to the door.

"Another couple of weeks."

"You usually have them hauled by now."

Anita eased back into the kitchen when she heard concern in Cal's voice.

"I'm burning through money like crazy. Going to Lancaster tomorrow maybe to look at some heat pumps. I was hoping to squeeze in another week or two of fishing."

"It's getting pretty cold on the bay for fishing."

Dusty stopped with his hand on the door. "The lobsters don't know that."

"It gets dangerous when ice starts forming on your boat and equipment. You've got more than yourself to think about now."

Fatigue marked Dusty's face. "I know. That means I gotta pull Josh from working on the house for a few days."

"What's he working on?"

"Bathroom, I think."

"I'm free next week. I'll do that."

"Dusty, can we go? I'm tired?" Sarah whined.

"In a minute, Princess. Are you sure? I thought you were still working at the Tolsters'," he said to Cal.

"They can wait. I'll come by tomorrow when you get home and have a look at what needs to be done."

Dusty frowned. "I appreciate the help, but I don't want you losing the Tolster job. From what I hear they're planning on renovating the entire house."

"It only takes you a couple days to haul traps, right? I'll tell him I'm waiting on material or something."

"Okay. Thanks, Cal. Guess I'll see you tomorrow. 'Night, Anita."

Anita put her arm around her husband's waist

as they both watched Dusty strap the children into their seats and drive away. "Mr. Tolster is going to be disappointed when you don't show up next week."

"Tolster doesn't have a brother working his boat too late in the season."

She laid her head on his shoulder. "He's good with Sarah and Brendon, isn't he? For some reason, I didn't expect him to be."

Cal turned and wrapped his arms around her. "I think we've all underestimated my brother. Now, what was that you said earlier? Something about me being, I believe the exact words you used were, *incredibly sexy?*"

Tell him now. She pulled back far enough so she could look into his eyes. "I want a baby, Cal."

His face hardened. "This is exactly why I don't think you're ready to babysit those kids. Oh, come on, hon. Please don't cry." He stroked her arms. "You know I'd love for us to have a baby, but I'm not going to risk your life. Just thinking about the possibility makes me sick."

She sighed. Not that again. "I'm strong, and I'm ready. I am not my mother. Haven't you listened to anything the doctor said?"

"I did. I also know it wasn't his wife we were talking about, but mine. I need more time, Anita. I'm not ready to take that step yet."

Anita tried to bury her disappointment. Would he

ever be ready to take a chance and let her get pregnant? She couldn't imagine living without Cal, but she also couldn't imagine not having children. She prayed it wouldn't come down to having to choose between the two, because she couldn't say for sure which one she'd pick.

CHAPTER NINE

DUSTY TURNED OFF his truck and studied his house, which was lit up like a hotel with no vacancies. His electricity bill was going to kill him. He groaned as he reached for his lunch box. He'd put a push on, hauling traps for the past two days and trying to beat the storm that was forecast for tomorrow. With Josh and Andy's help, he'd managed to pull all his lobster traps in record time, but he'd pay for it with aching muscles. All he wanted was to crawl into bed and have a good night's sleep. For the first time in months, he didn't have to get up before the crack of dawn.

He probably would, anyway. It was his favorite part of the day, especially now that he got to share it with Teressa. He often went to bed soon after the kids crashed and missed spending time in the evening with Teressa, but now that he'd hauled his traps for the winter months, maybe they could have a date like he'd suggested in the beginning.

Had it really only been three weeks since Teressa and the kids had moved in? He grunted as he swung out of the truck. Felt like a lifetime.

When he'd pulled into port a couple hours ago, he'd been happy and relieved to finally have the fishing season behind him for another year. As he unloaded the last of his traps, he kept thinking of the great supper Teressa would have waiting for him, and how she liked to sit with him at the table while he ate on the nights he was late getting in. She'd tell him about her day, and he'd soak her up.

She always smelled so good, sweet and spicy, and he never got tired of watching her, especially when she got all worked up about something. Even when they were kids, he'd gone out of his way to provoke her just to see her eyes spark and watch how her freckles stood out against her white skin.

If she hadn't gotten pregnant with Sarah, Teressa could have gone anywhere in the world and become a famous chef, but she cooked his supper every night and sat at his table. Most nights he counted himself pretty damned lucky.

Of course Sarah also sat at that same table, always clinging to a part of his anatomy, his leg or arm or literally hanging around his neck. He didn't know how he was going to fix that, but she was driving him crazy and something had to be done. Same with Brendon. The kid could not spend his life crying in dark corners. It creeped Dusty out. Things had to change, but he hadn't a clue how.

He tried to slip into the house unnoticed, but Sarah, as usual, flew out of whatever room she'd been in and attached herself to his leg. He wished his radar on the boat worked as well.

"Dusty!"

He sighed, patted her on the head and tried to sit down on the chair to take off his boots. Just once he'd like to walk into his own house and be left alone for a few minutes.

"Sarah, I'm tired tonight. Can you let go of my leg, please?"

"But I've been waiting and waiting for you."

Where was Teressa? He noticed Sarah listened to her mother a hell of a lot more than she listened to him. What did he have to do to make Sarah understand he was serious without scaring her by shouting? Which was exactly what he felt like doing. He'd already terrorized Brendon. He dragged them both over to the chair and managed to sit.

"I'll take your boots off for you."

He got that little girls did stuff he was never going to understand, but no matter how he looked at it, having someone fawn over him wasn't right. Plus he was bone-tired and didn't want to deal with her right now.

"No," he said louder than he'd intended. And immediately felt guilty as Sarah scrambled to her feet, her bottom lip trembling.

"Where's your mother?"

"In the b-b-basement doing the laundry."

His laundry, probably. Hadn't she listened to a

word he'd said the other day? Brendon decided to poke his head around the corner of the living room, looking at Dusty as if he were a monster that had risen from the depths of the ocean.

"Can't any of you get along for a few minutes without me refereeing?" Teressa shot up out of the basement like a missile and aimed straight for him.

"Time out." Dusty made a *T* with his hands. "Could we talk? Alone?"

Teressa cocked her head to one side and studied him. After a minute she sighed. "You're right. We need to talk. Although I'd feel much better if I could shout at someone right about now."

"We'll talk first, and then if you want, you can shout at me. How's that?"

"Far too reasonable for my lousy mood. Bedroom?"

"I thought you'd never ask."

When he closed the bedroom door, he moved over to the window and as far away from Teressa as he could get. It didn't make sense that he got a charge out of her being snippety with him, but he did. Nothing he'd like better right now than to wrap his arms around her and kiss her. Then she'd have something to shout at him about. After she kissed him, of course. "Help me out here. What's up with Sarah?"

"She's a little girl, and her world's been turned all around. She's holding on because she's afraid."

"Of what?"

Teressa sagged against the door. "Of losing you, I think. It's the only thing that makes sense. She doesn't know her own father, and by leaving my parents' place, she essentially lost her grandparents. That's a lot of loss for a little girl."

"So, take her to see her grandfather."

"I will."

"When?"

"Soon. Okay?"

"Good."

He stared out the window at the black November night and massaged the back of his neck. "I know it probably doesn't look like it, but I'm trying with Sarah. I never realized how much I like independent women until now."

Teressa sniffed.

"What?"

"Nothing." She rapped her fist against her thigh.

"When you say it like that, what I hear is *everything*."

"We're pretty dependent on you at the moment," she murmured.

Dusty hooted. "You're so independent, it's a pain in the ass sometimes. You don't need anyone."

"That's not true. I need you."

"For what? To make more work for you? FYI, I don't try to be a slob. I just am. And I know it doesn't look like it, but I'm trying to pick up after myself. It's just you get there before I do most times."

"What are you saying? That I should lower my standards instead of you raising yours?"

Dusty hid his smile. What a firecracker. "Maybe we could meet somewhere in between."

He watched her turn that over. "Maybe," she finally conceded.

He ambled across the room toward her. "Not so easy having to budge on things, is it?"

"Guess not."

He hooked a finger through her belt loop and tugged her toward him. "Don't suppose you care to make it up to me by kissing my hurt better?"

She pulled away. "We're having a serious conversation, Dusty."

"When do we get to have fun?"

"Fun?"

"That's where you laugh and don't worry about anything for more than five minutes. Fun."

"I should go back to the kitchen. I think I hear Brendon sniffling. You know what that means."

"Yeah, prelude to a meltdown. The other half of the dynamic duo. Does he always cry or is it just me?"

"He came that way."

"Seriously?"

"Seems like. I keep hoping he's going to grow out of it, but no luck so far."

"So, it's not just me."

"No."

"Why didn't you tell me that before?"

She shrugged. "I don't know. Why would you think it was you that made him act that way?"

"Because I went ape-shit on him with the car thing, and I haven't got a clue when it comes to kids? To me they're like tiny aliens."

She laughed. Dusty caught the sound and held on to it. "I guess we should talk more often," she said.

"No kidding." He leaned toward her before she could open the bedroom door and kissed her softly on the mouth. "Let's go out to dinner tomorrow night."

She didn't pull away like he'd expected. "Like a date?"

He rubbed his nose against hers. "Yeah."

"Could we just stay at home and watch a movie or something? The thought of driving all the way to Lancaster exhausts me."

Dusty buried his disappointment. He'd wanted her all to himself for a change. "Sure. We'll get the kids drunk on vodka so they'll fall asleep early."

"Ha-ha."

Teressa opened the door, but didn't leave the room. "I need you," she said. "I think of you off and on all day and save up bits of gossip to tell you. I like that I'll see you at the end of the day, even though the kids may be crying or we're both exhausted. And I love our mornings together. It's just…we need to be careful how we fit the pieces of our lives together. I'm afraid if we rush one part, we won't get the rest right."

"You know what's really weird?" he said.

"What?"

"I know what you mean, and I agree. That's gotta be a first." He huffed out a laugh.

She smiled. "Come on. Let's go face the music."

He decided to take a few minutes for himself before returning to the kitchen. That had been a sweet—but too short—interlude with Teressa. He had to make more of an effort to take her out on a date. That was okay, wasn't it? To not always want Sarah and Brendon around?

He hadn't thought about it before, but he actually understood what Sarah was going through. He'd lost his mother when he was only a few years older than Sarah was now, so he knew what it felt like to have people you love disappear. The worst part of his mother's death for him was he'd never know if she meant to come back for him. Not knowing had left a hole in his life; a hole he'd carefully avoided looking directly into.

He wasn't repeating history by pushing Sarah and Brendon away, was he? He kept his distance because he felt overwhelmed and needed room to breathe, but what if they saw it differently? What if they thought it was them, not him, who were the problem? Much like he'd believed his mother's desertion had been his fault. He'd never forgive himself if he hurt Teressa's kids. They deserved so much more from him than he'd been willing to give up to this point.

The smell of supper cooking chased away his morose mood when he walked down the hallway to the kitchen. His mother had left twenty-four years ago. She was nothing more than a faded memory. But Teressa and Sarah and Brendon were right here, and it was time to start thinking of someone other than himself.

THREE DAYS LATER, Teressa tried to settle into the front cab of Dusty's truck, but she couldn't get comfortable. She knew Dusty was up to something, and it was killing her that she couldn't figure out what. She'd already tried asking him, but all he'd mumbled was something about needing help choosing the new bathroom fixtures.

"Are you sure it's okay to leave Sarah and Brendon with Anita? She just had them a few days ago," she asked in a last-ditch attempt to avoid the town trip. She didn't like surprises.

"Did she act like she didn't want the kids?"

No, Anita had looked excited, and healthier than she had for a long while. Teressa supposed if she knocked around a big, clean house by herself all day, she'd be happy for a diversion, too. Geez, she'd probably never get the chance to know what that felt like for…she counted on her fingers…another twenty years if she was lucky.

Twenty years. It sounded like a life sentence. She'd be almost fifty. *Oh, my God.*

"What's wrong? Are you okay?" Dusty put his hand out as if to shield her. "You've gone all white. Is it the baby?"

"I just realized I'll be almost fifty by the time this baby grows up."

"I bet you'll be the sexiest fifty-year-old mom around."

"Dusty." She swatted his arm.

"What?"

"The point is my life will be over."

"Really? Someone should tell Pops his life is done then. He's sixty-eight. Sometimes I think he moved into the senior apartments because of that nurse, Ada."

"No way!"

"Anytime I drop by unannounced, it seems like she's at his apartment or they're hanging out together in the main building. I think Pops has got the hots for Nurse Ada." He snickered.

"She's a lot younger than him."

"So? You have to admit, Pops is pretty awesome."

True. Pops Carson looked good for his sixty-eight years, and despite his heart attack a few months ago, had the vitality of a much younger man. She studied Dusty beside her in the driver's seat. He'd probably age as well as his father had. She hadn't thought much beyond the next few months, but she suddenly realized the idea of growing old with him was a comforting thought.

"Are you sure you're okay? You still look…different. You'd tell me, right? If you didn't feel well?"

"I'm fine." She caught his hand and placed it on her belly.

He glanced at her stomach. "I don't feel anything. Am I supposed to?"

She smiled and covered his hand with hers. "Not for another month or more. The baby's moving inside, we just can't feel the movements yet."

"When do we go for the first ultrasound?"

We. Her mother had accompanied her to the other ultrasounds. Going with Dusty was going to be a pleasant experience compared to that. At least he wouldn't accuse her of being a slut. Doing most things with Dusty was pleasant. She'd been so wound up with all the changes in her life, she'd actually forgotten she got to share this pregnancy and birth with one of her best friends. If he didn't let her down.

"In another couple of weeks. I have the date written down at home."

"Is that when we find out if it's a girl or a boy?"

"That's right, and if we'll have twins."

"Twins?" He snatched his hand away. "There aren't any twins in my family."

A giggle escaped her. "Kidding. I hope," she added. "Which are you hoping for, boy or girl?

"Dusty?" she asked when he didn't reply.

"Give me a minute." His voice sounded raw with emotion. "Talking about it makes it seem so real. I hadn't really thought… Wow. A boy, I guess. No, a girl." He looked at her, a sense of wonder on his face. "It doesn't matter, because it's our baby. We're going to need another room and baby stuff."

"I've got some baby clothes, and people have showers and give us things we need."

"I can afford to buy my own child whatever it needs."

"It's okay, Dusty. People like buying baby clothes. Haven't you ever heard of a baby shower?"

He frowned. "I guess."

"Don't worry. We'll still have to buy things. Why are we stopping here? This isn't the hardware store." She eyed the bank from the parking lot Dusty had pulled into. It was the same bank where he'd tried to get her to open a joint account with him. She was staying within a budget she knew she could cover with her own wages. If there was money in his account to buy building materials for the house, great. If there wasn't, they could go without. She'd mastered the art of frugal living years ago.

She didn't like the way Dusty avoided looking her in the eyes right now. What had he done?

"I asked the lawyer to meet us here to save time. I've got a couple of forms I need you to sign," he said.

"Forms," she repeated.

"I'm deeding half the house to you."

The vein in her forehead began to pulse. She blinked her eyes, trying to bring the brick bank building into focus. "You what?"

His house. He was giving half his house to her. A hysterical laugh rolled up her throat. Which half?

Dusty finally looked at her. Glared at her. "I don't want any argument on this. The lawyer says I can deed you half the house whether you sign or not. Signing the forms makes it easier for you if something happened to me. That's all."

"Why?" Damn it. She would not cry.

"Because I can't stand the idea of someone having the power to kick you out of your own house. You deserve your own home, Teressa, and so do Sarah and Brendon. And I don't want you feeling like you have to do stuff for me because you're staying at my house. I want it to be *our* house."

"Dusty." She stopped and cleared the tears out of her voice. She didn't know how to react. She was overwhelmed, and scared silly. It was too much; she should have seen this coming.

Owning a house together was almost worse than

getting married. By accepting his offer, she was committing to a long-term relationship, and she wasn't sure… She was already responsible for so many people.

Dusty brushed a lock of hair behind her ear. "I think we're going to be okay, don't you?"

She covered her face. "I don't know. I want us to be, but…I don't know. Neither of us are perfect, and it's hard enough to make a relationship work with just two adults. But with two kids and another one on the way? Those aren't good odds."

"If we break up, we'll do what other couples do and sell the house and start over," he said patiently. "But as long as we're together, I want things to be equal between us. I don't ever want you to feel you don't belong. That's important to me. Look, can you not make a big deal about this? Can we just go in there and sign the papers?"

She stared at the pointy toes of her cowboy boots, which she'd thought were so cool in the secondhand shop. Now they just looked stupid and out-of-date. "People don't give me things. Especially big things like houses."

She attempted a smile as she felt a leap of excitement. *Her* house. Well, *their* house. "I don't feel right accepting your offer. Thank you, Dusty. Not just for the offer, but for understanding how hard it is for me to depend on you."

His shoulders twitched. He hadn't liked that last

part. Dusty was the kind of guy who'd probably love to have a woman starry-eyed in love with him; one who'd let him be the man of the house. Instead, he was stuck with bossy, independent her.

"Do you still think you might move away some day?"

"I don't know. The chance to do so is becoming more and more remote."

"I don't want you to be unhappy, but I don't think I could handle you moving away and taking our child with you." He stared straight out the windshield.

"That's why you want my name on the deed of the house? You're afraid I'll leave?"

"I was moving stuff around the basement the other night, and one of your boxes fell over, and I saw a couple certificates from the cooking courses you took. You never told me you were at the top of your class." He glanced sideways at her. "And some letters, too. Replies from all over the world. That's what made me take a closer look. The stamps. You applied for a job in Scotland three months ago."

He turned in his seat to face her. "I can't let you go, Teressa. Now that you're having my baby, I can't handle the thought that Duke would suffer because you left him behind or he grew up thinking his father didn't care enough about him to go with him. I know what that feels like. It's not something you ever recover from, you just learn to live with it. So I tried to think what I could do to make you happy so you won't leave. Other than falling in love with me, that is." His poor attempt at a smile came out crooked, and Teressa had to hold herself back from reaching for him.

She opened her mouth to refuse his offer, but her throat ached from emotion and no words came out. Dusty had been referring to his mother. She hadn't realized that was an issue for him, and her heart ached for the little boy he'd been when Jane Carson left town. She'd always assumed because Pops was such a terrific parent, he'd made up for his wife running away. She'd been wrong.

And now Dusty was stuck with another woman wanting to leave. What a nightmare.

But she still had her own doubts about their relationship. Dusty was almost always dating some woman, and she was using the word *dating* kindly, but he never stayed with any one of them for long. What made her think he'd changed? Would he be eager to move on in a few months, like he always did? She wanted to believe he was ready to settle down and have a family, but wanting didn't make it so. He was trying; she'd give him credit for that.

In a way, giving her half ownership of the house was easy for Dusty. It wasn't as if the house was a home that he loved and had invested much of himself into. He hadn't done a thing to it until she'd moved in. She wasn't trying to belittle the gesture, but put it into perspective and not lose her head—or her heart.

Being generous came easy to Dusty. Giving her part ownership of the house so she didn't feel dependent on him was a grand gesture. But could she trust him to be there for her and the children for longer than a few months?

"Giving me part ownership of the house won't guarantee anything, Dusty. I don't want to accept your offer, but I'm going to, because I agree with you. We seem to have come to the part of taking the next step. You know, the three month-six month milestone. Only our relationship is accelerated, because of…Duke? Seriously? Duke?"

Dusty leaned over and kissed her gently. "Thank you."

"Got something to show you in my truck," Cal said the next day. Dusty followed him outside.

"These are from Mrs. Tolster's kitchen. They're almost brand-new. I know because I installed them two years ago." Cal opened the tailgate on his truck to show Dusty the cabinet doors stacked neatly inside. "She said to give them to charity. I figured you could use them for your kitchen."

Dusty reached inside the truck back and pulled one out. So now he was a charity case. Great. "Are you sure it's okay to give them to me? They must cost at least a couple thousand."

"I could take them to the Habitat for Humanity store or the Sally Ann and let you buy from them, or you can accept your good luck that you have a brother who's looking out for you."

"Gotcha. I'll take them. Thanks, Cal." He grabbed an armload and headed toward the house.

Cal followed him with another armload. "You'll have to buy hardware for them, but I'll order the hinges because I can get them cheaper than what you pay in the stores."

"Thanks. Teressa's going to love these. God knows, she deserves the best kitchen. I'm gaining weight from the dinners she cooks."

"Where are the lady of the manor and the heirs apparent?"

"Heirs apparent. Good one. Brendon's getting his hair cut at Wilder's barber shop."

Ever since he'd told Cal and Pops about putting Teressa's name on the deed, Cal had been poking fun at him about getting kicked out of his own house and being homeless. Dusty had to admit the thought had occurred to him before he'd contacted his lawyer. Even his lawyer had questioned the wisdom of exposing himself, so to speak. But if he didn't have faith in his and Teressa's relationship, what chance did they have at a future together?

Putting her name on the deed hadn't been so much about him or even them. It drove him crazy that Teressa had so little backing her up. He had so much—a family he loved and who loved him, a job he couldn't imagine not doing, friends and now a kid on the way. *A kid.* Every time he thought about his son or daughter emotion welled up inside him, and he felt as if he was drowning. He wasn't used to feeling that way and didn't know what to do with the weird energy. If he didn't know better, he'd almost think his hormones were going wacko on him, like he was pregnant.

He understood meeting on equal ground was important to Teressa, and it was the only way he could think to make that happen. He'd been hoping to remove at least one of the obstacles in their way. When he saw those letters asking her to take a job halfway around the world, he'd panicked. He'd told her he didn't want her to leave because of the baby. But he also couldn't imagine his life without her in it. Now that they were living together, he liked the idea of having her in his life every day.

"Dave Wilder's a quiet man," Cal said.

"Teressa and the kids aren't very close to him. But she needs her family."

"She doesn't need her mother."

"Everyone needs a mother, Cal."

They stared at the cabinet doors stacked against the kitchen counter. The only time he and Cal had talked about their mom was when Sylvie forced them to. After all these years, Dusty still got a rotten feeling in his gut when he thought about her leaving him behind.

Cal took off his ball cap, ran a hand over his hair and resettled the cap on his head. "Anita was pretty worn-out from looking after Sarah and Brendon again. You've got to find someone else to help with the kids. What happened to Carmen?"

"Carmen's still around, I think. Teressa usually takes care of arranging for the babysitter. I probably don't pay as much attention as I should." He sat at the kitchen table. "Anita's looking a lot better these days. It's a shame she can't help Adam with the wedding. Teressa says he's freaking out big-time."

"I thought we settled all that."

"I guess there's a bunch of details he has to take care of. Flowers and shit. Stuff." He made a face. "I'm trying not to swear anymore."

"You guys have to back off and leave Anita alone. She's not well."

"What's wrong with her?" Cal had loosened up a bit the past few weeks, but Dusty could tell he was still carrying something big on his shoulders. Cal had helped him out more times than he could remember, and he wouldn't mind returning the favor. He'd do anything for his big brother.

They both turned when the outside door opened, letting in a gust of cold air. "Smells like snow out there," Pops said as he shed his jacket. "Got the coffee on, son?"

Cal pulled out a chair for him. "I thought the doctor said only one cup a day."

"You're turning into an old fussbudget." Pops turned to Dusty after he sat. "And I suppose you don't have any beer in the house?"

Dusty grinned. "Nope."

"Wusses. Are those Mrs. Tolster's cupboard doors?" Pops nodded at the stack.

"Yeah. Cal brought them. I was just asking him what's wrong with Anita. He thinks she's too tired to help Adam with planning the wedding." He ignored Cal's killer glare. It was hard, even for his tight-lipped brother, to keep stuff from Pops. Maybe they'd finally get him to talk.

CAL CURSED UNDER his breath as Pops leaned his arms on the table and settled his concerned gaze on him. Hell, now he was in for a grilling. "I was wondering the same thing. You and Anita have been struggling for quite some time. What's the problem?"

Cal's jaw tightened. "I don't feel comfortable talking about it."

"With your family? You know we have your best interests at heart."

He stared at the door, wishing he could get up and walk out. "She had a miscarriage and lost our baby."

Pops stood and went over to Cal and put his arms

around him, and for a minute, Cal let himself relax in his father's arms. "I'm sorry to hear that. She's going to make a great mother, you know." He patted him on the back and sat down again.

"I didn't even know she was pregnant." Cal stared at the floor as the words hung in the air. "I knew something was wrong. But I thought she wanted a divorce and didn't know how to tell me."

His stoic look crumbled as he gazed at Pops. "What kind of lousy husband am I that my own wife can't turn to me at a time like that?"

"You're a good man, Cal. Did she say why she kept it from you?"

Cal folded into a chair, his legs no longer capable of holding his weight. "Her mother had several miscarriages, and apparently…" He dragged in a breath. "She died in childbirth. Anita had never told me that, because her mother's death was always a forbidden topic in her family. Can that happen these days? Do women still die giving birth?"

"I guess," Pops said. "What does the doctor say?"

"That idiot. He says she's fine, and that I'm overreacting. But it's not his wife at risk, is it?"

"Is she at risk?" Dusty asked. "Just because her mom had a problem, doesn't mean Anita does. Maybe the doctor's right. Maybe you are overreacting."

Cal fixed him with a glare. "How would you feel if Teressa lost your baby?"

"Christ." The color drained out of Dusty's face.

Cal nodded. "Exactly."

Pops frowned at Cal. "You do know you're the best thing that ever happened to Anita, right? Her father would have sucked the life right out of her if you hadn't come along. Don't make the same mistake he did. Anita loves you, but you can't smother her. You've got to give her room to breathe."

"So if she wants to try for another baby, I should let her?"

"I think you should both go back to the doctor and listen with your heads, not your hearts this time. Calculate the risk and figure out if it's worth it."

"And let her help Adam with the wedding," Dusty added.

Pops looked at him, obviously fighting a smile. "One problem at a time. Are you okay, Cal? Want to talk about it some more?"

"No. You're right, I haven't been thinking about what Anita wants. I'll ask her to schedule another doctor's appointment. Or see a different doctor, if she'd agree to that. I know we need to move on with our lives. It's just…if anything ever happened to her, I don't know what I'd do."

"What's the problem with the wedding?"

Grateful for the distraction, especially about something that wasn't his problem, Cal relaxed. It had nearly killed him confessing to his father how he'd screwed up. But as usual, Pops had set him on the right path and boosted his ego a bit, too. He knew Anita had been miserable with her life when he met her, and that she had delighted in so many little, inconsequential things since coming to live with him. Like hanging around the house in pajamas Sunday morning or leaving the dirty dishes until the next day because their passion for each other took precedence over a clean house.

"Sylvie's making Adam do everything, and he hasn't a clue about anything. Me, neither," he added.

"I'll help him."

"But you're the father-in-law."

"I'm also the father of the bride, and I've got the time."

Dusty snickered. "Can I be there when you tell Adam?"

"Don't you ever grow up?" Cal said.

"Believe it or not, I'm trying."

The oven dinged, and Dusty got up to look inside. "Lasagna. Yum. You guys want to stay for supper? It looks like Teressa made enough to last a week."

"Love to, if Teressa doesn't mind," Pops said.

"I'll call her."

"No need. She just pulled up," Cal said, looking out the window. "Where you going?"

Dusty shoved his feet into his boots. "To help her bring the kids in."

"Uh-huh." Cal winked at Pops. "And to beg the missus to let him invite people over for supper."

"Shut up."

"Boys," Pops admonished.

Dusty and Cal grinned at each other. It felt like old times.

"Call Anita. We've got tons of food, honest. I'll make a salad to go with the lasagna."

Feeling better than he had for a long time, Cal punched in Anita's number. Family suppers were the kind of thing she went nuts for. And after hanging out with his family, maybe it would be a good time for them to talk about starting one of their own.

DUSTY SLIPPED OUT the door and hurried over to the minivan. Halfway there, he realized there was a man sitting in the front seat beside Teressa. Teressa rolled her window down. "I invited Dad to eat supper with us. Whose trucks?"

"Cal and Pops. They're staying for supper, too. We've got enough, right? I'll make a salad. Hey, Mr. Wilder." He smiled at the thin, gray man.

She raised her eyebrows. "Sure. There are a couple baguettes in the freezer. We can do garlic bread, too."

"I got my hair cut, Dusty," Brendon chirped as he tumbled out of the backseat.

Dusty squatted down. He couldn't remember Brendon voluntarily telling him anything before. "You look good, kid."

Brendon grinned at him. "Grampy cut it. He wants to go see the whale, too."

Dusty stood. Why had he ever mentioned the damned whale? A kid as small as Brendon wouldn't understand if the whale decided not to show, plus it was getting close to the time for the last of the whales to migrate south for the winter, and there weren't as many around. He hated disappointing people, and he seemed to be doing that a lot these days. Whether they saw a whale or not, he'd make sure Brendon had a good time.

He put his hand on the little boy's head. "We'll have to check the weather. I think tomorrow is supposed to be a nice day, so we'll probably go then. You got any friends you want to bring?"

Brendon leaned back to look up at him. "Anita and Grampy. Mom can come, too, if she wants."

But no one Brendon's age. Weird kid. At his age, he'd had a posse of friends already.

"Grampy cut my hair, too," Sarah said.

"It looks nice, Sarah." It would look better if Wilder had cut more of the wild curls off, but no way was he going there.

She leaned against him. "Will you carry me to the house?"

"Sarah!" Teressa scolded.

"How about you take your grandfather in and show him the house," Dusty suggested. "Your mother and I will be there in a minute."

Teressa stood beside him as they watched the three of them walk to the house. Dusty draped an arm over her shoulders. "I take it the visit went okay?"

She leaned her slender frame against him. "It was great. Except for the part when he called Linda to say he was coming here for supper."

"She must have hated not being invited."

"I guess, but there's not much I can do about it right now."

He pulled her into an embrace. "Give it time. She'll come around." He kissed the top of her head. "Hope you don't mind I asked Pops and Cal and Anita for supper."

"Don't be ridiculous, it's your—" Chuckling, she buried her face in his jacket.

He laughed with her. "Yeah, I went there, too. Teressa?"

She looked up.

"You're feeling okay, aren't you?"

"You mean with the pregnancy?"

"Yeah. No more twinges or anything?"

"I'm fine, Dusty. Stop worrying." She slipped her

arm through his, and they started walking toward the house. "You've got yourself a genuine brood mare. Hips like mine were designed for popping out kids."

He ran his hand over one hip then squeezed her behind. "That explains why I get so turned on looking at you."

She tried to swat at his hand. "Behave yourself."

He laughed. "Or what? You're going to make me go to bed?"

She laughed with him. "What's gotten into you?"

He stopped by the door. Other than he was excited about everyone getting together for supper at his and Teressa's house? "I realized today what a lucky man I am. I want us to get married."

With a sinking heart, he watched her face close up. She was going to say no. Again.

"Dusty. Please. We've been over this. Why do you always pick the most inappropriate times to propose to me?"

"Why not? We've got a lot going for us, Teressa. All you have to do is say yes."

"Because…" She looked everywhere but at him. "I know this is going to sound stupid, especially coming from someone like me, but I don't want to get married because it's the right thing to do. I want to get married because I'm in love."

And there he had it—the truth. He hunched his

shoulders and yanked the door open. Teressa didn't love him. Had no intention of ever loving him.

What else had he expected?

CHAPTER TEN

JEANS WERE MADE to be worn by men like Dusty. Her arms full of dirty dishes, Teressa admired the view from behind as he loaded the dishwasher a few hours later, after everyone had left. He was in incredible shape, and as much as she liked how his jeans molded themselves to his tight behind, she wouldn't mind seeing more. Or less. Like no clothes. They'd only had one night of getting naked together, but she'd never forget the feel of his satin skin stretched over muscles that rippled under her fingers as she explored his body.

"That was nice tonight." She shoved the dishes on the counter.

Dusty chuckled. "Wish I'd gotten a picture of Adam's face when Pops offered to help with the wedding. Any more of that pumpkin pie he brought?"

"All gone." She moved behind him and put her hands on his waist. "You have a really nice family."

He straightened. "I like them. Adam fits right in, don't you think?"

She moved in closer, pressing her body against

his. She loved the way his muscles rippled with movement. "I thought his eyeballs were going to pop out when Pops started talking about the wedding. Makes sense for your dad to help, though."

She slid her hand around to his front and slipped it up under his T-shirt. Heat shot through her as she traced the line of hair down his belly to his waistband.

He grabbed her hand. "What are you doing?"

"What do you think I'm doing?" His ass muscles tightened as she rubbed against him from behind.

He grabbed both her hands this time, pulled them out from under his T-shirt and turned around. "I'm not in the mood. I'm tired."

Teressa laughed, amazed he'd managed to say that with a straight face.

When she gripped the bottom of his shirt, he squeezed her hands. "I'm serious. I'm not interested."

Dusty was *always* interested. "Want to tell me what's going on?"

He stepped away from the dishwasher and folded his arms. "I'm good enough to have sex with, but not good enough to marry. Is that it?"

"Oh, my God." She covered her mouth with her hand. "Do you hear yourself? Who are you, and what have you done with Dusty? Besides, who said anything about having sex? I was just trying to cop a feel."

"Funny. Not. I meant it when I said we should get married. I don't want Duke to think we didn't want him. We need to get serious about having a real relationship, because kids need stability. But you're not even interested in discussing us and what we're doing. Plus, this is a small town we live in. I worry the kids at school are going to start making cracks to Sarah and Brendon about us not being married."

This was so not the way she'd imagined the evening going. She gazed longingly at the beautiful picture Dusty made standing in the kitchen. The top of his hair was bleached almost white by the sun while underneath, the color looked as dark as his shadowed jaw. She liked his ocean-blue eyes more when they sparkled with humor, but even serious they were a beautiful color. This grim Dusty was a different person from the one she knew, and she wasn't sure where he'd come from. She'd imagined them cuddling up on the couch and talking about the dinner and who said what to whom. It had all sounded so cozy in her head when she'd thought about it.

"You're not calling our child Duke," she said. "It's too big of a name for a baby. And I'm not going to get married while I'm pregnant. I don't care if I'm being selfish, that's how I feel." She also didn't like being rejected. It stung. "Heaven knows what people already say about me, but they are not going to say Dusty Carson married me because he knocked me up. I know this is hard to believe, but I still have some pride left."

"That's just an excuse. Anyone who knows you realizes you're smart and successful, and that you've got it all together. What you mean is you don't want to marry *me*." He put his hands on his head and spun around. "I'm so stupid. I thought you just needed time to adjust to being pregnant again and to the idea of getting married. But that's not it at all. It's marrying *me* that's the problem. And you know what's really pathetic? I know where you're coming from. I screw up with your kids more often than I get things right. And they run hot and cold with me. Some days I feel like I'm barely tolerated around here. Obviously, Sarah and Brendon take their cues from their mother. You can't kid a kid," he said bitterly.

Teressa slowly sank into a chair. What had she thought? That she could have everything her way? That Dusty would be there for them always whether she married him or not? He'd move on at some point, because he'd want a family of his own. She'd been taking advantage of her oldest and best friend, and he'd called her on it. She was so ashamed of herself.

It wasn't just her life she'd be gambling with. She had Sarah and Brendon to consider, and as Dusty had pointed out, he struggled to like her children.

Her shoulders dropped under the weight of fac-

ing the truth. Marriage was a trap. She knew that
sounded about as cynical as a person could get,
and that was why she didn't say it out loud. Every
day she struggled for control in her life. Tried to
make the kids behave and be happy, tried to make
the café a better business, tried to hold on to her
sanity and make a home out of the shell of a house
Dusty lived in. If she got married, another person
would want a piece of her, and life would swallow
her up completely. How could she possibly explain
that to anyone and have that person still like her,
never mind love her?

She was so lost. She wrapped her arms around
herself. "Maybe we all need more time."

"If something happened to you, who would get
the kids?"

"What?"

"Who would be responsible for Sarah and Brendon? I've already talked to my lawyer about having
full rights to my own child, but what about them?"

"When were you going to tell me?"

"About talking to the lawyer? You're acting like
I did something wrong. He's my child, and I want
everyone to know. The usual way is to marry the
mother, but short of that, I get my name on his
birth certificate and we share custody fifty-fifty.
I've named you, then Cal and Anita as guardians."

She tried to imagine what it would feel like to
have someone tell her she couldn't see her own

child when she wanted. "I'd never interfere between you and this child, Dusty."

"But you won't marry me, either."

She looked away. Damn it, he didn't have to look so betrayed. "Not right now." Especially if he wanted to marry her only because of the baby. It wasn't enough for her, she wanted more.

"What about Sarah and Brendon?"

"I…I don't know. My parents are their legal guardians, but if Corey or Stan wanted custody if I died? I don't know."

"Seriously? After what happened with Stan? That's not good enough, Teressa. You have to do something about taking care of Sarah and Brendon's future."

"Nothing's going to happen to me."

"Let's hope not. Call my lawyer. He'll help set up whatever you want."

"You're right. I should have taken care of that when Brendon was born." She stared at her hands. "I hate thinking like that, but I'll call him next week. Thanks."

He gave a curt nod. "You might want to rethink having your parents as guardians, as well. They're getting older, and it would be tough on them, having to bring up two small children. And your mom isn't the easiest person to be around." He yawned. "I'm going to crash. I've got a lot on my plate for tomorrow."

Teressa sat in the kitchen by herself and listened

269

269

269

269

269

269

to the house settle for the night. She and Dusty would be okay. They'd had disagreements before and had made amends. She hadn't meant to hurt him, because she loved him, just not the way he wanted her to. She wished things could go back to the way they were before she'd gotten pregnant, when being friends had been almost enough. But when had she ever gotten what she wished for?

DUSTY KEPT ONE arm around Brendon's waist to keep him from slipping off the captain's seat. His father had held him in the very same way when he'd been Brendon's age. Dusty's heart lightened. Wouldn't it be something if Brendon wanted to be a fisherman when he grew up? Not that he wished the harsh lifestyle on anyone, but it was true that the sea got in some people's blood. It was in his and his father's.

If he was away from the sea too long, things got out of balance for him and his world turned sour. He glanced at Pops, who stood at his shoulder in the wheelhouse, like he had when Dusty was growing up and learning how to handle the boat. Maybe someday he, too, would get the chance to pass on his knowledge of the sea. He'd never allowed himself to think along those lines because there was no heir to this throne. He grinned at the idea. But now, maybe there could be. If Brendon was still interested in ten years or so, he'd start teaching him. Or maybe his own child. It didn't matter which kid, and that surprised him. What had surprised him was how Brendon and Sarah had expanded his world and made him look at life differently.

"You have to keep both hands on the wheel," he instructed Brendon as they cruised out of the narrow channel. "And keep her between the red and green buoys. Otherwise you'll run her aground."

"Can I make it go faster?" Brendon asked.

Dusty laughed and looked over at his father. How many times had he asked Pops the same thing? "Sure can. Push this lever here."

Brendon giggled as the boat lurched forward.

"Slow down," Teressa shouted from the back of the boat.

The unexpectedly warm day sparkled like a rare jewel, and the whole family had decided to come. They'd set out lawn chairs to sit on in the space where Dusty usually stacked plastic bins filled with lobster. He'd scrubbed the boat as best he could to get rid of the fishy smell. Old *Out & About* sparkled in the sunshine right along with the day.

Dusty and Brendon turned to grin at Teressa. Instead of smiling back, she got a weird look on her face, one he'd never seen before. Her stomach was probably acting up.

Dusty turned back to the wheel. He'd noticed black circles under her eyes this morning when they'd rushed around to get ready to go. She'd been pretty quiet, probably because she was still ticked off about him not being his usual accommodating self last night. He'd never said no to Teressa, or any other lady, really, but that was beside the point. He'd been hurt that she hadn't even considered marrying him and had struck back the only way he knew how. Maybe if he'd acted like an adult and got her to talk more about why other people's opinions were so important to her they could have worked out their differences. Although he didn't think that was the only reason she turned down his proposal. If it had been, she could easily have set a date in the future.

They needed to sit down and discuss their problems. His reaction may not have been the most mature, but he'd made her stop and think for a change instead of her usual shucking him off as an idiot. He wasn't an idiot, but he knew she thought of him as a lightweight in the emotional category. He rolled his shoulders and widened his stance as they rode over an ocean swell. He'd always thought there was nothing wrong with keeping things light and easy, but he seemed to need more than a good laugh and a few drinks these days.

"You've gone quiet, son. Anything wrong?"

Dusty glanced at Pops standing beside him. "Things are good. Guess I need another cup of coffee."

"When are we going to see a whale?" Brendon asked.

Pops winked at Dusty. "You're the look-out," Pops said. "You've got to skim your eyes over the water, like this." He shaded his eyes with one hand and moved his head back and forth. "You're looking for a big, big fish breaking through the water or water sprouting up. That's the whale breathing, and boy, does he have bad breath."

Brendon giggled. "He should brush his teeth! Mommy!"

Teressa entered the small cabin. When she stood beside Dusty, he put his arm around her shoulders. She'd only been on his boat a handful of times, which was odd now that he thought about it. Even old Beanie had been out with him more than she had.

"You feeling okay?" Her skin had a translucent look to it today that made her freckles stand out.

She smiled weakly. "A little queasy, maybe."

Dusty slowed the boat down and rubbed her back. Why hadn't he guessed all these years that she got seasick? More to the point, why hadn't she told him? "Pops, we need a cup of the cure over here."

"I assume you mean my ginger-tea cure, not the rum-and-Coke one."

Teressa laughed and leaned against Dusty. "Ginger tea sounds delicious."

"I've got a thermos full right here." He pulled

a stainless thermos out of a knapsack and poured her a mugful.

"What else do you have in that knapsack?" she teased.

Pops eyes sparkled. "I wasn't kidding about the rum and Coke. But I also have plain old crackers. You'll want to munch on a few of those."

"And you need to steer the boat," Dusty added.

"I don't know how."

"Brendon and I will teach you." He shifted until Teressa stood between his arms. "Head for the red buoy, but keep it on your left. Once we're past that, we're out of the channel and in the open."

Dusty lifted his hand from the steering wheel.

"Dusty! I can't do this."

"Yes, you can, Mom. I'll help you." The boat wiggled as Brendon steered back and forth.

"For heaven's sake." Teressa gripped the wheel and brought the boat under control. "Where is that red buoy?"

"Right there." Brendon pointed.

"Eleven o'clock," Dusty added.

"Huh." She glanced at Dusty. "That's clever. Thanks, Pops," she said as he handed over his ginger-tea cure.

Dusty watched her sip the ginger tea while keeping her eyes on the horizon. Her stomach would soon settle. "I'm going to check on the others."

"You're leaving me?" Teressa squeaked.

Dusty hesitated in the doorway of the cabin. It'd be nice if she needed him as much on land as she thought she did out here. "You're doing fine. Eyes on the horizon, keep just to the left of the red buoy. I'm not going far, and you've got Pops right there."

A minute later, he slumped into the lawn chair beside Cal and accepted a mug of coffee from Adam.

"Got a new captain," Cal commented.

"Yup." He sipped the hot brew. He'd wanted to hover over Teressa, making sure she was okay, but forced himself to go to the back of the boat. She didn't like to be fussed over, plus, as hard as it was, he was sticking to his guns. If she didn't want to marry him, fine. But he wasn't going to pretend he was happy about her decision.

Didn't mean he didn't feel like kicking something, though. He'd been waiting forever to get her in his arms, and the only time she'd encouraged him had to be right after she turned down his marriage offer. Damned right he was taking her rejection personally. Teressa would realize soon enough he was serious about marrying her. And if she didn't want to be in a relationship with him, he'd start thinking about moving on, because, damn it, it hurt knowing she didn't think he was good enough to marry.

He turned his attention to Teressa's father, who'd

barely said a word since they'd cast off. "How you doing, Mr. Wilder?"

"Fine. Fine." He bobbed his head. Hard to believe the mild-mannered man was Teressa's father. The fire must have come completely from her mother's side.

Sarah left Anita's side and planted herself in front of him. "I have to pee."

He smiled, wondering what Teressa would have to say if he let her try to pee over the side of the boat, the way most males did. He grunted and shoved to his feet. "Come on."

"You just sat down," Sylvie said. "Do you want me to take her?"

Sarah leaned against his leg and popped her thumb into her mouth. He put his hand on her head. "Thanks, but I'll show her how to use the toilet. Come on, Princess."

"I know how to use a toilet."

"This one's a bit different. It's called a head, for starters."

A minute later, Sarah wrinkled her nose, her face turning white. "It stinks down here."

Man, if she puked he'd have to clean it up. Teressa wouldn't last two seconds belowdecks, and cleaning up after a sick kid wasn't something you could ask anyone else to do. "Tell you what. You pee, and I'll flush it. Okay?"

Sarah went in and closed the door. Dusty waited a couple of minutes. "Sarah? Are you finished?"

"I don't feel so good," she said in a tiny voice.

"Are you done going to the bathroom?"

"Yes."

Now what? He whipped the door open. Sarah swayed on her feet as she tried to turn on the tap. He picked her up and rushed up the three steps to the deck and over to the side of the boat. Poor little tyke. "I'll get a wet cloth for your hands. If you feel like being sick, lean over the side of the boat."

"Troubles?" Sylvie crouched down by Sarah.

Relieved for the help, Dusty stood. "I'll get a wet cloth so she can wipe her hands." He looked down at Sarah's white, pinched face. Just because she was sick didn't mean she had to look so sad. Why couldn't females just say what they wanted straight out? What was it with making him feel all these emotions?

He scooped Sarah into his arms and patted her back. "Maybe you could get that cloth, Syl? And a cup of ginger tea."

He tucked one of Sarah's wild locks of hair behind her ear. "You're just like your mom, Princess. You need to get your sea legs."

She laid her head on his shoulder and sighed. "I feel good like this."

"Seasick on a boat?"

"No, silly. With you. It makes me feel better."

Up until now, every time Sarah had clung to him, he'd only thought about how much he hated her hanging on to him. It hadn't occurred to him she was doing it for a reason. Although Teressa had tried to tell him, hadn't she? Understanding why Sarah was doing something made it easier to handle somehow.

When Sylvie appeared with the cup of tea, he set her down in a chair beside her grandfather. "Sylvie has a cup of ginger tea for you. Careful, it's hot."

He turned toward the pilothouse when the boat slowed down.

"There she blows," Pops yelled, and then he laughed. "I always wanted to say that."

Dusty looked in the direction Pops was pointing and saw a water sprout from a whale. "You see that, Brendon?" he called.

Brendon kneeled up on the seat. "What?"

Dusty rushed into the pilothouse, spared a glance for Teressa, who had regained her color, and snatched up Brendon. "It's the whale. She's come to say hello to you. You got her in Neutral, Pops?" Sometimes the whales dove under the boat, almost as if they were playing with it. It was best to disengage the propeller until the whales moved farther away.

"Aye, aye, Captain."

Dusty rolled his eyes. Pops had taught him everything he knew about handling a boat, fishing and the ocean. And a good deal about life, too. He needed to sit down and talk to his father about what was going on with him and Teressa. Pops would probably have some insight to why she didn't want to get married. The only thing he could come up with was she thought he was a lousy bet. Maybe she was right. Maybe he wasn't good enough for her.

Years ago, she'd been anxious to leave Collina. She'd wanted to be a chef in Paris, and there'd been no question of a future between them. He'd been relatively happy until Teressa got pregnant, and they had to look at their relationship more closely. If he thought about his life, he was still content with his lifestyle. He could change in some ways, but give up living in Collina and not working on the ocean? He couldn't imagine doing anything else. Didn't want to. But if that was the only way he could be with his child, he'd make that sacrifice.

He took Brendon out to the side of the boat. "Watch out there and just keep your eyes moving along the surface of the water."

Brendon wrapped one arm around Dusty's neck, his tiny body trembling. A second later, Sarah attached herself to his leg. "I can't see, Dusty."

He managed to pick her up with his other arm, and a humpback whale broke the surface, and then dove back down.

"I saw'd him." Brendon's body shook with excitement.

"Me, too," Sarah sang out.

Dusty felt a swell of pride as if he'd personally arranged to have the whale make an appearance. "Keep watching. Maybe she'll breach for us today."

"What does that mean?" Sarah asked.

"It means she'll come right up out of the water." As many times as he'd seen a humpback breach, it never failed to amaze him. Forty to fifty feet long, and weighing at least eighty thousand pounds, it was a miracle the huge animal could thrust itself out of the water in one mighty leap.

"You look loaded down. Want me to take Brendon?" Cal appeared by his side.

He didn't. He loved sharing the moment with both kids. But his arms were aching from the load, and he was going to drop one if he didn't unload.

"Look, Dusty!" Brendon shrieked. The whale breached about twenty yards off the stern. "I saw'd him! I saw'd him!"

"Me, too, buddy." Spontaneously, he kissed Brendon's cheek. When Brendon grinned at him, they connected in a way they hadn't before, as if they were seeing each other clearly for the first time. Dusty saw a young boy brimming with energy and curiosity; Brendon just needed the confidence to reach out and experience what life had to offer him. Like he was doing right now.

No matter if he continued living with Teressa and the kids or not, he and Brendon would always have this moment between them, because the boy had claimed a piece of his heart.

Cal slipped his arms around Brendon and pulled him into his arms. "Come on, little man. Dusty needs a break."

Dusty winked at Brendon and tousled his hair. He caught Teressa watching him with a puzzled look on her face as she stood in the pilothouse with Pops, sipping her tea. He'd have thought after all these years she knew everything about him there was to know and there were no surprises between them. But he spent more time on the water than on the land, and it wasn't often she got to see him in his element. He hoped she liked what she saw, because working on the ocean was a part of him he wasn't willing or able to change. But there were other things he needed to.

He'd been careless over the years, distracted by his own life, and he wanted it to be different between them now. He needed to treat her with greater consideration. He wanted to be a man who deserved to be loved, and he wanted to be a father to her children. All of them.

OF COURSE SHE wasn't jealous of her own son. It was ridiculous to even consider the idea. Teressa watched as Cal took Brendon out of Dusty's arms. The way Dusty looked at Brendon, as if he loved him, stirred up all sorts of emotions. Jealousy was not one of them. For heaven's sake, Dusty had looked at her with affection plenty of times. But love?

She gripped the steering wheel of the boat, although they were idling in Neutral and turning the steering wheel had no effect. What she wanted to do was go outside and stand beside Dusty and be part of whatever was happening between him and her children. But she'd felt awkward around him since last night. She didn't understand where they stood with each other at the moment; certainly in a place they'd never been before. She didn't like the uncertainty. Dusty was…well, Dusty. She'd always relied on him being there for her on one level or another.

"Adam and I were wondering if you could recommend someone to make the wedding cake," Pops said.

Teressa dragged her attention away from the scene outside. "I'll make it," she offered spontaneously.

Pops tilted his head. "I didn't know you did wedding cakes."

"I took a course in cake decoration a million years ago. I'd love to make Adam and Sylvie's cake for them, if you trust me. Does the wedding have a theme?"

"A theme." Pops laughed. "Do we need one?"

"Not really." She grinned. "I guess a pumpkin-shaped cake wouldn't work, eh?"

"How about a little house with seashells around it? Something like that?"

"I love the idea. Maybe I can even get an easel in there. I'll try making a sketch of it. Mind you, it'll look like the kids drew it. I don't have Sylvie's talent."

Pops slipped his arm through hers. "You don't need her talent. You have your own."

"That's sweet of you to say." And far from the truth.

"I'm not trying to be nice, Teressa. I'm telling you something important."

She squinted against the glare of the sun on the water and tried to read Pops's expression. He'd always been friendly, and had even had a serious discussion with her before he agreed to sell her a share of the café that had been in his family since he'd bought it for his wife. Jane Carson had not been a content person and had lost interest in the café a couple years after Pops bought it. It came as no surprise that he wanted to make sure history was not about to repeat itself.

Honestly, if she'd had an alternative, the café would have been the last place Teressa would have considered buying into. Mostly because it was in her hometown and given the opportunity she'd leave in a heartbeat. Much like Dusty's mother.

Huh. She hadn't made that connection before. Dusty always seemed so certain about where he belonged—it was a joy to watch the graceful way he moved around his boat—it had never occurred to her he felt insecure about anything. Was he afraid she'd leave like his mother had? Hadn't he said the very same thing when he put her name on the deed to the house? And more important, could she honestly tell him she wouldn't?

Pops took her arm. "You're a much bigger part of this community than you realize. People around here depend on you."

She snorted. "To make them a bowl of soup or a pie."

"That's right." He nodded. "When someone needs to get out of the house or take a break, they know they can always go to the café, and you'll have something to nourish their body. And sometimes—" his eyes twinkled "—you give them a little zing to make them laugh or to stop feeling sorry for themselves. Whatever it is they need, you zero right in on it."

She grinned. "And I thought that was called being a bitch."

Pops's expression turned kind. "You've got a big heart, Teressa. I've never known you to let anyone down."

"Except my mother." And Dusty. She glanced toward the back of the boat, where everyone was standing, watching for another whale sighting. Dusty held Sarah on his hip and Brendon had wormed his way back to Dusty and was now sitting on his wide shoulders, her son's spindly legs dangling over Dusty's chest. For a man who'd been a confirmed bachelor a few weeks ago, he certainly looked comfortable with her children. As they did with him. When had they started to grow into a family? What had she done?

She took a step toward them, but reined herself in. If she wasn't going to marry Dusty, she'd have to move out of his house soon, because her children were falling in love with him and the longer they stayed, the more they'd suffer when they did leave—the more they'd all suffer when they left. The thought made her heart ache.

She studied the different colors of the ocean. The water was a light blue close up, but farther out, it turned a deep navy.

"You haven't exactly escaped unscathed, either. Sometimes life happens," Pops said.

"You want to know if I plan on hurting Dusty."

Pops raised his shoulders in resignation. "Whether he's aware of it or not, he's always picked women he knew wouldn't stick around. It doesn't take a genius to figure out his mother's decision to leave us marked him. I guess I'm wondering if he's interested in you because he knows deep down, he can count on you to leave, too."

Interested in, not loved. Dusty had never said he loved her, had he? Maybe, like Pops was suggesting, Dusty knew their relationship would never amount to much, just like all his other ones. How could she blame him?

She'd never taken their relationship seriously. His friendship, sure, but there had never been any point to thinking beyond a few good laughs together. She had a family to take care of and that hadn't fit into his happy-go-lucky world.

But now they were having a baby, and that changed everything. Now they had to take their relationship seriously, but was there anything between them other than a fondness left over from their childhood? Was Pops saying he thought Dusty was in love with her for all the wrong reasons? She worried Dusty was talking himself into loving her because he wanted them to be a family. That wasn't enough, and they both knew it.

She turned to Pops, who stood by her side, waiting for an answer. "I can't tell you what you want to hear, Pops. I wish I could say we were in love, but Dusty and I still have a lot to figure out."

"You better hurry up, because Brendon and Sarah have already made up their minds." He nodded toward the back of the boat, where his son was holding her children.

Her stomach clenched. The harder she tried, the more out of control her life became. She wanted more. She wanted it all—love and lust and friendship—

and she wouldn't settle for anything less. She'd had to settle all her life. But she refused to settle when it came to marriage.

CHAPTER ELEVEN

A FEW DAYS LATER, Teressa stiffened when Dusty snuck up behind her in the café kitchen and laid a rose on the counter. She snatched it up and spun around to find him standing far closer than she'd thought. His wide shoulders blocked the view of the rest of the kitchen. Adam had the afternoon off—more wedding preparations—and other than Tyler, who was doing heavens knows what in the dining room, she was the only one working.

She shoved the rose toward him. "What's this?"

He smirked. There had been a lot of that going on lately with him and the kids, and it was driving her nuts. "A rose."

"I know it's a rose. Why are you giving it to me?"

He let out an exaggerated sigh. Or maybe it was heartfelt. She'd been trying harder to be nice since her talk with Pops the day of the whale sighting. She couldn't stand Dusty being mad at her. Things had thawed between them, but they weren't as easy around each other as they used to be.

And if she was being honest, all three, Dusty and Brendon and Sarah, had been super annoying

the past week. They'd be talking and giggling—
giggling!—but would stop the minute she walked
into the room. There'd also been way too much
whispering going on. At first she'd tried to be a
good sport, happy that Dusty seemed to be getting
along with her children so well. But she finally
had to admit that she was jealous of the easy ca-
maraderie that had blossomed among the three of
them. She felt left out of her own family, and she
didn't like the feeling. Now Dusty was sucking up
to her for some reason.

"Because a pretty lady was selling roses outside
the liquor store and I wanted an excuse to talk to
her. Or—" he smiled "—because I wanted to give
you a rose."

She sniffed. "Thank you. I think. What were
you doing at the liquor store?" God help her, she'd
sounded exactly like her mother when she uttered
those words. What was happening to her?

"Buying some beer for Pops and Cal. We're
going to the hunting camp tonight." He hesitated,
his brow wrinkling. "I thought I might ask Brendon if he wanted to come, too. I think he'd like to
hang out with the guys. And maybe your dad," he
added. "He doesn't seem like the kind of guy to
hang out, but then maybe no one ever asked him."

It was exactly the kind of thing she always
wished would happen; that the children would have
a real father who would take them on adventures.

But it hurt to think her little boy was growing up and wanted to spend time with men instead of her. She blinked back tears. "Are you going to drink beer, too?"

Dusty sighed again. "Teressa, do you really think I'd take Brendon to the hunting camp and tie one on?"

"No. Sorry." She felt stupid because she wanted to wail her heart out. She couldn't help but feel as if her little boy was starting to like Dusty more than her.

"Hey." Dusty put a finger under her chin and lifted it up until she had to look directly into his beautiful blue eyes. "What's going on with you?"

She folded her arms around her waist. "Nothing."

"Except you looked like you'd lost your best friend when I said I wanted to take Brendon to the hunting camp with me." His eyes lit up. "You're jealous."

"I am not. I'm just…" She stopped to swallow her tears. "He's my little boy, and he's never… I've never…"

Dusty pulled her into his arms. She took a deep calming breath and exhaled, her tension melting away. For the first time in weeks, she felt as if she didn't have to hold on tight or everything would fall apart. She inhaled again, just to breathe in the smell of him.

"You're going to miss your little boy," he said.

Tears brimmed in her eyes. "I know I'm being silly, but I can't help myself. Things are changing too fast."

"I didn't mean to upset you, Tee. If you don't want Brendon to go with me, that's okay."

"I want him to. It'll be good for him. It's just… he's only three."

"I won't drink, and I'll bring him home tonight if he wants."

"I know you'll take good care of him. It's okay. It's just my hormones acting up."

He laughed down at her. "I don't suppose they're *acting* acting up, if you know what I mean."

"I feel weepy, that's all."

"Too bad because you feel damned good in my arms."

"I'm fat and my face is all splotchy from crying."

When his gaze dropped to her breasts then to her belly, her skin turned sensitive from his hungry look. "That's not what I'm seeing." He grinned.

She pouted, feeling ridiculous but not able to stop feeling sorry for herself, either. "I thought you hated me. Besides, I'm not wearing anything lacy today. Nothing interesting to see here."

"I don't hate you, Teressa. And FYI, interesting would be if you wore nothing at all. Everything else is just window dressing in my opinion."

She couldn't help but laugh at him. He sounded

so earnest. "I'm getting bigger everywhere. Nothing fits."

"So buy some new stuff."

"Maybe." She didn't want to discuss money. Her own money was stretched to the limit, paying the mortgage on the café and covering the children's expenses. At least she didn't have to pay rent.

He dropped his arms and stepped away from her. An edge crept into his voice. "If you'd let me open that joint account like I wanted to, you'd have enough money."

"Right."

"I noticed the other day that the kids need new winter jackets, too. You should take them shopping."

"I will. Soon." As soon as she'd saved enough to buy them jackets and boots.

He looked as though he wanted to say something else, but changed his mind. Instead, he smiled. "Don't suppose I can talk you into making a pot of your famous chili? Pops is bringing breakfast, and Cal's got the munchies covered. I said I'd bring supper."

"When are you going?"

"I don't know. As soon as Brendon gets out of day care, I guess. I want to go for a walk in the woods with him before dark."

"You have to tell Carmen you're taking him."

"Already did." His expression turned guarded

when she frowned at him. "What? I said I had to ask you first. I've still got to phone her."

She'd managed to shove Carmen to the back of her mind the past couple of weeks. But she always seemed to be around wherever Dusty was. "When did you see her?"

"She went to town with me today."

"Excuse me?"

"I, ah…I needed her help with some…stuff. So she came with me. But she's home now," he added. "She's picking Sarah up after school."

"What did you need help with?"

Dusty started fiddling with the rolling pin she'd been using when he came in. "Stuff."

She took the rolling pin away from him. "What kind of stuff?"

He stuck his hands in his pockets and studied the wall above her head. "I can't tell."

She pulled her stool over in front of him, sat and crossed her arms. "I think you can."

"It's a secret."

"Even if I'm not ready to get married, I don't appreciate you hiding things from me. Especially if it involves you spending the day with a beautiful woman."

He picked up the rose, snapped off the stem and tucked the flower behind her ear. "Okay, but you've got to act surprised. The kids and I are planning a surprise birthday party for you this weekend. Carmen helped me buy the decorations for the party because both Sylvie and Anita were too busy."

Teressa dug her fingers into the edges of the stool. Otherwise, she'd fly apart into a million different pieces. "Oh, Dusty," she managed to say before her tears took over.

When he scooped her into his arms a second time, it felt like such a safe place to be. She rested her head against his chest and let her tears flow. She'd missed him so much the past few days.

"Sarah and Brendon said you've never had a birthday party, and when I tried to remember, I couldn't think of one, either." He rubbed soothing circles on her back. "They're so excited, Teressa. I wanted to tell you, but I promised them I wouldn't. If you don't act surprised, you'll ruin everything."

"I'm sorry."

He laughed. "For what? Being pregnant?" He grabbed a handful of tissues from the box on the desk behind him and handed them to her. "Those are good tears, right? You're not upset, are you?"

"No." She blew her nose and wiped the tears away. "I was jealous because you were having such a good time with Sarah and Brendon, and they didn't seem to need me, and neither did you. I'm used to being the center of their universe. It's stupid, but my emotions are all over the place these days. I'm not making much sense." She wiped her eyes again and tried to smile. "I don't know why

I'm so weepy. I didn't feel like this when I was pregnant with Sarah and Brendon."

"That's because you can this time."

"Can what?"

"Be weepy. You were on your own before, except for your mother. But you've got me this time." He took her hand. "I like to think me being around helps a bit."

He did a ton of little things for her and the kids. But even if he didn't, just knowing he was there for them was enough. His fitting into their lives had happened so gradually, she'd almost not noticed.

She squeezed his hand. "I know I don't always make it easy for you, but that's because I'm used to taking care of everything myself. I'm not very good at sharing."

He brought her hand up to his mouth and kissed it. "The past month has been a steep learning curve for me, too. But you know what? I think we're making progress, Teressa. Sometimes, we almost feel like a family."

She ran her hand along his jaw, loving the feel of his rough beard against her palm. She stood on tiptoe and brought her mouth close to his. "You're not going to ask me to marry you again, are you?"

"No, ma'am." He slid his hands down her back and over her behind. "You want to get married, you'll have to do the asking. Besides, we don't have to be married to be a family."

She loved feeling the way she did right now, warm and safe in Dusty's arms. Heat burned through her the minute she pressed her lips against his and felt his answering pressure, and she loved that even more.

"Geez, how come every time I walk into the kitchen someone's kissing someone else these days?" Tyler whined as he hovered just inside the door.

When Teressa laughed, Tyler looked surprised. Hmm, maybe she should try laughing more often. "Who else is kissing in my kitchen?"

"Adam and Sylvie, duh. And…" He frowned. "You were in the bathroom the other day, crying or whatever, and Pops came into the kitchen to find some more butter for that nurse from the seniors' home. She followed him in, and I caught them cozying up inside the walk-in cooler." His frown looked fierce. "That's just not right. What if he had another heart attack?"

"At least Ada would know what to do." Dusty laughed.

"Dude, he's too old to be fooling around like that. You've got to tell him to cool it."

"More importantly, why didn't you get him the butter to start with?" Teressa said, pretending to scold him. Tyler was the worst waiter she'd ever worked with, but his mother was the best hairdresser in the village, and Teressa had been going to her since her teens. If they fired Tyler—not that there was anyone to replace him—his mother might cut her off. And Tyler kind of grew on a person after a while.

"I tried. Honest, boss. I think he wanted to impress the hot nurse."

"Her name's Ada," Dusty said.

"Yeah, well she's still hot. Does she just look after the old people at the seniors' center or if, like, I got sick, would she come to my house?"

Teressa laughed at the same time Dusty did. "I'm pretty sure she only works at the center." Teressa turned back to the pie dough she'd rolled out before Dusty had interrupted her. "She's a little old for you, anyway. What happened to Melissa?"

Red blotches stained Tyler's face and neck. "She dumped me."

"Sorry to hear that." Dusty patted his shoulder. "You've gotta go through a few to find the right one."

"Is that what you did? You dated like a gazillion babes and ended up with Teressa. 'Course she's pregnant."

Teressa's stomach plummeted. She wrapped her hand around the rolling pin, but made herself loosen her grip. Tyler was just a stupid kid who didn't know anything about life beyond their village.

And she did? She was as small-town as him,

although inside, she didn't feel that way. He was only repeating what everyone else was saying, that Dusty was making the best of the situation. What if everyone was right? What if she was the ultimate charity case?

Dusty put his arm around her shoulders. "I didn't end up with Teressa. I chose her. She's the one who doesn't want to marry me. I keep hoping I'll convince her to have me, though."

Oh, hell. Did everything Dusty say these days make her cry? "Let go." She shrugged off his arm. "I've got work to do." She didn't want him to save her or spare her feelings or whatever he was trying to do. She wanted to be his equal in every way, not the old lady who lived in a shoe, who had so many children....

She'd finally started thinking of the house as hers, or partly hers, and had even added a few personal touches, like hanging the awesome painting in the living room that Sylvie had given to her a few years ago. She loved that painting and was proud to own a Sylvie Carson original, but had never had a wall big enough to hang it on except the bedroom in her mother's old carriage house. Now the painting absolutely shone on her living room wall. She'd like to buy a rug to reflect the colors in the painting but that would have to wait. First she had to buy Sarah and Brendon new winter coats.

The point was she thought of the house as home,

and that was progress of a kind, right? Maybe if she was patient, more things would fall into place as easily.

"Good luck with convincing her to marry you," Tyler snickered as he grabbed his jacket and slid out the back door.

"So, where were we?" Dusty said from behind her.

"Back to work is where I am." She was going to ruin the piecrust if she kept rolling it over and over again. She didn't know why she felt so prickly. It was getting harder, not easier, to be around Dusty these days. Boundaries kept disappearing. She was just too damned comfortable, and it didn't pay to feel that way. It was a sure bet that things were going to fall apart.

She shivered when Dusty ran his finger along the nape of her neck. "What's this about you crying in the bathroom all the time?"

"Stop that." She swatted at his hand. "Tyler's exaggerating. It's nothing."

Dusty crowded her. "I like touching you. I think you're throwing out those things. Pheromones."

Teressa laughed; she couldn't help herself. "What do you know about pheromones?"

Dusty settled his hands on her hips. "I know they make you sexy. Or make me think you're sexy. Same thing."

"Where did you hear about them?"

"Looked them up online."

Teressa looked at him over her shoulder. "Why would you do a thing like that?"

"I was reading about being pregnant and changing hormones, and I saw an article about sexy hormones, so…" He shrugged.

"You're so predictable."

"Is that a bad thing?"

She hesitated, and then continued cutting the piecrust into manageable pieces. "No, it's nice. I don't like surprises."

"Good thing I told you about the party, then. But you're going to act surprised, right?"

"I've had a lot of practice over the years pretending to be surprised. There's a large container of chili in the freezer. You can have that batch to take to the camp." She wiped flour from her hands. "Do you have extra clothes for Brendon? His sleeping bag and his pajamas? Don't forget his stuffed pig."

"What kind of kid has a stuffed pig? I'm going to buy him a bear or a tiger."

"Go ahead, but he loves that pig."

"So, do I get a kiss before I go?"

"Aren't you bringing Brendon to see me before you leave?"

"No. You'll cry, and then he won't want to go. Oh, come on." Dusty laughed. "I didn't say that to make you cry."

She scrubbed the back of her hand across her

eyes. "I know. I'm okay. But go." She waved at the door and turned back to work when she heard him leave the kitchen. How many times had work saved her in the past?

She lined pie plates with crust as she listened to Dusty dig in the deep freeze for the chili. She could tell when he hesitated by the door, but he left without saying anything else. Small wonder. She'd cried all over him and snapped and snarled at him. She could give lessons on how to repel a man. She didn't mean to push Dusty away. It could be she was even ready to be a couple now, which was kind of ironic because there was a good chance it was too late.

"WHERE'S MOMMY?"

"Working." Dusty made a mental note to buy the little dude a knapsack. Teressa wouldn't object to that, would she? He chucked the garbage bag filled with a sleeping bag and kid paraphernalia in the back of his truck. He'd answered that question a hundred times already. "Can you climb up into the truck?"

Brendon squinted at him, looking as if he was a hundred years old and trying to assess the situation. For Christ's sake, you'd think he was a child abductor the way the kid was carrying on.

"Your mom said it was okay to take you to the hunting camp," he said once again. "Pops and Cal are coming, and your grandfather is, too. Up you go." He swept his hand in front of him. He could have easily picked up Brendon and put him in his car seat, but he wanted him to climb into the truck by himself. If Dusty couldn't convince him to do even that, he might as well forget taking him all the way out to the camp. They'd just have to turn around and come right back.

Brendon sighed like an old man. Dusty sympathized. "Okay, but my mom better not get mad." He crawled into the car seat Dusty had installed in the backseat weeks ago. It hadn't taken him long to realize what a monumental hassle it was to move Brendon's car seat from one vehicle to another. By the time the kids outgrew the seats he'd be worrying about them driving by themselves. Parenting was turning out to be one long worry.

Dusty climbed in and started the engine.

"I need my pig. Where's my pig?" Brendon looked on the edge of tears.

Dusty turned off the motor, got out and dug in the garbage bag until he found the stupid pig. "Here." He tossed it to Brendon and started the motor again. "What's with the pig?"

Brendon hugged the stuffed animal. "I like him."

"Why?"

"'Cause."

He supposed that was as good an answer as anything else. He pulled up in front of the barber shop and honked his horn. Brendon's father, Stan, strolled out of the shop at the same time. Dusty cursed under his breath and stared straight ahead to avoid eye contact. A minute later, Stan knocked on Brendon's window. Reluctantly, Dusty lowered the automatic window.

"Hey, son. How are ya?" Brendon cringed when Stan reached inside and ruffled his hair. Every protective instinct Dusty possessed roared to the surface. The hair on his arm actually bristled. He'd already terrorized Brendon once. This time he'd keep it together if it killed him.

"I hear insurance agreed to replace your car," Dusty said.

"Yeah, but this time I'm buying a truck."

"Got a haircut?" Dusty said to make an effort to be friendly.

Stan ran his hand over his crew cut. "Old man Wilder doesn't mind giving out a freebie once in a while. We've been friends for a while."

"Really?" It seemed like an unlikely friendship. Mr. Wilder was such a mild-mannered man, much like Brendon, actually.

"How about you? You friends with the old man?"

"I don't know him all that well."

"He doesn't mind helping out here and there. He'd do anything for that daughter of his and his grandkids." Stan smirked, his bloated face twisting into a cunning look. "I'm a little short today. Don't suppose you could spot me a fiver?"

Instead of grabbing Stan by the scruff of his neck and dragging him through the window to plow his fist in his face, Dusty forced himself to smile. "Sorry. I don't carry cash anymore. Gotta go." He fluttered the gas pedal. "See you around."

Stan stumbled backward when Dusty pulled away from the curb. Probably not the best move, but it was either leave right away or get out of the truck and punch the slimeball in the face. Teressa needed to talk to the lawyer about getting that insect out of their lives.

He was tired of excusing Stan's behavior. A free haircut once in a while seemed fairly innocuous, but did Stan also ask Teressa's father for money? He'd have to ask Pops for advice on how best to approach the situation. He didn't want to embarrass Mr. Wilder. He pulled his cell phone out of his pocket and dialed the barber shop to let Mr. Wilder know he'd be a few minutes late picking him up. After Stan had enough time to clear out, Dusty planned to swing back and pick up Wilder.

He glanced over at Brendon, who was wiping his runny nose with his hand. Dusty flipped open the glove box and pulled out a package of clean wipes. "Can you open one of those yourself?"

"I think so." Brendon went to work on opening one with his little fingers. Maybe it would distract him from that unfortunate encounter with his father. He hated that Stan could lay claim to Brendon. Donating sperm did not make a man a father.

"Dusty?"

"Yeah?"

Brendon had opened the package and was wiping his face and hands. "Can you be my daddy?"

Aw, hell. What was he supposed to say to that? Dusty's heart squeezed tight, like the kid had reached into his chest and yanked on it. "I want to be, and in a lot of ways I can. Like right now, me taking you to the camp and going for a walk in the woods. That's what dads do with their sons. But I don't know if I can be your legal father."

"Will you ask?"

Dusty smiled. "Yeah, I will. We should do something to seal the deal of us being best buds, what do you think?"

"Kiss my pig!" Brendon squealed and stuck the old, worn stuffed animal under Dusty's nose.

Oh, man. He closed his eyes for a second. If anyone saw him kissing the frigging pig they'd never let him forget it. He looked one way, then the other, to make sure no one had pulled up beside him and quickly kissed the pig's nose. "Your turn."

Brendon kissed the pig fifty times and cuddled it all the way out to the camp. By the time they arrived, Dusty had begun to wonder if he should have brought Sarah instead.

Three hours later, Dusty stuck another couple of logs into the stove and closed the door. He was glad he'd bought the new stove last year, the kind with a window in front to watch the fire, because it was slowly sinking in that being able to afford extras—and the list of what that included grew daily—was now a luxury that belonged to his past. Someone should give a guy some warning about being cut off from having money to spend. It wasn't that he begrudged the kids the things they needed, but... Okay, so he was selfish. Who knew? He worked hard, but really, life had been pretty damned easy so far. Hell, he'd just moved out of home less than a year ago. Kind of pathetic when he thought about it.

After a walk in the woods earlier with Brendon and Mr. Wilder—he'd insisted on Dusty calling him by his first name, Dave—Dusty realized Brendon was probably going to take after his grandfather and be a biologist. That meant at least four years of university they'd have to pay for.

Dave had surprised all of them—him, Cal, Pops and Adam—with the depth of his knowledge of local plants. Dusty had forgotten he'd worked as a biologist for the provincial government. As Pops pointed out, Dave should be passing that knowledge on to school-age kids. Even at three years old, Brendon had held on to his every word. Who'd have guessed old Mr. Wilder was an expert on all the plants Dusty had seen all his life, but couldn't identify. He was looking forward to another hike in the spring when there were more plants, because the frost had killed off a good number last week.

"You've got the old camp fixed up pretty good, son." Pops pushed back from the table with a groan. "Someone put that chili away. I can't stop eating it."

"Me, too," Adam agreed. Dusty couldn't believe he'd forgotten to tell Adam about the get-together. Showed how much he had on his mind lately. Pops had let him know, though. Dusty snickered. Instead of hunting for deer, they'd sat around eating, telling stories to Brendon and debating the pros and cons of a sit-down dinner as opposed to finger food for Adam and Sylvie's wedding. If he and Teressa ever got married, he wanted to elope.

"Good thing I fixed the old camp up last year," he said to Pops. "Teressa says we'll be about fifty by the time the baby grows up, so pretty much what you see is what I get."

"What did you decide about that heat pump for the house?" Cal asked.

"I'm getting it in a couple of days. You ever install one of them?"

"Nope."

"Wanna help me with mine?"

"Nope."

"Can't say I blame you. Seems like all I do these days is try to figure out how to install something or how to fix it."

"Quit whining. I'll give you a hand installing the heat pump," Cal said. "A lot of people want to buy those pumps. I could probably pick up some extra cash if I knew how to install them."

"So you'll make all your mistakes with mine," Dusty said, partially joking, but mostly not.

Cal grinned. "Exactly."

"Let me know how it works out," Adam added. "Sylvie and I will probably be looking for a new furnace or something for the big house."

Dusty perked up. "Why? Is Sylvie pregnant?"

"No. Good thing, too. My house is big enough for the two of us, but I wouldn't want to add anyone else. Beanie's still got the bathroom at the big house ripped apart, and now he's all excited because you've been talking about a second bathroom in your basement. God knows when he'll get ours done. Tolsters want one, too, I hear."

"Trust me, I need my second bathroom more than you need yours," Dusty grumbled. He'd been so desperate a couple of mornings, he'd considered erecting an outhouse in the backyard.

"I got to pee, Dusty." Brendon tugged on his hand.

"Okay." Dusty took his tiny hand in his. "You ever used an outhouse?"

"No." Brendon sounded doubtful. "Can I pee outside instead?"

"Yes, you can. You know why?" He opened the door and ushered the small boy out in front of him.

"Why?"

"Because there are no women around. We can fart and we can spit and we can pee outside until we go home."

"How come we can't do that at home?"

"Because women don't like it, and we want them to like us. Do you remember how to pee outside?"

"Yes."

Dusty knew it was ridiculous to be proud of the way Brendon took a leak on his own, but that didn't stop him from grinning his approval. After Brendon was done, he slipped his hand into Dusty's again. "Why do we want women to like us?"

"Because…they smell nice."

Brendon's eyes grew round. "They do! Aunt Anita smells really, really nice."

Dusty laughed. "So does your mom."

Brendon popped his thumb into his mouth. Crap. He had to blow it by mentioning Teressa. And he really didn't think Brendon should be sucking his thumb without washing it first. Kids were a lot of work. You had to watch everything you said around them, and everything they did.

"Do you know how to play poker?" Light and warmth spilled out of the cabin when Dusty opened the door. It smelled good inside, a mix of wood smoke and the lingering scents of chili and coffee.

"What's poker?"

"Kid, you've got so much to learn. Bring any money with you?" Dusty teased.

"I've got this much." He held up all five fingers, and then folded one down.

Dusty put his hand on Brendon's thin shoulder, and—not for the first time—was amazed at how frail he was. "That'll buy you about a thousand toothpicks. Wash your hands at the sink. Come on, boys." He pulled a chair up to the table. "Brendon's my good luck charm and he's going to help me clean you out."

Dusty grinned at his brother. Cal had taught him how to play poker and how to put someone in a headlock, and had also let Dusty practice driving, using Cal's first truck. He'd almost burnt out the clutch, learning how to shift gears. He hoped Brendon would be as great a big brother to the child he and Teressa had made. He cleared the sudden lump in his throat and started dealing the cards.

Later that night, Dusty killed the headlights of the truck as he and Brendon rolled into their yard. Brendon had fallen asleep earlier, but when he'd woken to go to the bathroom, he asked to go home. Dusty didn't have the heart to refuse him.

More asleep than awake, Brendon rested his head on Dusty's shoulder when he picked him up and carried him into the house. He liked hanging out at the camp well enough, but for the first time, he'd been anxious to get home and not just because of Brendon. If anyone knew how to look after themselves, it was Teressa, but he still didn't like leaving her and Sarah on their own. Brendon kissed Dusty on the mouth when he tucked the kid into his bed. It was an innocent little peck, but damn if he didn't feel Brendon's genuine affection. He still wasn't comfortable calling it love, because when someone loved you, like when a kid loved you, well… that was something a person shouldn't take lightly. Just because Brendon was small didn't mean his emotions weren't as genuine or as important as an adult's.

He slipped into Teressa's bedroom next door to the kids' room, eager to see Teressa, even though he expected to find her sound asleep. His mind went blank when he stared at her empty, made-up bed.

After a minute of staring at the tidy blankets, he stumbled out into the living room. She wasn't there, or in the kitchen or the dining room.

He snuck back into Brendon's room. Sarah was safely tucked into her bed, sleeping with total abandon, the way kids did, her limbs sprawled every which way, her mouth open.

Bathroom. He raced down the hallway, but knew before he opened the bathroom door that Teressa wasn't in the dark room.

He rubbed the hard lump in his chest. What if she'd run away? His mother had. But Teressa? No way. As long as he'd known her, which was forever, he'd counted on her being there. He'd hated that she'd gotten pregnant with Sarah all those years ago, but a part of him had been relieved she couldn't leave town like she'd planned. He'd always felt guilty for feeling partially relieved at her misfortune.

He forced himself to move forward. His bedroom was next, then the basement and then...he didn't know. Just that he'd keep looking until he found her.

His breathing loosened the second he saw her asleep in his bed. *Christ*. He sank down on the edge of the bed, careful not to disturb her as he tried to drag oxygen into his starving lungs. She was right here, where she belonged. Everything was okay.

In the morning, they'd wake up and have breakfast together, and Sarah would hang on to him half the morning, and Brendon would tell his mother about learning to play poker, and Teressa would pretend to be mad at him because he taught her son how to gamble.

He sunk his face into his hands. If anything happened to any of them, he'd go berserk. He was more than committed to his little family. He was in love with them. What if, in the end, he wasn't good enough for them, and he lost them?

CHAPTER TWELVE

"DUSTY?" TERESSA ROLLED over and without thinking of the consequences for once, laid her head on Dusty's denim-clad thigh. "I'm glad you're home. I missed you."

Dusty brushed her hair off her face. Inwardly she purred at the abrasive feel of his work-roughened fingers against her cheek.

"That explains why you're wearing my old T-shirt."

She smiled sleepily when she heard the laughter in his voice. "Did Brendon have a good time?"

When he leaned against the head of the bed, she pushed up enough to snuggle against his chest. His arms banded around her, and she traced her fingers through the hair on his arm. His muscles grew taut beneath her touch.

"Yeah. He likes your dad a lot. We've got to figure out a way for them to spend more time together."

She wiggled to get into a more comfortable position. "My mother probably gave him hell when he went home."

"Hey, Teressa?"

"What?"

"Could you not, you know, wiggle like that?"

She tilted her head back and smiled up at him. "Or what?"

"Or I'm going to start getting ideas."

She slid her hand under the flannel shirt he was wearing. His stomach felt as hard as a rock. She loved his body. He sucked in a sharp breath when she found his nipple and tweaked it. "You have the most beautiful body."

Without warning, Dusty flipped her on her back. His huge body hovered above her, one of his powerful legs thrust between her thighs. The sparkle in his eyes darkened with intent. "Don't tease me, Teressa. I passed my due date for sex a few weeks back."

She ran her hand over his shadowed jaw and cupped his cheek. Using her thumb, she traced the outline of his mouth. A groan escaped from deep in her throat when he bit the fleshy part of her thumb. "Make love to me, Dusty. I need you."

A smile slowly spread over his face, and he dipped his head and took her mouth with his. Gently. She slid her hands up over his heavily muscled shoulders. He felt so good, so familiar, which didn't make sense, because they'd only made love once before, the night she got pregnant.

He teased her mouth open with the tip of his

tongue and demanded more, his hand covering her breast. Her T-shirt bunched up around her waist, and she wrapped her legs around him. She couldn't get close enough to him. She needed his weight and his strength and his laughter and his loyalty. She needed to see his sparkling blue eyes and the quiet way he smiled at her first thing every morning. She wasn't sure it made sense, but sharing that first cup of coffee with him in the morning was one of the reasons she was falling in love with him.

He withdrew long enough to shuck his clothes and strip her T-shirt off. He hovered above her, examining every inch of her body, a smile on his face. Her body flushed at the close scrutiny. Not able to abide the building heat inside her, she arched up, pulled him to her and held him in her arms. Held him close and hard. And when she opened herself to him, his kiss deepened while he slowly entered her.

She took him deep inside her, and that, too, felt familiar. She'd been watching him fall in love with her children the past few weeks, but had been so busy fighting her own feelings for him that she hadn't recognized what was happening. She loved him for loving them almost as much as she loved him for being who he was. She'd always loved him.

When she called out his name, her body exploding with pleasure, he covered her mouth with his to smother the sound. He pushed her hair back off her face, kissed her eyes, her forehead, made soothing sounds deep in his throat until her breathing returned to almost normal. Then slowly, rhythmically, as if they were dancing, he made love to her. When she felt pressure build inside her again, she wrapped her legs around him once more and rode out the storm with him as he emptied himself into her.

"God, Teressa." He rested his forehead against hers, both of them breathing harshly. "Making love to you is unbelievable. You're so beautiful and responsive." His large hand covered most of her stomach. "Are you okay?"

"Better than okay." She held his hand in place. "Feel that?"

"What?" he whispered.

"The baby. Do you feel him moving around?"

"No way." Dusty kept his head on her stomach. "Oh, my God. I felt it. Him. The baby. Hello in there."

"You're tickling me. Stop that."

His hand crept from her stomach down to her pelvis.

She caught his hand in hers. "That didn't last long."

"Can't help myself. Saw your curls." When he raked his fingers through her damp curls, her hips came up off the bed. "I should have asked before. Making love doesn't hurt him, does it?"

"No. It's good for him, because making love to you makes Mommy very happy. And that makes the baby happy."

"Excellent." He blew on her damp curls. "I think Mommy is going to be very happy agàin in just a few minutes."

She startled herself when she giggled. "A few minutes? You think highly of yourself."

He wiggled his eyebrows. "You may not know this about me, but I have impressive powers of seduction. I'd be honored to show you just how persuasive."

She arched her body in a full-length stretch. "Do your worst."

An hour later, sweat-soaked and boneless, Teressa sank into Dusty's arms as he spooned her from behind. There was no awkwardness between them. They made love as if they'd memorized each other's body years ago.

"DUSTY."

With a satiated smile on his face, Dusty rolled over and sleepily reached for the woman of his dreams. He could have sworn he'd just fallen asleep, but if Teressa was willing to continue where they'd left off—he paused to savor exactly what they'd been doing not so long ago—then he'd find the stamina to oblige her. No problemo.

He patted the empty space beside him, cranked

one eye open. Teressa sat up against the headboard, her legs pulled up to her chest. When he heard her sniffle, fear slammed into him.

She'd changed her mind about them.

"Teressa?" He snapped on the bedside light and grabbed her ankle. "What's wrong, Tee?" *Please say nothing.* Let it be hormones, that's all. He rose up on one elbow and supported his head, which suddenly felt like a ten-ton ball of iron. It wasn't hormones. She wouldn't have gotten half-dressed just to cry about nothing.

"I'm bleeding and I have cramps."

His heart stopped. They shouldn't have had sex. He should have been gentler, and for sure he shouldn't have— "Bleeding...where?"

"My vagina. I've been having cramps all week, but I thought it was from standing up too much at work. I don't know what to do, Dusty."

Feeling helpless, he watched the strongest woman in the world break apart as she covered her face with her hands and sobbed. Dusty crawled over to her and wrapped his arms around her shoulders. "I'm going to call your mom and dad to come over to look after the kids. We'll drive to the hospital. It'll be quicker than waiting for an ambulance." He kissed the top of her head. "You don't have to do anything except curl up and wait for me. Tell me what you need, and I'll get it for you."

Teressa's sobs sounded as if they were ripped

from the bottom of her soul. "Come on, honey. Crying that hard can't be good for the baby."

"I'm…I'm afraid I'm going to lose it. I should have…should have paid more attention. I'm a rotten mother."

He squeezed her shoulders again then rolled out of bed. "We're not going to lose our baby. You're young and healthy, and the best mom in the world. We can talk about all this later. I'll get you a towel and call your parents."

They couldn't lose the baby. Not only because he was already in love with the little tyke, but he also worried the baby was the only thing keeping him and Teressa together, and just barely at that. Teressa had drawn the line years ago, her on one side, him on the other. He'd accepted that they'd never step over that line, but in the past few months he'd allowed himself to start thinking of Teressa differently. Like maybe he wouldn't mind so much if the line disappeared. So, he'd stepped over it the first chance he got. It was only after she got pregnant that she made an effort to have a relationship with him beyond friendship. He knew it had been a struggle for her, and if there wasn't a baby, there may not be a "them," either.

Dusty considered waking Sarah and Brendon before they left, but decided against it. After calling Teressa's parents, he went back to the bedroom and gathered up what he thought Teressa needed.

By the time she'd managed to struggle into some clothes with his help, her parents were at the door. Dusty caught them before they knocked.

"Where is she?" Linda, Teressa's mother, tried to push her way past him, her face white and strained. He grabbed her arm to stop her.

"First off, the kids are still asleep, so please keep your voices down. Second, Teressa's in the bedroom. She's really upset. Don't upset her more."

Linda pulled her arm away. "She's my daughter, for God's sake. Of course I won't upset her."

Dusty didn't say anything, but raised an eyebrow as he stood solidly between Linda and the bedroom.

"Should I make some tea or coffee for you to take to drink on the way?" Mr. Wilder asked.

"Thanks. Teressa loves her tea." He turned his attention back to Linda. "You can talk to her for a minute, then we've got to go. I'm going to start the truck so it warms up."

Five minutes later, he wrapped Teressa in a blanket and carried her out to the truck. "You okay?"

Teressa gave him a weak smile when he climbed into the driver's seat. "I don't feel sick. I'm just scared. Why did you phone my mother instead of Sylvie or Anita?"

Dusty pointed the truck toward Lancaster and picked up speed. "Adam and Sylvie are working day and night to get ready for their wedding."

"I just bet they are." When he heard her soft

snicker in the dark cab, he smiled and relaxed. Teressa always got his stupid jokes.

"What is it with weddings?" he asked. "Do they make everyone horny?"

This time, she giggled. "It's romantic, seeing two people so much in love," she explained.

Like we are. Dusty didn't say the words out loud. Were they? Or were they, at best, resigned to making the relationship work? For sure, the sex part worked just fine. But he'd always known that. He also knew it wasn't enough.

He shifted uncomfortably in the bucket seat. She hadn't said she loved him or even that she thought they had a chance as a couple.

"What?" When had Teressa grown so sensitive to his moods?

"Nothing. I called your mother and father because they're your family. They needed to be the ones to help."

"Sometimes you're brilliant."

"Only sometimes, eh?"

She laughed again. "No one's smart all the time. I think the older you get, the smarter you get."

"Or maybe you've just gotten to know me better." It was an odd thing to say, because they'd known each other almost their entire lives. But once Dusty hit his teenage years he hadn't slowed down long enough to say more than an occasional hello to her. And after she'd gotten pregnant with Sarah, the only place he'd seen her was at the café when she was working.

"I've known you forever, Dusty Carson."

"Yeah, but we didn't hang out together after a while."

She was quiet for a minute. "That's true. I never looked at it like that."

"Me, neither. Tell me a secret," he suggested, spontaneously.

"A secret?"

"Yeah, tell me something you've never told another person." He grinned to himself in the dark. As far as distractions went, that was a good one. He didn't want Teressa worrying about the baby until they had to.

When she was quiet for a couple of minutes he wondered if his ploy had failed. "I wanted to ask you to my senior prom, but you started going steady with Carol, so I didn't."

"Carol." He narrowed his eyes. He kind of remembered her.

"Oh, my God, don't tell me you don't remember her. Everywhere I looked, you two were making out."

"Ohhh, Carol. Right."

"Are you smiling right now?"

He doused his grin. "Nah. You should have asked me, anyway. I might have gone with you. Who did you go with?"

"Billy Tomalsin."

"Okay. I remember that." Even back then, he'd had a weird need to protect Teressa. Billy liked to brag about his dates. When he suggested he'd gotten to second base with Teressa on prom night, Dusty had plowed his fist into Billy's big mouth. He'd gotten in a lot of trouble for that fight.

"Your turn. Tell me something I don't know about you."

"I beat up Billy after he took you home prom night."

Teressa swatted his arm. "That was you?"

"Yes, ma'am."

"No one would talk about it. Why did you do that? He never asked me out again."

Good. "I probably had a few too many beers and felt like getting into a fight." Even now he couldn't bring himself to embarrass her by telling her what Billy had said. Dusty had threatened to beat up everyone at the late-night bonfire if he ever heard another word about Billy's date with Teressa.

"It's okay with me if you want a beer once in a while."

He covered her hand that rested on the console between them. "I might have one when this baby is born. Are you still getting cramps?"

"A bit."

"We're almost there. We'll be fine."

"I hope so."

He heard tears in her voice and wondered if she just meant that she hoped the baby would be fine or if that hope extended to their relationship, as well. The next few hours could make a big difference in their lives, because if there was no baby…well, they'd see. He was a little rusty with praying, but he thought this might be the time to start trying.

CHAPTER THIRTEEN

TERESSA HATED HAVING Dusty in the small cubicle with her while the doctor examined her. She felt so…exposed. It wasn't that she didn't want him close by, but out in the waiting room would have worked better for her. By the look on Dusty's face, it was safe to assume he wasn't enjoying himself, either.

The doctor stood and pulled the sheet over her. "All your symptoms—bleeding, cramps and swollen ankles—are not unusual for pregnant women, but I think it's a good idea if we take an ultrasound and see what's going on in there. Have you had one yet?"

"No. I have an appointment next week." She pressed her legs together.

"Okay. We'll do one as soon as we can get a technician in here. I'm also going to keep you in the hospital for a few days for observation."

Teressa sat up. "I can't. I have children and a job."

The doctor pulled up a chair and sat beside the bed, his back to Dusty. He hadn't wanted Dusty in the room, either, because technically, he wasn't a relative. "How much do you want this baby?" he asked her.

She heard Dusty suck in a breath. She knew how he felt, as though someone had just punched him, because she felt the same way. "More than anything."

The doctor nodded. "Good. The baby's probably fine, but you need to stay here for at least two days until we run some tests. And be prepared when you do go home, you're going to be spending more time in bed than you probably want to. Which reminds me…" He turned to face Dusty. "Having sex is not a good idea until after the baby is born."

Dusty flushed as red as a cooked lobster. "I just want Teressa and the baby to be okay."

"Of course you do." He turned back to Teressa. "We'll get you moved into a room, and then take you down to the lab to do an ultrasound. If you get cramps or start bleeding again, let the nurse know. I'll see you when we get the results from the test."

Teressa lay back on the bed and closed her eyes. She was almost too tired to even feel guilty. Without coming right out and saying it, the doctor had implied having sex had caused the bleeding.

Dusty came close to the edge of the bed and gently pushed her hair off her forehead. She probably looked like a disaster. "I'm so sorry, Teressa. I should never have touched you."

"I had cramps off and on all week and didn't go to the doctor's. If it's anyone's fault, it's mine." She kept her eyes closed, the effort to open them beyond her.

"Can I get you anything?"

A nurse came into the cubicle with a wheelchair. "It looks like you get to be our guest for a few days, Mrs. Wilder. If that handsome husband of yours would like to push your chair, I'll show you where we're moving you to."

Wearing a light blue V-neck sweater that hugged his chest and old, worn jeans, Dusty did look handsome. And she looked like a hag. Didn't matter. All she wanted was to crawl into a bed and sleep. Maybe the doctor had a point about bed rest—for two days. After that, they'd see.

"Can you phone my parents?" she asked after they'd installed her in a room. Another woman, asleep, or pretending to be, was in the other bed. The nurse had pulled the curtain closed between the beds to give them the illusion of privacy.

Dusty pulled a chair over to her bedside and sat. "Sure."

"Aren't you going home?"

"And leave you alone? No. I want to be here for the ultrasound, too."

"And then you can go home."

"Why are you so anxious to get rid of me?"

"I'm not," she whined. "I'm so tired I can't think."

She was ashamed of how she was acting, but she couldn't seem to help herself. She was exhausted, and something about Dusty had always made it easy for her to not have to pretend to be stronger or smarter or anything other than exactly what she was. Feeling as vulnerable as she did right now, she was afraid she'd do or say something she'd regret. Would it be so bad to let someone take care of her for a change?

"Right." He got to his feet, his face grim. "I'll call your parents, and I'll wait in the family room down the hall."

"You'll need a list for the kids." She started counting on her fingers. "What time they have their bath, what each one will or will not eat, what they have to take to—" Dusty covered her fingers with his hand.

"We'll manage, Teressa. Stop worrying."

"Easy for you to say."

"You think any of this is easy for me?" He looked deep into her eyes. "Is it for you?"

She squirmed, dismayed that she hadn't given him the benefit of the doubt. Dusty had changed a lot in the past few months, but especially the last month, and she needed to start acknowledging that to him and to herself.

If she lost this baby…well, she'd known all along the only reason he was with her was because she was pregnant. If there was no baby, the incentive for staying together was gone, right? At least, for Dusty it would be. All along she'd assured herself she could handle him leaving her, but she wasn't certain that was true anymore. She did know he'd break Sarah and Brendon's hearts if he left.

Two hours later, Teressa envied Dusty as he paced the room while she was stuck in bed. The room was thick with anxiety, hers and Dusty's, as they waited in her room for the doctor to arrive with the results of the ultrasound.

They both stiffened when the doctor strode into the room, several papers in his hands. Teressa searched his face, but she couldn't pick up any clues from his neutral expression.

"How are you feeling now?" the doctor asked her as he dug in his breast pocket for his glasses.

A hundred percent worse. "Okay. No cramps."

He nodded his approval. "Good. Well, I've got… news. Let me show you."

He lined up the papers on the bedside tray. "Have a look at this one." He pointed to the first printout of the ultrasound. "There's your baby."

Dusty's hair brushed her cheek as he leaned forward with her to look at the image. "That's our baby? It's so small."

"Not to worry. It will grow fast. Especially if Mom here stays off her feet. Now, look at this one. Do you see it?"

"Oh, my!" Teressa slapped a hand on her mouth. It couldn't be.

"What? I don't see anything." Dusty sounded as if he were hyperventilating.

The doctor handed the paper to her. "I'll let you do the honors, Mom."

Teressa tried to swallow her tears as she kept her eyes on Dusty's terrified expression. "We're having twins."

"Twins?" He looked from the doctor to her, a weird, strangled look on his face. In slow motion, his legs folded up and he crumpled to the floor.

"Oh, my God." Teressa leaned over the side of the bed, trying to reach him. "Is he all right?"

"I'll check. Stay where you are." The doctor squatted down beside Dusty's large body sprawled on the floor and felt his pulse. "I guess it's true, the bigger they come, the harder they fall. You can stop crying. I don't think he's hurt." He straightened Dusty's leg out of an awkward angle. "Believe it or not, he's not the first man I've had faint when they hear they're having twins. I don't suppose he's felt nauseous lately."

"Now that you mention, he has. Why? Is something wrong?"

The doctor stood. "I suspect your big, tough guy has couvade syndrome."

For the second time in as many days, Teressa felt the earth shift beneath her feet. She'd always thought of Dusty as strong and healthy. He couldn't be sick. "What is that?"

Dusty started to stir, and the doctor offered his hand to help him sit up. "Sympathetic pregnancy," he said. "Hey, big guy, how are you feeling?"

"What happened?" Dusty's eyes immediately sought hers.

The doctor clamped a hand on his shoulder. "You fainted. Can you stand up now?"

"Yeah. Thanks." Dusty climbed to his feet, looking sheepish. "First time that's happened."

"I'm guessing it's the first time you've had twins, too."

"Twins." Again he sought her gaze. She blinked back more tears. He'd said *twins* as if it was the most beautiful word in the world. "We're having *two* babies, Teressa."

She pulled the sheet up to her chin and fought the urge to melt under his proud gaze. Just wait until he had to get up in the middle of the night for not one, but two babies. If she carried the pregnancy to term, that is. Panic slid through her. Of course she'd go full-term. Like Dusty said, she was young and healthy. *Two* babies. Oh, my.

"Do you know the sex?" she croaked.

"You'll know with the next ultrasound. I'll notify your ob-gyn, and she can set it up. You still have to stay here for at least two days." He started writing on her chart. "I'm recommending you stay off your feet for a good portion of each day. But I think it would be good for you to walk a half hour twice a day. Or break that down into fifteen minutes four times a day."

He put the chart in the slot at the bottom of the bed. "I've requested a couple tests to be done today. Did you say you have children at home?"

Teressa let out a sigh before she could catch it. "Two. Sarah's six and Brendon's three."

The doctor turned to Dusty. "I hope you're ready to take on the lion's share of the work around the house. And you." He frowned at Teressa. "Get as much rest as possible while you're here. I'll see you in a couple days before we release you."

After the doctor left, Dusty kept his back to her as he stood at the window and stared outside. It was light enough now to see the outline of the buildings on the hill below them. Her heat fluttered. He'd changed his mind. He'd finally come to his senses and was going to run, and he was trying to find the courage to tell her. She'd known all along he'd back out when the going got rough. *Two babies.* She started crying. She couldn't do this.

"Hey." Dusty turned and moved over to her when he saw her tears. "What's wrong? Are you okay?"

"I can't do it. I can't have another two children. I just can't," she sobbed.

Dusty lifted up the blanket. "Move over."

"What are you doing?"

"I'm getting in bed with you. Move it."

She scooted over as far as she could. Dusty kicked off his work boots and climbed onto the bed and slid his arm around her shoulders. She laid her head on his chest, relaxing to the sound of his heartbeat.

"What were you thinking about at the window?" she asked. Might as well get it all out in front of them so she knew what she was dealing with.

"I was thinking of how life can change so quickly. No matter how hard you try, it can get away from you. At least we've got each other."

"Do we?"

"I may be going out on a limb, but I assumed we'd continue living together at least for now."

"I thought you were plotting ways to run away."

He looked down at her. "You're kidding, right?"

"There's a small chance I could have a miscarriage."

"That's not going to happen, Tee. You're going to be fine as long as you follow the doctor's orders."

If only it was that simple. How about if she also opened her heart and invited Dusty in? What if she took the chance, and he said no?

CHAPTER FOURTEEN

TERESSA SETTLED INTO the passenger seat of the truck and stole another look at Dusty. Was it her imagination or did he get better looking every time she saw him? It must be true that absence makes the heart grow fonder, because she hadn't seen him since Sunday night, when he'd brought the kids to visit her at the hospital. Yesterday afternoon he called and in a harried voice said he didn't think he could make it to town and was that all right? She wanted to ask him what was so important he couldn't visit, but bit her lip and told him she was fine. Then she careened between feeling desperately lonely and worrying what kind of trouble Dusty had gotten into now. Surely if Sarah and Brendon weren't okay, someone would have phoned her.

Anita had dropped by for an hour in the afternoon and tried to assure her that everything was fine at home, and Pops had arrived around suppertime with Ada, who had brought her homemade chicken soup. The soup tasted almost as good as her own recipe.

"Everything okay at home?" she asked Dusty again.

Dusty sent her a sardonic look as he pulled out of the parking lot. "For the tenth time, everything's fine. I got Sarah and Brendon off to school and day care this morning. Adam cooked supper last night and ended up staying to eat. That was nice. Cal and Anita dropped by the night before. I think I heard Tyler say something about cooking supper for us tonight. Don't worry." He grinned. "Adam said he'd supervise."

"It sounds like Grand Central Station at our place."

"I think it's good for Sarah and Brendon to have lots of family around. I've been watching them get to know everyone better. I think Sarah's over me. She's crushing on Cal now, and I've gotta tell you, it's a hoot watching him handle her."

She sniffed. "Apparently, no one missed me. That's good, I suppose."

Dusty pulled into the parking lot beside them and put the truck in Neutral. Before she realized what he was doing, he cupped her face with both hands and kissed her long and hard. When he finally released her, he calmly put the truck in gear and pulled back into traffic. It took her several tries before she caught her breath.

"Before we get home I should warn you Sarah's moved into your room because she missed you, but I don't think she's going to give up the room without a fight." He threw her a smile. "How do you feel about sleeping with me? I love the idea of falling asleep with you beside me every night. Besides, we'll need to keep the twins with us for the first few months, or so Ada says, and my room is the only one big enough for all four of us."

Heat stirred deep in her belly. She had no problem sleeping with Dusty. If she just had herself to think about, they probably would have "slept" together eons ago. But she still worried that losing the twins was a possibility. If that happened, then what?

She'd had a lot of time to think in the past two days. She finally admitted Dusty fit into their lives perfectly. He loved Sarah and Brendon, and they loved him. The only thing that held her back from committing herself to Dusty was her hang-ups. She couldn't even use the excuse that he was irresponsible, because he had changed so much in the past few months. But there was still something there, and not just with her, but with him, too.

He'd never said he loved her. Could he be holding back because *he* didn't trust *her?* And for her part, could she honestly tell him marrying him was enough for her? That she wouldn't regret giving up her dreams once and for all and be happy to live in Collina?

She forced herself to concentrate on what he was

saying. Oh, yes, sleeping together. "You remember the doctor said no sex, right?"

"Yeah, about that. I called him. He's mostly worried about penetration because…I don't know. The floor of your vagina is thin? Does that sound right to you?"

"Possibly. What if I lose the babies?" she blurted out. Damn. She could have approached that topic in a more gentle way.

A vein pulsed in his jaw. "You won't."

"But what if I do? The twins are the reason we're together. You'd be free to leave."

She immediately felt bereft when he pulled his hand away from hers. "You still don't get it, do you? Maybe you're right. Maybe we don't belong together."

"I have to think of the children," she barely managed to say past the rock in her throat.

Dusty was silent for a few minutes. He might as well have been sitting in another vehicle rather than right beside her. She felt walls going up all around her.

"You're not being reasonable when you think Sarah and Brendon have to rely entirely on you. There are a lot of people who love them, and if you'd let them get closer to the kids and spend more time with them, everyone's life would be richer. Not everyone is like your mother. It's possible to love Brendon and Sarah and not expect anything in return. If you decide you don't want to marry me, I'll accept your decision. But the twins are going to know what it's like to be part of a big family. I won't have it any other way. I'd hate to think Sarah and Brendon would miss out on all the fun."

He still hadn't said anything about loving her. Feeling bruised inside, Teressa shrank down into her winter coat and stuffed her cold hands in her pockets. Dusty didn't understand. Aside from the help her mother had given, which always came at a price, she'd been solely responsible for Sarah and Brendon. And now he was telling her the way she was raising them was wrong. Was it possible he was right? That all she'd had to do all these years was ask for help?

Good thing she'd had a couple days of rest in the hospital because she was exhausted already, and she wasn't even home yet.

When they finally pulled into the yard, she shoved aside her depressing thoughts. She'd expected pandemonium when she walked into the house, but it was eerily quiet. "Where are Sarah and Brendon?"

Dusty put her overnight bag on the floor. "I told you, school and day care."

"Of course." She felt out of sorts, like a visitor in her own home. She hung up her coat and slipped off her shoes. "The house looks okay." The floor was a little crunchy under foot and there were dirty dishes stacked in the sink, but she supposed it looked like a house where busy people lived.

"Sarah swept the floor this morning. I think she missed a few places. And Brendon was supposed to put the dishes in the dishwasher, but he couldn't find his sneakers, so we had to look for them instead."

Nothing was done up to her standards and yet the house was still standing.

Dusty hung up his jacket and kicked off his boots, but went back and nudged them into the closet. He grimaced at her. "I'm learning. Want a cup of tea?"

"Sounds good." She started leafing through the mail stacked on the counter. "What's with the tent in the living room?"

Dusty laughed, and the house suddenly came to life. "That's an experiment gone bad. First night, I thought the kids could use a little distraction, so we pretended we were camping. They kind of got overexcited. I'll put it away as soon as you go to bed."

"I'm not going to bed." She'd been lying on her back for two days. Her muscles screamed for exercise.

"Yeah, you are. Doctor's orders." He came up behind her and scooped her into his arms. "I bought you a present." He carried her into the bedroom and set her carefully on the edge of the bed.

"What?"

He handed her a bag from Victoria's Secret.

"I really don't think I'm in the mood—"

"Humor me. Need some help changing?" His eyes sparkled.

He was doing it again, making her fall in love with him. She wanted to. She wanted to give him her heart and say, *take care, it's fractured.* "Give me a minute," she said in a husky voice.

He hesitated, but finally left her alone.

She dumped the contents of the bag onto her lap and held up the beautiful nightgown Dusty had bought for her. It was dark green silk with an empire waistline, so she'd be able to wear it when her belly grew bigger. She pulled her clothes off and let the nightgown drift over her. It fell to just above her ankles and covered her modestly enough that she could wear it around Sarah and Brendon, but the way the folds of material clung to her full figure left no doubt she was a woman. Wearing it made her feel beautiful.

She sniffed back tears. Dusty had bought it for her, not for him. He knew she'd hate having to stay in bed and in his way, was trying to make her feel better about being confined. She lay back on the bed and closed her eyes.

Dusty was right. Sometimes she forgot to think about herself and what she wanted. For years she'd played the same old tired scenario in her head. She was young and successful and living in an exotic place far away from here. But she was no longer that young girl. She was a woman, and she wanted to be loved for exactly who she was, not the person she thought she should be. Is that what Dusty had been trying to tell her all along? He loved *her?* Warts and all.

She was a coward, afraid to reach out for what she wanted. What would it take to shake her out of the hole she'd dug herself into?

A WEEK LATER, Teressa had half an hour to get a grip, pull herself out of her depression and think about the bride, Sylvie, who absolutely glowed today. She wanted to be the one getting married, but she still hadn't found the courage to ask Dusty to marry her. She wanted what Sylvie had. To be in love and to be loved.

Teressa moved to stand behind her friend and look at her reflection in the mirror. "Your gown is perfect. You look fantastic. Just like we planned when we were kids. Remember?"

Sylvie had surprised them all when she'd insisted on a traditional wedding. She was the artist, after all. Teressa had expected almost anything except traditional. But Sylvie had made the right choice. Her long, white gown laced up the back, showcasing her slender back and shoulders. Blond curls spilled out irreverently from beneath the traditional bridal veil.

Teressa's lip trembled as a wave of nostalgia rose inside her. They'd planned their weddings together when they were twelve years old. Not many years after that Sylvie moved to Toronto to study art, and it had taken her far too many years to find her way home. But she was finally getting her wedding. Unlike Teressa, who had pushed away the only man who could possibly love her, because she was so demanding. Just like her mother.

Sylvie laughed a beautiful golden sound. "I'd forgotten about us making those plans," she said.

A few months ago, Teressa hadn't thought it possible her friend could be as happy as she was today. She'd been so lost, but she'd finally put it all together, and Teressa thought of Adam as Sylvie's reward for being true to herself. If there was a lesson in there for herself, she failed to see it.

"Listen." Teressa smiled at Sylvie in the mirror. "If you have any second thoughts about Adam, let me know. I still think he picked the wrong woman."

If it hadn't been so apparent that Sylvie was the center of Adam's world, Teressa wouldn't have dared joke. But Sylvie and Adam were made for each other. Any fool could see that after being around them for five minutes.

What did people see when they looked at her and Dusty? An ocean of trouble? Not that there was any *her and Dusty*. They merely cohabited a home, being overly polite and solicitous to each other. If

Dusty asked her in that gentle tone he'd adopted lately if she wanted one more cup of tea, she was going to scream.

She forced her mind back to Sylvie and her wedding. In a few minutes, Pops would arrive with the car to pick up the bride and the bridesmaid and take them to the church, where Dusty was waiting right now as Adam's best man. "I'm so happy for you, Sylvie. You deserve to be happy."

Tears welled in her eyes again, and she swung away and pretended to be fascinated with the bouquet of flowers sitting on the coffee table in Sylvie and Adam's living room. She *had* to stop crying.

"Are you okay, Teressa?"

"Of course." She wiped an errant tear away with her fingertip before turning around. "I'm a little weepy," she confessed. "Hormones, you know?"

Sylvie looked at Teressa's waist, which the exquisite blue velvet dress Sylvie had ordered made for her, emphasized. It was the last design Teressa would have chosen, it was too short, too tight, but when she'd put it on, she'd felt…beautiful. Womanly. The top showed a bit more cleavage than she felt comfortable with, but no one was going to be looking at her, anyway.

"You're allowed to feel weepy. Stay away from the punch, though. I think Tyler had plans to spike it."

"I'm going to start teaching Tyler how to cook," Teressa said.

"Are you?"

Although Sylvie owned a third of the café, Teressa often forgot to discuss her plans with her partners. "Unless you or Adam have a problem with that," she conceded. It was Sylvie's wedding day after all. "He's going nowhere, and needs a trade. Plus, now that Adam and you are getting married, Adam will probably want more time off to go with you when you have to travel for art exhibits."

"I think it's a good idea to train Tyler. You're right, he needs something to make him employable." Sylvie picked up a pearl earring and put it on. "But Adam and I aren't planning on traveling a lot."

"But you could if you wanted to."

"Yes, but we won't. We love it here."

But Sylvie could leave anytime she wanted. She could go to Paris, London, Rome. Anywhere. "Why?" Teressa asked.

"Why what?" Sylvie slipped on the second earring. They both looked at her reflection in the mirror.

"Why would you stay here when you can go anywhere you want?"

Sylvie looked thoughtful for a minute. "It's interesting to visit different countries and cities, but for me, what matters most is the people. I feel loved here. Like I matter. You can lose yourself in a big city if you don't have anyone else."

Teressa frowned. "I guess that makes sense." A

corner of her mouth quirked up. "I saw Oliver on my way here. He looked yummy." Oliver was Sylvie's agent and once-upon-a-time lover. Refined, sophisticated and handsome in a cultured way, he was the complete opposite of Adam, who looked like a brawler. But the longer you knew Adam, the less you noticed his rough edges, and Teressa didn't know a kinder person.

Except Dusty. The words whispered through her mind. She shook them off.

"How did Adam feel about inviting Oliver to the wedding?"

Sylvie turned from the mirror to look at Teressa. "Not great. But he needs to see for himself there's nothing between Oliver and me other than he's my agent. Actions speak louder than words. And speaking of actions, how did you get my brother to finally grow up?"

Teressa opened her mouth to quip *which brother?* but realized Sylvie was serious. "You think Dusty's changed?"

"How can you even ask that? He gave up drinking beer, which he loves. And he never once complained about doing it." Sylvie narrowed her eyes. "What names are you considering now?"

"I finally talked him out of Duke. So now it's Luke. I've always liked that name."

"And for a girl?"

"Emma, but…"

"What?"

"I've always loved the name Daisy. It's such a fun-loving name."

"So tell him."

Teressa shrugged. "He's earned the right to name our babies."

"I have to tip my hat to you. I never thought he'd grow up. Who would have guessed he'd be so good with children? And your house. Wow. It's really looking good. He's been working hard, hasn't he? Usually when he's done fishing for the year, he slacks off."

Teressa felt clammy, as if she might throw up.

Sylvie hugged her. "It's going to be okay, Teressa. You two will find your way."

"You're going to make me cry again, and today is supposed to be about you, not me. But thank you for being such a good friend." She blinked rapidly to clear away her tears. "You know I love you, right?"

Sylvie beamed a radiant smile at her. "Of course you do. We're family."

Teressa struggled to swallow her tears as they smiled at each other. Sylvie was her oldest friend in the world.

As they turned toward Pops, who had just opened the door, she realized that wasn't true. Dusty had made friends with her the first day of school. Her family had just moved to Collina, and she hadn't met anyone yet. Dusty was a big kid, in grade three, and for some reason decided she needed protection from the older kids. She'd forgotten about that. In one way or another, she supposed he'd been looking out for her ever since, although Dusty had never made a big deal about it.

"There's my beautiful girls," Pops boomed. "Don't the two of you make a picture. I hope you're ready to go. Last time I saw Adam he looked like he was going to faint. Hard to tell if it was because his tie was strangling him or if Oliver had arrived." Pops laughed.

He looked pleased when both women laughed. "You're looking very handsome, yourself." Teressa patted his arm.

"Thank you." Pops glanced briefly in her direction, but really only had eyes for his daughter. No wonder. She'd never seen Sylvie look so happy.

"I'm going to make one last trip to the ladies' room." She climbed the stairs to the second floor as much to use the bathroom as to give Sylvie and Pops a few minutes of privacy before they left.

Once inside the spacious bathroom Adam had designed, she sank onto the toilet and rested her head against the wall beside her. She was already exhausted, and she still had the wedding and reception to get through. She wasn't sure she'd survive the whole ceremony, especially with the damned persistent backache she'd had the past day or so.

She should have followed the doctor's instructions and gone for more walks. But when was she supposed to fit those in?

She eased off one high heel, massaged her foot, then slipped the shoe on again and stood. Okay, she took a deep breath. She could do this. She refused to even consider letting Sylvie and Adam down. At best, maybe she could slip away from the reception early.

"I've got Sylvie tucked safely into the car. Now your turn." Pops waited for her at the bottom of the stairs.

"I hope I didn't keep you waiting." She gratefully took his arm. The stone walkway to the car was uneven, and she had almost zero experience wearing high heels.

"We're right on time. How are you feeling, Teressa? I haven't been able to get in a visit with you lately."

Pops used to swing by the café in the quiet time between breakfast and lunch, and they'd sit down and talk for half an hour with a coffee. They'd discuss what was happening with the café, with Sarah and Brendon, with herself. She realized now she missed his visits and wondered why he'd stopped coming. Of course, he no longer owned the small restaurant. And rumor had it he was spending time with the nurse at the seniors' center. But Teressa worried he'd stopped because of her tumultuous relationship with his son.

"I'm pregnant." She smiled at him as she stated the obvious.

"I don't know anyone who does pregnancy more beautifully than you do."

"You're going to make me cry."

"At the risk of spilling more tears, I saw the wedding cake. It's amazing. I can't believe it's the first one you've ever made."

"Thanks, Pops. I loved making Sylvie and Adam the cake. I'm so happy for both of them."

They stopped at the door to the car, and he hugged her carefully. "I want you to know no matter what happens, I'll always see you as my other daughter. I know it must be hard for you, but I'm so happy you're having Dusty's babies. I can't wait for grandchildren."

"Oh, Pops." She didn't bother to hide her tears this time.

"There now." He handed her a clean hankie. "Didn't mean to make you cry."

When Teressa slipped into the backseat beside Sylvie, Sylvie took her hand and held it all the way to the church. Teressa had no idea if Sylvie was giving or asking for support, but it felt as if the exchange was equal. How dare she wish for more when she already had such wonderful friends?

DUSTY FIDGETED AS he stood beside Adam at the front of the small church. Why had Adam agreed to torture himself this way? Waiting for his bride to show up was hard enough on a guy, but when Oliver walked in and took a seat halfway down the church, Adam looked as if he was going to hurl. He and Sylvie should have eloped and had a party afterward. Standing up in front of everyone, wearing suits and ties, waiting, like, forever, sucked.

But in a way he understood why Adam had agreed to a traditional wedding. His soon-to-be brother-in-law would do anything for Sylvie. Just as Dusty would for Teressa. The difference was Teressa didn't want anything to do with him. He rolled his shoulders, the suit jacket tight across his back.

Adam had already told him Beanie would finally be finished with the plumbing at the old family home in another day or so, and if Dusty wanted, he could move back home. It was Sylvie's house now, but Adam and Sylvie were happy living next door in Adam's house for the time being. Of course they'd still be renovating the old house, but he'd been living in the middle of renovations at his own house, so same old, same old.

Except he'd be alone. Sylvie had asked if he minded that they extend the same offer to Teressa, and it had damned near killed him to agree. To his relief Teressa declined, saying Sarah and Brendon had settled nicely into Dusty's home and she didn't want to move them again so soon.

Adam shifted beside him. Dusty could tell he felt as fidgety as he did. He started humming "Me and Bobby McGee" until Adam elbowed him. "Cut it out," Adam murmured.

"Looks like everyone's here, but the bride," Dusty said out of the corner of his mouth.

Adam pulled on the knot in his tie as if it was choking him. "She'll be here."

Dusty noticed Adam had raised his voice at the end of the sentence, as if it was a question. "No doubt in my mind. You guys are solid gold."

Adam smiled. "Thanks, man. It's killing me standing up here."

"Looks like you're saved. Here she comes." And then he felt as strangled as Adam had a minute ago.

When Teressa followed Sylvie into the church, Dusty staggered back a step, his breath leaving him in one big whoosh. Teressa looked so beautiful, her blue dress clinging to her like a second skin. He spared a quick look for his sister. Yeah, she looked good, but Teressa looked so…ripe. And…and… pregnant. Like a goddess.

She glanced at him briefly when she stopped behind Sylvie, and then moved to stand to the left of Sylvie. He'd assumed she'd be standing next to him.

He'd managed to miss the one rehearsal they'd held because Sarah had been sick that night, and they had to choose which one of them could attend because, like everything else that happened around here, almost everyone in the village had gone to the rehearsal, whether they'd been invited or not, and they couldn't find a babysitter.

He swore he could smell the sweet, spicy scent that was uniquely Teressa's from where he stood on the other side of Adam. Dusty raised his hands to shove them in his pockets, then dropped them by his sides as he endeavored to pay attention to what the officiant was saying. He wanted to stand beside Teressa and hold her hand in his. Well, he wanted to touch a lot more than that, but considering he was standing at the front of a church with pretty much everyone he knew sitting in front of him, he'd settle for holding her hand.

But he didn't have the right to even do that. He'd tried the best he could to make them work, but they were stuck, and he didn't think they could get unstuck. He no longer had any idea how to make Teressa love him. But he'd always known that was a losing proposition.

He tried to give the wedding his full attention, feeling like a shell of a man inside, but whimpers from the pew right in front of him made him wince. Uh-oh. He'd avoided looking at Sarah and Brendon for this very reason. He hadn't seen much of either of them the past few days, and if they missed him half as much as he missed them, of course they were going to make a fuss. Too bad it had to happen in the middle of Sylvie and Adam's wedding.

He should have thought ahead and asked to hang out with them for an hour or so last night. But he hadn't gotten to the point where he could accept that he was only going to be a part-time dad, although that was the way things were shaping up. The thought of the three of them living in his house without him tied his gut into knots. He loved that they were safe and had their own space, but he wanted to live there with them, too.

Sarah quickly progressed from sniffles to outright crying, and Teressa's mother was making almost as much fuss as Sarah, trying to keep her quiet. Now he knew where the little girl inherited her drama-queen genes from.

He glanced at Teressa for guidance, but she was staring down at her feet, biting her bottom lip, probably attempting to hold back either a smile or tears. Aw, hell. Tears it was. He saw one lone tear trickle down her cheek.

He shifted his gaze to Sylvie and held up his finger. The second she winked, he stepped down from his post as best man, snatched Sarah off the pew and returned to stand beside Adam with the little girl in his arms. A collective sigh went up from the church as Sarah patted his cheek, kissed him, then laid her head on his shoulder. What they didn't hear was her whisper, "I love you."

They also didn't hear his heart breaking. He clenched his teeth to hold in the emotion that clogged his throat. No way could he look at Teressa right now, or he'd break down completely. When had he turned into such a wimp?

When he'd fallen in love with his little family. And yes, damn it, they belonged to him.

The officiant had smoothly continued on with the ceremony when the commotion started again. Brendon, this time. He didn't wait for Dusty to save him, but made a break for it all by himself as he dashed up the two steps to Dusty and clung to his leg.

Dusty blushed, and then laughed when the congregation started laughing. He took the small boy's hand in his and squeezed gently as he winked down at him. It had taken a lot of guts to break free from old Grandma and join them at the altar.

The tension ran out of Dusty as Brendon gripped his hand with both of his small ones. He nodded at the officiant, who had stopped this time, shrugged at Sylvie and Adam and avoided Teressa's eyes. She was probably glaring daggers at him at the moment, anyway. They'd sort it out later. Right now what mattered was Sylvie and Adam's wedding.

And that the kids loved him, even if their mother didn't.

OH, DEAR HEAVENS! Anita clenched her hands together in her lap. Dusty was the kind of person who grew on you, so she sympathized with Sarah and Brendon. She knew Dusty had taken a big step back from the children the past few days, but she had a pretty good idea why, and she had to agree with him. Teressa was being pigheaded about her and Dusty's relationship.

When Anita first met Dusty, she wasn't sure they'd ever be friends. But she knew he'd argued with Cal about shielding her too much from…well, life. If she ever needed someone to champion her cause, Dusty was the man to go to.

Sarah's hissy fit didn't surprise her, but Brendon having the nerve to run to Dusty did. Anita blinked back a tear, not the only tear in the church right now, she'd bet.

Cal slid his arm along the back of the pew behind her and leaned in close. "Are you okay?" he murmured.

She shivered as his breath tickled her ear, and she leaned against him. She could barely wait for them to be alone to tell him her decision. A few weeks ago Cal had come home and talked to her, really talked to her, about having a baby. She agreed to try another doctor, because she was confident the doctor would tell them the same thing; that it was okay for her to try to get pregnant. Yesterday, the ob-gyn had given her the go-ahead.

She'd planned to tell Cal last night when she'd

gotten home from town, had even bought a bottle of champagne to celebrate, but she'd made the mistake of dropping by her father's office before leaving the city. According to his secretary he'd been too busy to see her. She couldn't imagine how he'd react when he found out he may someday be a grandfather. Not that she'd planned to tell him last night. She'd only wanted to see if he was okay. But she'd been so upset by her father's refusal to make time for her that she decided to wait until she felt stronger emotionally to tell Cal her news. *Please let him be as excited as she was.*

She slipped her hand into her husband's big, rough hand. "I'm fine. Look at your brother. Who would have guessed he'd be so good with children?" Would Cal be as loving? Sometimes, he seemed so remote.

She watched Adam and Sylvie exchange the vows they'd written and slip rings on each others' fingers. Brendon's nose started running, and Dusty let go of his hand to dig out a hankie from his pocket and pass it to the little boy. Sarah finally raised her head from Dusty's shoulder to watch Adam and Sylvie kiss.

Teressa looked as if she was going to faint.

"Let's see if Sarah and Brendon will walk out with us. Teressa looks like she needs an arm. Dusty should help her."

Cal's mouth twitched. "When did you become the local matchmaker?" he asked as they stood and clapped, watching Adam and Sylvie walk down the aisle.

Anita leaned forward and took Brendon's hand. "Hey there, big boy. Want to walk me out of the church like the grown-ups do?"

Brendon stuck his thumb in his mouth and nodded as he slipped his hand into hers. She waited until Cal had pried Sarah away from Dusty. She had no idea what Cal whispered in Sarah's ear, but she giggled and finally let go of Dusty and went into Cal's arms. Cal nodded his head toward Teressa, who was stuck in place at the altar. Dusty was by her side in a flash.

Anita smiled to herself as she watched Dusty naturally curl his hand around Teressa's waist and rest it on her swollen belly. Teressa sagged back into him as if a load had suddenly lifted off her shoulders. They followed Teressa and Dusty out of the church and into the bright clear December day.

Anita addressed the little girl now looking comfortable in Cal's arms. "Sarah, I need your help finding another pair of shoes for your mother. Do you mind going home with me to find something more comfortable for her to wear?" Walking behind Teressa, Anita had noticed that Teressa's shoes were causing her trouble.

"I'll get Dusty's truck keys and give him ours,"

Cal said. "He has the kids' car seats in his truck. We might as well drive that. Sarah, you stay with Anita."

Anita laughed. Cal wasn't giving Sarah the chance to attach herself to Dusty just yet.

She noticed Dusty refused to let go of Teressa as he dug in his pocket for his keys and accepted their set from Cal. He smiled across the parking lot at Anita, but she could see it was an effort. Poor man. Knowing that Teressa was afraid to commit to him, Anita was on his side.

Up until a few months ago, Dusty hadn't been the most reliable person around. But people changed. She should know, because she'd changed in a big way since letting Cal into her life. And she was about to change even more. How exciting was that?

After the children were settled in the vehicle, Anita caught Cal's arm and pulled him to the back of the truck and kissed him.

He slid his hands around her waist and pulled her into him. "I'm bringing you to more weddings." He laughed.

"It's not the wedding." She looked around at the crowded parking lot. This was not the place she'd imagined telling him about her good news. But she couldn't keep it to herself any longer.

"The doctor says we can try for a baby."

Cal stilled, his eyes turned darker and serious. "Really?"

"Really. I saw Dr. McAllister yesterday. He says I'm fine, and we can expect a normal pregnancy when and if I get pregnant. I was going to tell you last night, but then…you know, my father upset me, and I…" She grabbed his hands. "Be excited for us, Cal. I want this baby so much."

"You were going to tell your father before you told me?"

She stepped back. "The only person's approval I need is yours, Cal. I remembered him saying my mother kept a diary, and I wanted to ask him if I could borrow it to read."

Cal would probably always struggle with his dislike of her father, but she often let herself daydream of the day her husband and her father overlooked their differences for the sake of their family.

Cal cupped the back of her head with his hand. She closed her eyes when he kissed her forehead. "He won't give it to you, honey. You know how he is."

"Tell me you're happy about trying for a baby."

He smiled his beautiful crooked smile that had stolen her heart the first time she'd met him. "Of course I am. I'm going to worry about you every step of the way, though, when you do get pregnant. Get used to it."

She laughed. "Like I'm not already. You'll have to get used to me telling you to back off."

"I like it when you're bossy."

She leaned into him. "Good thing. I'm going to practice on you, because I doubt I'll ever be able to discipline our child. I hope he looks like you."

Cal laughed. "He? Getting ahead of yourself, aren't you?"

"He. She. Doesn't matter to me."

Cal took her hand in his. "And the doctor really said everything was good? That you're all right?"

"Yes."

"You have to promise to tell me if you're not, Anita."

She squeezed his hand as she stared into his eyes. "I promise."

The promise felt as serious as a wedding vow. She'd made a terrible mistake, hiding her miscarriage from Cal. But thank goodness he'd understood, because he knew she'd come from a household full of secrets. She hadn't even known how her mother had died until she started her period. The boarding school where she was living must have called her father, because he appeared a few days later, informed her that her mother died in childbirth and she, too, could be at risk, so it was necessary to always take precautions not to get pregnant. Then he left, and she had no one to help her put that information into perspective. Her sex life when she got older, what there was of it, was a disaster. The two men she'd slept with had told her she was frigid, and the man she'd become engaged to, her father's protégé, hadn't cared. He was marrying her to get closer to her father, or her father's money to be precise. But Cal...Cal had shown her what making love was like with someone you loved. She couldn't wait to have his baby.

"You're not going to cry all the time like Teressa does, are you?"

"I don't know. Teressa has a lot to cry about at the moment. I don't."

"No, she doesn't. All she has to do is see what's right in front of her nose. The kids know how solid Dusty is. Teressa needs to smarten up."

"Speaking of the kids, they've been unusually quiet."

Cal craned his neck to look in the side mirror. He laughed and waved. "I suspect they've been watching us in the mirrors."

"We should get going. They'll sit still for only so long."

Cal caught her hand before she could turn back to the truck. "So, ah, does that mean it's okay to start trying right away?" His eyes glowed.

She laughed. "I like your enthusiasm."

"How long do we have to stay at the reception?"

"Cal." She pulled her hand free and headed for the front of the truck. "Until the end. We're family."

Cal climbed into the front seat and closed the door. "Whatever you say, Mrs. Carson. But I think I feel a headache coming on."

"Brendon's gotta pee," Sarah announced.

"You'll have to hang on, bud. We're stuck in traffic at the moment."

"He knows how to pee outside. Dusty taught him how. He taught me, too, but it doesn't work for girls."

Cal burst out laughing as Anita tried to smother a giggle. She didn't think Teressa would approve of them encouraging Sarah to tell their family secrets. "I'm sorry I missed that one." Cal smiled at Brendon in the rearview mirror. "If you get desperate, Brendon, say the word and you and me will run for the bushes, okay?

"Man," Cal continued, half under his breath. "The things my brother gets up to. He never fails to amaze me."

Anita settled back into the truck seat with a happy sigh. She and Cal were going to try to have a baby, finally, and Cal was okay with that. After losing the other baby at two months, he hadn't wanted to try again. But they were on their way to their happily-ever-after now. So were Adam and Sylvie. If only Teressa and Dusty could see their way clearly and realize they were made for each other. It wasn't too much to hope that maybe someday soon they would.

CHAPTER FIFTEEN

SHE WAS EXHAUSTED, and her feet were swollen from wearing the stupid heels. Teressa didn't have an ounce of energy left over to deal with Dusty, or the kids or her parents right now. *Not one ounce.* She sank into a winged-back chair situated in an alcove created by a turret.

The Waterside Inn was at least two hundred years old and full of nooks and crannies where one could curl up and read a book or have a glass of wine and watch the snow come down. Not that it was snowing out today. It was almost cold enough to, but bright sunlight spilled through the windows behind her, warming her near-bare back.

Adam and Sylvie had decided against a sit-down dinner for their reception. There were lots of comfortable chairs and group settings where people could visit with each other as the waiters circulated amongst the crowd with platters of finger food. Thank goodness Adam and Pops had decided to hire a catering company from town to supply the food. Otherwise, she'd have felt obligated to step in and offer to cook. The MacAfees ran a beautiful inn, but weren't renowned for their food.

Not that anyone would have let her cook. She was going to scream if one more person told her to go lie down. "Here you go." Dusty brought the cup of tea she'd requested, and a plate full of tiny sandwiches and pastries. "I'm going to grab a coffee. Be back in a minute."

Teressa tried to smile at him, but her facial muscles had seized up. Between her fatigue and the ache she got in her chest every time she looked at him, she wasn't in a happy place. At all.

She thought she'd die of mortification when Sarah made a scene at the wedding. But when Dusty had stopped the ceremony to pick up Sarah, she felt as if someone had knocked her feet out from under her. One minute she was standing on solid ground, and the next, her whole world turned inside out. She was in love with Dusty Carson. She could hardly breathe, thinking of the depth of feeling she felt for him. It was as if a floodgate had opened, and she was awash with love for him. At the moment, she couldn't imagine why she'd thought she didn't love him.

If they hadn't been heading to Adam and Sylvie's wedding reception, she would have begged Dusty to take her straight home and make love to her. She'd seen him dressed in a suit before, but when she walked into that church today and saw him, so handsome, so solid, standing at the altar smiling at her with his heart in his eyes, she realized she'd made a terrible mistake. Instead of concentrating on what was so right about Dusty, she'd been looking at what was wrong. As if she, herself, was perfect. She snorted. God help her if she was too late to repair the damage done.

She leaned back in the chair and passed a trembling hand over her hair, hoping she didn't look as disheveled as she felt. Not that it mattered. Dusty was interested in every other person in the large room, except her.

"Brought you a change of shoes." Anita sat in the chair beside her and pulled a pair of Teressa's flats out of the bag she held.

"You're my savior. Thank you so much."

"You'd do the same for me."

"Except I can't imagine you having anything as remotely unsightly as swollen ankles."

Curious, Teressa watched as the corners of Anita's lips curled up. She looked as though she had a secret, and Teressa knew better than to pry. Anita would tell her when she was ready to share.

"I love the wedding cake. It's a masterpiece."

"I had fun making it. Have you and Sylvie discussed a Christmas event for the café?" she asked Anita, more to keep her by her side for a few minutes than out of interest. Sylvie's "events" always made more work for Teressa. Anita was their PR person.

"Not yet, but it would be fun to stir things up after Christmas. Do you have any ideas?"

"Ideas for what?" Tyler pulled a footstool in front of Teressa and sat.

Teressa sighed. It would never occur to Tyler, or anyone else here, that a conversation might be private.

"An after-Christmas event at the café," Anita explained.

"That'd be great. It's always so boring after the holidays," Tyler said. "What are we doing?"

Teressa and Anita glanced at each other. Anita looked as amused and irritated as Teressa felt about Tyler's assumption that there was a "we."

"No idea," Teressa said. "Any suggestions?"

"We could have a mystery weekend," Tyler offered. "You know, like we pretend someone's been killed, and then everyone has to solve who the murderer is."

"Those always sound like so much fun," Anita agreed.

"What sounds like fun?" Cal appeared behind Anita and put his hand on her shoulder. Teressa noticed Anita's expression soften as she reached up and covered his hand with hers. Not so long ago, Anita would have turned stiff as a board if Cal showed any public display of affection.

"Putting on a mystery weekend after Christmas," Tyler announced.

"Like someone pretends to get killed?" Cal tipped his head to one side. "Might be fun."

Usually Cal censored anything that demanded Anita's time. "Maybe we should go on a mystery weekend to see how it works," he suggested.

Anita beamed up at him. "Great idea. How about it, Teressa? Do you think you and Dusty would be interested in something like that?"

"I would," Tyler interjected.

"No one asked you," Cal said bluntly.

"It was my idea."

"So?"

Teressa held back her laugh when she saw the hint of a smile on Cal's face. They were like a big, sprawling family, teasing each other and, occasionally, hurting each other, as only family could do. Another blinding revelation struck her. She loved living here and couldn't imagine her life without seeing the folks from Collina every day.

"Tyler could babysit Sarah and Brendon," Cal teased.

"Oh, come on," Tyler objected.

Cal laughed. "I'm kidding. Actually, if you guys are serious about putting on a mystery weekend, I think you should attend one of those weekends with us, Tyler. I suspect you're smarter than you look, and it's time we started training you to do…something. This village has lost enough young people. We've got to start giving people a reason to stay."

"I agree," Pops said as he joined their group. "From what Sylvie tells me, Teressa is thinking of teaching Tyler how to cook."

Tyler swung around on the stool. "You are? Would I make more money?"

Teressa smothered a smile. "We'd have to discuss it. Come in early tomorrow, and we'll start with cooking breakfast."

Tyler frowned fiercely at her. "You're not supposed to work."

"I'll sit down the whole time. I promise." That might actually work, and she wouldn't feel so grouchy all the time and left out. Confined at home, she'd missed the work and the gossip and seeing friendly faces every day. Pops had been partially right when he said she was a central figure in the village. But what he hadn't mentioned was how important the people of Collina were to her.

"Wow! This is great. Thanks, guys. As soon as I get home, I'm going to go online and look up mystery weekends." For once, instead of dragging his feet across the room, Tyler flew. It had never occurred to Teressa that Tyler might be bored, not lazy. Seemed as if she was making faulty assumptions left, right and center about the people she knew.

"Make way. Gotta feed the pregnant lady."

Dusty took the chair Anita vacated as everyone drifted off. They were probably afraid she an'

Dusty were going to start fighting and didn't want to get caught in the middle of an argument.

Dusty loosened his tie and sat with his legs spread apart, his large hands resting on his thighs. Teressa caught her breath. He looked so gorgeously masculine. He was not in the least bit conscious of what a beautiful picture he made, sitting next to her with the sun spilling over his wide shoulders.

He glanced at the plate he'd brought her and placed it on the small table between them. "You should eat something. You probably didn't get a chance to eat much earlier."

She looked down at her hands. It was sweet that he was concerned about her, but she'd rather he thought she looked sexy. Her boobs were practically falling out of her dress, but he'd barely looked at her all day. She glanced at him from under her lashes. Now that she thought about it, he'd hardly spoken to her at all.

"Thanks for taking care of Sarah and Brendon during the wedding. I'm sorry they acted up."

"You don't have to thank me for doing anything concerning the kids, Teressa." His voice sounded rough. Angry.

She closed her eyes. She'd left it too late. He hated her. "Dusty—"

"Not here," he interrupted her. "I get it. They're not my kids. I know I'm not good enough for you.

Let's take a break and try to play nice for Sylvie and Adam's sake."

She slid forward in the chair and placed her hand on his knee. "I apologize for being so difficult. Can you ever forgive me?"

"For what? Saying the truth? Might as well face it, I'm not husband material."

"So, I guess if I asked you to marry me, you'd say no?"

Dusty froze, his coffee cup hallway to his mouth. He looked as if he was repeating the words in his head to make sure he'd heard her right. After a second he put the cup down as carefully as if it were a bomb.

Finally, he looked at her. She saw a flash of surprise, before caution chased it away. But she also saw his gaze heat up and soften.

His Adam's apple bobbed up and down in his throat. "Are you serious or is this some kind of wedding hangover thing? I think I've heard about that happening."

She laughed and slipped her fingers over the back of his hand. "No, Dusty. This isn't any kind of hangover anything. I've finally realized how much I love you, and I'm really, really sorry it's taken me this long to admit the truth to myself."

He puffed out his cheeks and expelled a lungful of air. "Can we go home now? I don't think you have a clue how beautiful you look today."

She laughed louder. "I thought you weren't looking at me because you hated me."

His gaze dropped to her breasts, and her body immediately responded. "That's not the reason. I wasn't sure I could keep my hands off you, and now I'm sure I can't." He stood. "Come on. You've got a bad headache and have to go home right now. Before you change your mind."

"What about Sarah and Brendon?" She couldn't stop giggling.

"Hell." He dropped back into the chair. "I forgot. Okay…" He looked around the room. "Cal and Anita can take them."

"Do you see them over there? Cal hasn't taken his hands off Anita since they walked into the inn. If I didn't know better, I'd say they're about to make a break for it themselves."

"That dirty dog. They are, too."

She pressed forward until her knees were rubbing against his. "You know, I hear anticipation… heightens the experience." She smiled and wiggled her eyebrows up and down. She couldn't believe she'd almost lost out on the chance to share her life with him. Dusty was so much fun.

"Mommy." Sarah burst into their private circle and leaned against Dusty's knee as she stood between his open legs. "I'm hungry."

Teressa smoothed down her daughter's wild

curls. "You sound more tired than hungry. Here, have some of these sandwiches."

"Name a date," Dusty interrupted.

"What?"

"Just in case it is a hangover thing, name a date right now."

"I'm not going to change my mind."

"I don't care. I need a date."

"Okay." She sat back. "A month after the twins are born."

Dusty's sudden smile chased away the grimness in his face. "Good. Now, as for you, Princess—"

Sarah started pouting. "Are you mad at me?"

"No. But it's not cool making your grandparents uncomfortable. You have to apologize to them."

"You're not the boss of me." She thrust out her bottom lip.

"Yeah, I am." She giggled when he tickled her. "I'm the boss of every princess around. Princesses are special people, and they don't hurt the people who love them."

"Will you come with me?" she begged Dusty.

Teressa watched his weathered face soften again. "Of course I will. Let's get it over with."

Her heart pounding in her throat, Teressa watched her beautiful, delicate daughter's hand disappear inside Dusty's big one as they made their way across the room to where her mother sat by herself. God. She'd come so close to being that lonely woman. But she had Dusty to save her. And Sarah and Brendon. And now, two new babies. She folded her hands on her belly. She had a family to take care of, and who would also take care of her. She was the luckiest woman in the world.

Nine months later

TERESSA WALKED OUT of the church beside her husband, who looked particularly handsome, wearing his good black suit and a baby over his shoulder. Her lips curled into a smile. Who could have guessed wild Dusty Carson would be such a wonderful, natural father. He'd mastered diapers the first day the twins were born, and always seemed willing to get up for the midnight feedings. The only time he wimped out was when one of the children cried. Tears demolished her big, tough guy.

She looked down at the baby in her arms, into the warm blue eyes of her son. Had she really once thought having two more children was beyond her? Every time she looked at both Luke and Daisy, she saw her husband in their sparkling blue eyes and blond hair. She squeezed her son's toes. She suspected both of them were going to lead them a merry chase. Thank goodness their father seemed to have an almost supernatural connection to them. He knew they were going to cry almost before they did. He could sense when they were asleep and when they woke up. Hopefully, that would someday translate into anticipating whatever kind of devilry they got into.

Sarah skipped up beside her as they walked down the stairs. Teressa couldn't believe how much her daughter had grown in the past year. Dusty's insistence that Sarah get her hair cut short had been nothing short of brilliant. Instead of unruly orange curls spiraling out from her head, a neat cap of soft curls framed her sweet, freckled face.

She'd already slugged her first boyfriend in the nose. Teressa had been mortified when Tommy's parents called to tell them about the mishap. Dusty, of course, had defended Sarah's actions, saying he'd have done the same thing, and then he'd made Sarah and Tommy sit down and talk about what happened. Apparently, Tommy had given Sarah his sister's bicycle for a present, but took it back when his parents asked where it was. She'd be keeping her eye on Tommy in the future.

"Can I hold Luke?" Sarah asked.

"It's better when you're sitting down."

"Mom, I'm not a baby. I know how to take care of my own brother."

"Yes, you do." She handed the one-month-old baby to her daughter, watching carefully that Sarah held on tight. She was proud of how much Sarah loved the twins.

"Need help here?"

Teressa hid her smile as her daughter fluttered her eyelashes.

"Hi, Cal," Sarah said demurely.

"Hey, Princess. That's a pretty dress you're wearing."

Not so long ago, Cal wouldn't have had a clue how to handle a little girl's infatuation. Dusty had been the same way, but he'd learned that little girls were almost harmless.

"Pretty dress you're wearing, too, Mrs. Carson." Cal kissed her cheek. "Welcome to the family."

"Thanks, Cal." Dusty had wanted her to wear a white wedding gown, but she'd chosen a midcalf beige, lace dress.

She looked around for her husband. He stood just outside the church, patiently letting a cluster of elderly ladies coo over Daisy. Brendon, as usual, wasn't far away from his father. Stan had signed the adoption papers, allowing Dusty to adopt her son just before the twins had been born. Sarah was the only one Dusty didn't have legal custody of, but they were trying to track down her father to ask if he would allow Dusty to adopt Sarah.

Teressa narrowed her eyes as the group of women twittered. Daisy obviously wasn't the only attraction they were cooing over. As if sensing her gaze, Dusty looked up and grinned in her direction. Electricity arced between them, and she looked around, amazed no one else noticed the sparks in the air.

They hadn't been able to make love for a while, and she was burning with impatience for the doctor to give her the go-ahead. Somehow it didn't seem right to not be able to make love on their wedding night. Last night while lying in bed, his arms around her, Dusty had told her in detail exactly how he'd make it up to her. She blushed as heat pooled in her belly. She couldn't wait.

"Can I hold Luke? I need the practice," Cal asked Sarah.

Sarah studied him. "Do you know how?"

"I think so. You tell me if I do it right." Luke settled into Cal's arms under Sarah's watchful eye.

Teressa watched Anita glide through the crowd toward her husband. Six months pregnant, Anita looked as svelte as ever.

Teressa's heart expanded as she thought how their baby would grow up with Daisy and Luke, and how much their Aunt Anita and Uncle Cal already loved the twins. She hadn't had anyone like that around when Sarah and Brendon were born. Her life was so much richer than it had been, and all she had to do was open her heart.

She turned around when someone touched her elbow. "Mother!"

Her mother's smile seemed almost genuine. "It was a beautiful wedding, Teressa. I'm proud of you. You have a lovely family."

Teressa bit back her sharp reply. It had taken a

ring on her finger for her mother to finally approve. But it was better than her mother's usual barbed criticism, she supposed. "How's the new condo?" she asked as she silently accepted Luke from Cal.

Her parents had sold the colossal old house Linda had inherited from her parents, and had bought a new condo in Lancaster. Linda looked, if not younger, more relaxed than Teressa had ever seen her.

"I love it. I can't believe I didn't sell that monstrosity years ago. I've met new people and even joined a gym, for heaven's sake. Did your father tell you he got a job cutting hair at the barber shop down the street from us?"

"He did." Her father didn't enjoy living in the city as much as Linda did. He drove all the way from Lancaster once a week to visit them, and Dusty had promised as soon as he finished the bedrooms in the basement, he was building her father his own room. Teressa suspected they'd be looking for a bigger house sooner than Dusty realized. She was lining up several different kinds of birth control, but she still worried she'd get pregnant again. She thought four children were more than enough, but Dusty argued that six sounded like a better number.

"Can I hold my grandson?"

"Of course." Teressa gently handed Luke to his grandmother.

Linda cooed at the baby. "You're a lucky woman, Teressa. Dusty's a good man."

"Funny," she said. "He says the same thing. How lucky he is because I'm a good woman." It had taken her a few months to finally believe Dusty when he said how lucky he was. They were both fortunate to have each other, as well as the children and their families and friends.

Tyler loped over to her, a goofy smile on his face. "I love this kid. My turn to hold Luke." He held out his hands.

Teressa's mother raised her eyebrows, but passed the baby to him without argument.

"Adam said I'm ready to handle the lunch special tomorrow," he said to Teressa as her mother walked away.

"Really? What did he say you could cook?"

"Pea soup."

She looked around for Adam. "Over my dead body."

"What's wrong with pea soup? Luke will eat some, won't you, boy?"

"Nobody likes pea soup, Tyler. It's summertime. Choose something lighter."

"Like the quinoa avocado salad I was just reading about in *Meals!* magazine?"

Teressa smiled. Adam hated quinoa. "Exactly that."

"Cool. Hey, Adam," he said to the giant man who approached them. Sylvie followed close behind him. "Teressa said I could make that quinoa salad I was telling you about. Here." He held the baby out to him. "Your turn."

Teressa and Adam and Sylvie watched Tyler speed off. "We've been played," Adam chuckled.

"That we have. But I'm on to him now. He won't get away with tricking me again," Teressa said.

"Hey there, Mrs. Carson." Teressa relaxed back into Dusty as he nuzzled her ear from behind. "I have a feeling Daisy's had enough. She needs some quiet time."

"Luke looks wide-awake," Adam said.

Dusty laughed. "That's because he's our party boy. But by the time we get him home, he'll be out like a light. Time to go. Brendon, my man." He tossed the car keys to the small boy. Dusty had talked Teressa into retiring her old minivan and buying a heavy-duty SUV. Nothing was too good when it came to the safety of his family. "Could you unlock the car and open the doors for us?"

Brendon pulled his pants up higher on his waist. "'Course," he said, and marched off.

Teressa and Dusty followed him after saying goodbye to Adam and Sylvie. "Think we can get the twins to sleep before everyone comes over?" she asked. They'd decided on having a small reception at their house because it was easier to get the twins down for a nap in their own beds.

"Maybe. Doesn't matter. There's sure to be someone who'll want to hold them. They're getting spoiled. It doesn't seem right that I have to compete to hold my own kids," he grumbled.

"The way I look at it is you'll have more time for your wife."

Dusty slipped his hand around her waist. "I always have time for you. Matter of fact, I don't know what I'd do without you."

She knew the feeling. Dusty had filled her life with love and laughter, and yes, the occasional argument, because they were both a little bullheaded. Which, in her opinion, made them perfect for each other.

"Let's go home."

A smile spread over her husband's face. "I like the sound of that."

* * * * *

LARGER-PRINT BOOKS!
GET 2 FREE LARGER-PRINT NOVELS PLUS
2 FREE GIFTS!

❦ HARLEQUIN®

Romance

From the Heart, For the Heart

YES! Please send me 2 FREE LARGER-PRINT Harlequin® Romance novels and my 2 FREE gifts (gifts are worth about $10). After receiving them, if I don't wish to receive any more books, I can return the shipping statement marked "cancel." If I don't cancel, I will receive 4 brand-new novels every month and be billed just $4.84 per book in the U.S. or $5.24 per book in Canada. That's a savings of at least 19% off the cover price! It's quite a bargain! Shipping and handling is just 50¢ per book in the U.S. and 75¢ per book in Canada.* I understand that accepting the 2 free books and gifts places me under no obligation to buy anything. I can always return a shipment and cancel at any time. Even if I never buy another book, the two free books and gifts are mine to keep forever.

119/319 HDN F43Y

Name _____ (PLEASE PRINT)

Address _____ Apt. #

City _____ State/Prov. _____ Zip/Postal Code

Signature (if under 18, a parent or guardian must sign)

Mail to the **Harlequin® Reader Service:**
IN U.S.A.: P.O. Box 1867, Buffalo, NY 14240-1867
IN CANADA: P.O. Box 609, Fort Erie, Ontario L2A 5X3
Want to try two free books from another line?
Call 1-800-873-8635 or visit www.ReaderService.com.

* Terms and prices subject to change without notice. Prices do not include applicable taxes. Sales tax applicable in N.Y. Canadian residents will be charged applicable taxes. Offer not valid in Quebec. This offer is limited to one order per household. Not valid for current subscribers to Harlequin Romance Larger-Print books. All orders subject to credit approval. Credit or debit balances in a customer's account(s) may be offset by any other outstanding balance owed by or to the customer. Please allow 4 to 6 weeks for delivery. Offer available while quantities last.

Your Privacy—The Harlequin® Reader Service is committed to protecting your privacy. Our Privacy Policy is available online at www.ReaderService.com or upon request from the Harlequin Reader Service.

We make a portion of our mailing list available to reputable third parties that offer products we believe may interest you. If you prefer that we not exchange your name with third parties, or if you wish to clarify or modify your communication preferences, please visit us at www.ReaderService.com/consumerschoice or write to us at Harlequin Reader Service Preference Service, P.O. Box 9062, Buffalo, NY 14269. Include your complete name and address.

HRLP13R

LARGER-PRINT BOOKS!

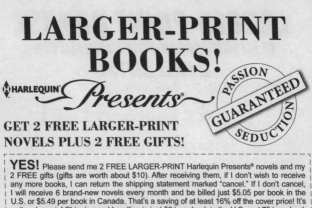

HARLEQUIN *Presents*

PASSION GUARANTEED SEDUCTION

GET 2 FREE LARGER-PRINT NOVELS PLUS 2 FREE GIFTS!

YES! Please send me 2 FREE LARGER-PRINT Harlequin Presents® novels and my 2 FREE gifts (gifts are worth about $10). After receiving them, if I don't wish to receive any more books, I can return the shipping statement marked "cancel." If I don't cancel, I will receive 6 brand-new novels every month and be billed just $5.05 per book in the U.S. or $5.49 per book in Canada. That's a saving of at least 16% off the cover price! It's quite a bargain! Shipping and handling is just 50¢ per book in the U.S. and 75¢ per book in Canada.* I understand that accepting the 2 free books and gifts places me under no obligation to buy anything. I can always return a shipment and cancel at any time. Even if I never buy another book, the two free books and gifts are mine to keep forever.

176/376 HDN F43N

Name	(PLEASE PRINT)

Address	Apt. #

City	State/Prov.	Zip/Postal Code

Signature (if under 18, a parent or guardian must sign)

Mail to the **Harlequin® Reader Service:**
IN U.S.A.: P.O. Box 1867, Buffalo, NY 14240-1867
IN CANADA: P.O. Box 609, Fort Erie, Ontario L2A 5X3

**Are you a subscriber to Harlequin Presents books
and want to receive the larger-print edition?
Call 1-800-873-8635 today or visit us at www.ReaderService.com.**

* Terms and prices subject to change without notice. Prices do not include applicable taxes. Sales tax applicable in N.Y. Canadian residents will be charged applicable taxes. Offer not valid in Quebec. This offer is limited to one order per household. Not valid for current subscribers to Harlequin Presents Larger-Print books. All orders subject to credit approval. Credit or debit balances in a customer's account(s) may be offset by any other outstanding balance owed by or to the customer. Please allow 4 to 6 weeks for delivery. Offer available while quantities last.

Your Privacy—The Harlequin® Reader Service is committed to protecting your privacy. Our Privacy Policy is available online at www.ReaderService.com or upon request from the Harlequin Reader Service.

We make a portion of our mailing list available to reputable third parties that offer products we believe may interest you. If you prefer that we not exchange your name with third parties, or if you wish to clarify or modify your communication preferences, please visit us at www.ReaderService.com/consumerschoice or write to us at Harlequin Reader Service Preference Service, P.O. Box 9062, Buffalo, NY 14269. Include your complete name and address.

LARGER-PRINT BOOKS!
GET 2 FREE LARGER-PRINT NOVELS PLUS
2 FREE GIFTS!

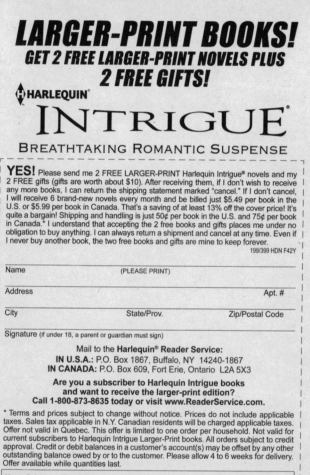

HARLEQUIN

INTRIGUE

BREATHTAKING ROMANTIC SUSPENSE

YES! Please send me 2 FREE LARGER-PRINT Harlequin Intrigue® novels and my 2 FREE gifts (gifts are worth about $10). After receiving them, if I don't wish to receive any more books, I can return the shipping statement marked "cancel." If I don't cancel, I will receive 6 brand-new novels every month and be billed just $5.49 per book in the U.S. or $5.99 per book in Canada. That's a saving of at least 13% off the cover price! It's quite a bargain! Shipping and handling is just 50¢ per book in the U.S. and 75¢ per book in Canada.* I understand that accepting the 2 free books and gifts places me under no obligation to buy anything. I can always return a shipment and cancel at any time. Even if I never buy another book, the two free books and gifts are mine to keep forever.

199/399 HDN F42Y

Name	(PLEASE PRINT)

Address	Apt. #

City	State/Prov.	Zip/Postal Code

Signature (if under 18, a parent or guardian must sign)

Mail to the **Harlequin® Reader Service:**
IN U.S.A.: P.O. Box 1867, Buffalo, NY 14240-1867
IN CANADA: P.O. Box 609, Fort Erie, Ontario L2A 5X3

Are you a subscriber to Harlequin Intrigue books
and want to receive the larger-print edition?
Call 1-800-873-8635 today or visit www.ReaderService.com.

* Terms and prices subject to change without notice. Prices do not include applicable taxes. Sales tax applicable in N.Y. Canadian residents will be charged applicable taxes. Offer not valid in Quebec. This offer is limited to one order per household. Not valid for current subscribers to Harlequin Intrigue Larger-Print books. All orders subject to credit approval. Credit or debit balances in a customer's account(s) may be offset by any other outstanding balance owed by or to the customer. Please allow 4 to 6 weeks for delivery. Offer available while quantities last.

Your Privacy—The Harlequin® Reader Service is committed to protecting your privacy. Our Privacy Policy is available online at www.ReaderService.com or upon request from the Harlequin Reader Service.

We make a portion of our mailing list available to reputable third parties that offer products we believe may interest you. If you prefer that we not exchange your name with third parties, or if you wish to clarify or modify your communication preferences, please visit us at www.ReaderService.com/consumerchoice or write to us at Harlequin Reader Service Preference Service, P.O. Box 9062, Buffalo, NY 14269. Include your complete name and address.

HILPI3R